Amathus

Armageddon

Cyberworld Publishing

www.cyberworldpublishing.com

This book is copyright © Gina Drew 2010
First published by Cyberworld Publishing in 2010.
Cover design by S Bush © 2010
Cover Photo - © Mega11 | Dreamstime.com
All rights reserved.
E Book ISBN 978-1-921879-00-5
Print ISBN 978-1-921879-01-2

Cyberworld Publishing
Jindalee St, Toronto, Australia

Koniotis Mysteries Series

Each book in this series stands alone, but they are also all connected in various ways and form the different parts of one story.

Laughter's Echo

Salted Away

Mouflon Brigade

Amathus Armageddon

Bogus Bills

Homewrecker

Amathus

Armageddon

Koniotis Mysteries - Book Four

by Gina Drew

Caitlyn's map of relevant places of importance in the Mediterranean

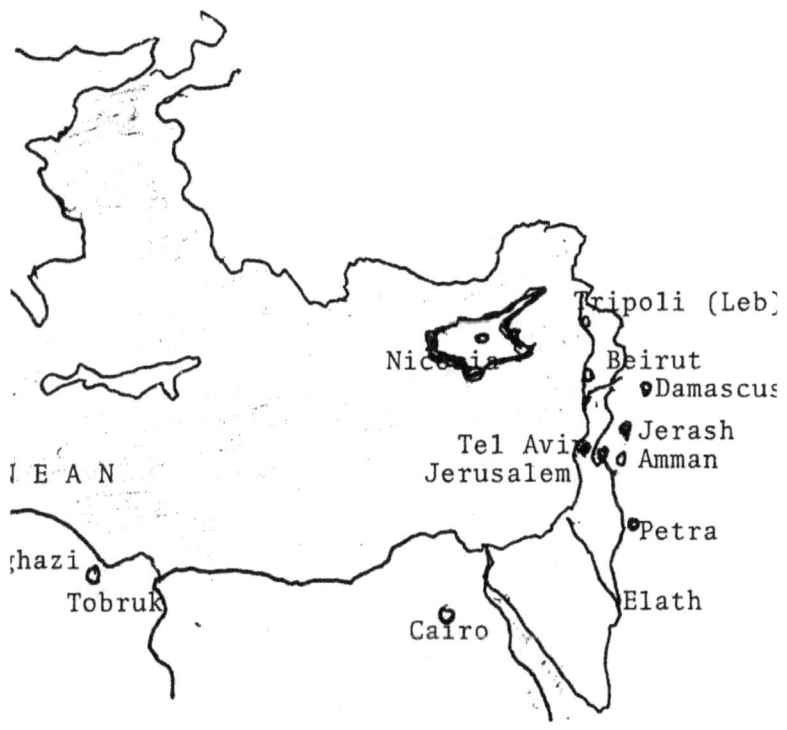

Tripoli (Leb)
Nicosia
Beirut
Damascus
Jerash
Tel Avi
Amman
Jerusalem
Petra
EAN
hazi
Elath
Tobruk
Cairo

Caitlyn's map of locations on Cyprus

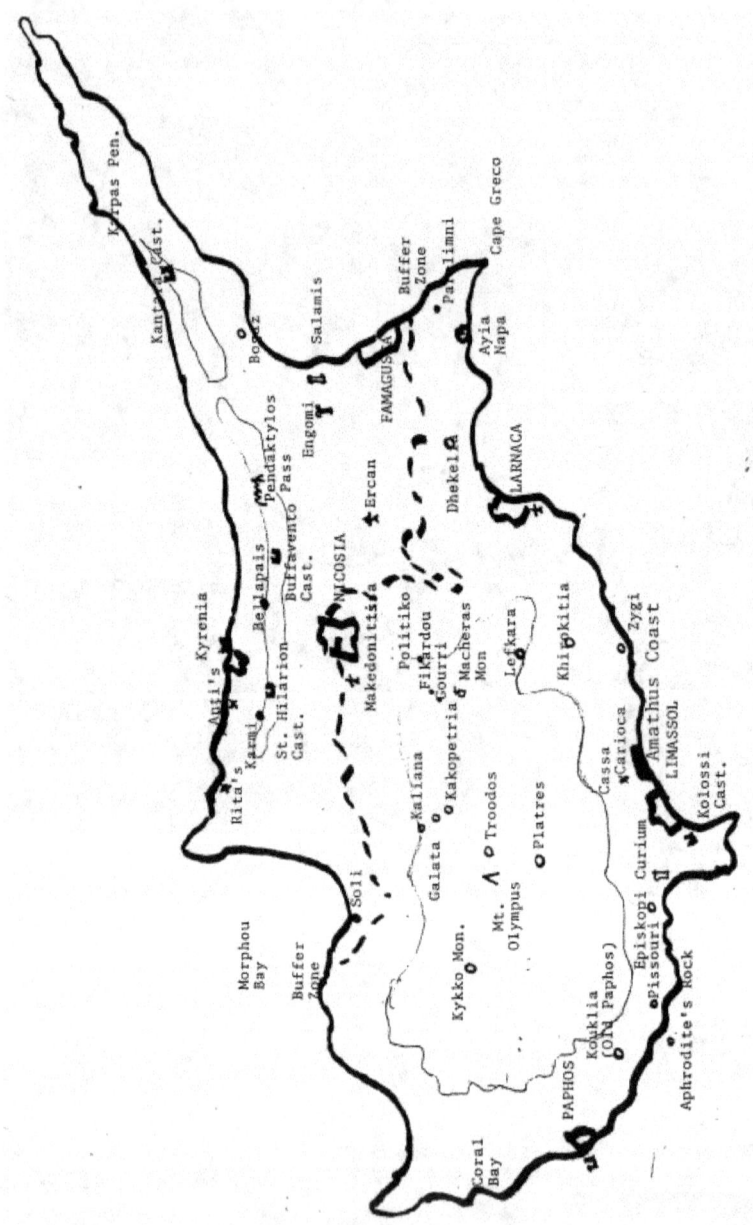

Caitlyn's map of central Cyprus

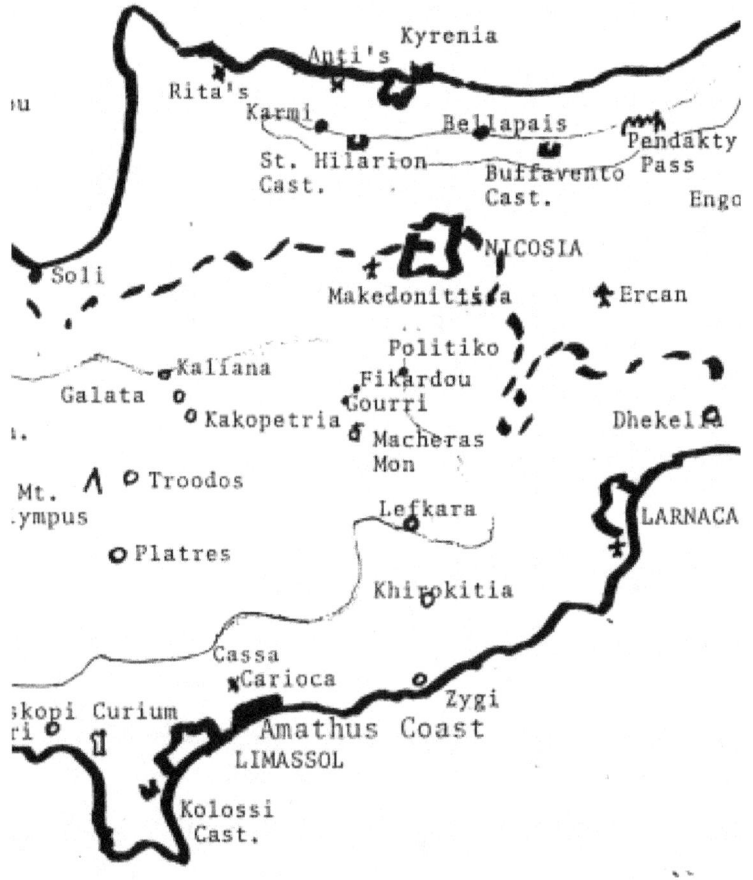

Caitlyn's map of Nicosia - Legend

A. OLD NICOSIA
B. TURKISH ZONE
C. MAKEDONITISSA VALLEY
D. MAIN UN BASE
F. STROVOLOS

1. Border Checkpoint
2. Ledra Palace Hotel
3. Central Prison
4. Stuart's Averof St. House
5. Syrian Ambassador's Residence
6. Turkish Cypriot Police HQ
7. Cyprus Museum
8. Greek Cypriot Police HQ'
9. UNICIS HQ
10. Koniotis House
11. Makedonitissa Monastery
12. International Fair Grounds
13. Markarios Stadium
14. Presidential Palace
15. Makarious Hospital
16. Hamilton Flat

Caitlyn's map of Nicosia

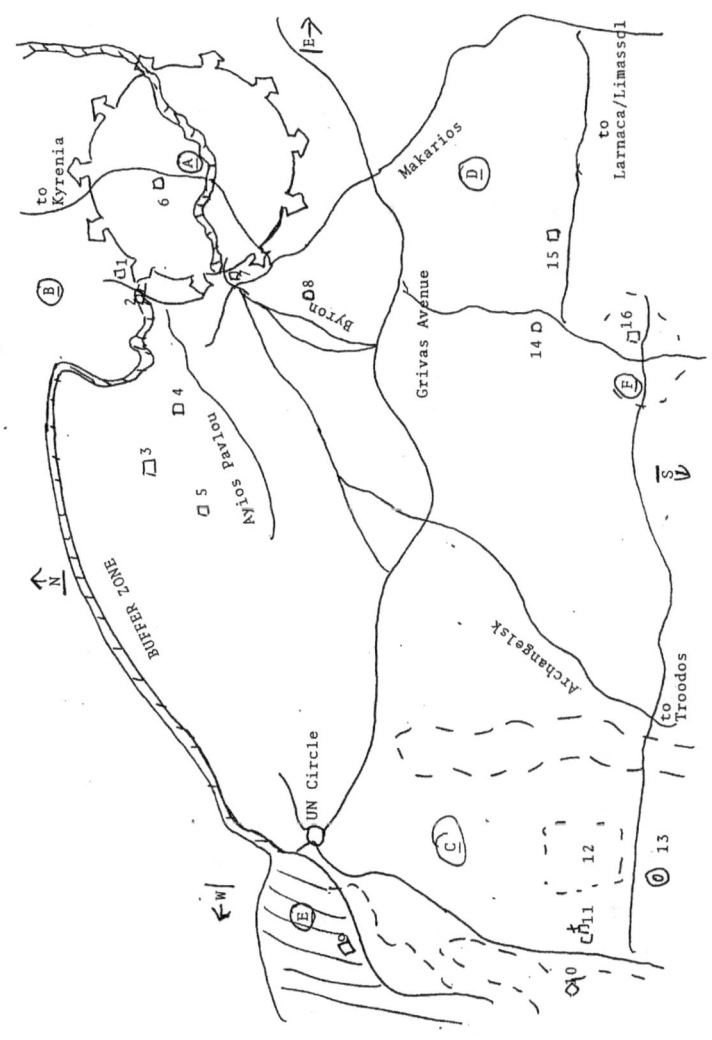

PRIMARY CHARACTERS

Ayman Abu Hani—*Former Lebanese ambassador to Cyprus*

Suzanne Abu Hani—*Wife of the former Lebanese ambassador to Cyprus*

Benjamin—*Ingrid Bittmann's secretary*

Ingrid Bittmann—UN *undersecretary for political affairs*

The Colonel—*Libya's leader*

Paul Conte—*American embassy in Jordan political officer*

Moshe Gilat—*Israeli Zionist and liberation war hero; husband of Israel's prime minister*

Rachel Gilat—*Israeli prime minister*

Stefan Gunnerson—*Swedish criminologist and agent of UNICIS, the United Nations International Crime Investigations Service*

Ginger Nives-Smyth Baldwin Remington Hamilton—*Wife of Willie*

Willie Hamilton—*retired British infantry major; now senior political and crime reporter for the* Cyprus Mail

Eric Isaksen—*The UN's roving mediator on international terrorism and crime*

Ahmad Jallud—*Anwar Jabril's nephew*

Thomas Jameson—*United Nations International Crime Investigations Service operations chief*

Caitlyn Spencer Koniotis—*American archaeologist in Cyprus; wife of Takis Koniotis*

Takis Koniotis—*Chief of UNICIS, the United Nations International Crime*

Investigations Service

Ellen Larkin—*Canadian high commission political officer*

Irene—*Takis Koniotis's aunt, and the Koniotises' nanny and housekeeper*

Demetris Mattas—*"Under the Grapevine" columnist for the Greek-language newspaper* Simerini

Munir Nahlawi—*Syrian ambassador to Cyprus*

Symeon Parikan/Salem Qazzar—*A Hizballah terrorist*

John Patterson—*Head of laboratory research at the United Nations International Crime Investigations Service*

Guy Piccard—*Long-lost husband of Eleni Piccard, Caitlyn's former mentor*

Jacques Piccard—*Former French ambassador to Cyprus; head of Piccard Shipping*

Maria Solonos—*Chief of Greek Cypriot International Investigations Division*

Spyros Steliou—*Cypriot police senior investigator*

Sergey Stepanov—*Security chief for the Israeli prime minister*

Alex Stuart—*British high commission political officer*

Dr. Theocharis Thoma—*A dentist*

General 'Abbas Sulayman—*Egyptian president*

Androulla Varnavidou—*Deputy to Greek Cypriot International Investigations Division Chief Maria Solonos*

Safa Ziya—*Deputy Director of the United Nations International Crime Investigations Service*

Chapter One

Jim's descriptions of the historical connections to the Cyprus landscape below brought thrilling images to Samantha's mind, opening worlds to her that she had never before experienced. This was her first trip to the Mediterranean—almost her first trip out of London. Jim, in turn, was primarily thrilled by the opportunity to touch Samantha's arms, hair, and breasts as he leaned over her to point out the various glories of the island.

But that wasn't completely true, he thought to himself. He was very happy to be back on the island where he had served his military stint as an electronics specialist on a hush-hush project at Episkopi, one of the three huge British sovereign military bases on the island's south coast. And he was particularly thrilled to be seeing the historic island from the air.

This was the first time he had been on a flight that had entered Cypriot air space north of Paphos on the west coast and flown over the Troodos mountains and past the southern port of Limassol en route to landing at the international airport at Larnaca on the southeast coast. As their airplane crossed the western coast, just below Morphou Bay, Jim pointed to a long ridge of sharp, rugged mountains, rising near the northwestern coast and then closely hugging the northern coast off into the hazy distance.

"Those are the Kyrenia Mountains. They are mostly limestone and were created because that is where the European and African continental plates meet. The edges of the plates have mashed together, and the edge of the African plate has been pushed up to form the mountains. They rise steeply enough on this side, but they show sheer drops of limestone cliffs on the upper levels when seen from the north. Very impressive, but we can't go there this vacation, I'm afraid. I told you the island has been divided by ethnic strife—Turks to the north and Greeks to the south—for the past twenty years and more. The Kyrenias are in the Turkish zone. In fact, all of the island we can see now is in the Turkish zone. The airplane entered Cyprus just below the Green Line."

"The Green Line?" Samantha asked. "I don't see any green line." She said it with a mocking smile, however. "Why do they call the line 'Green'?"

"We British are responsible for that. When the island was being partitioned during the colonial period the British administrator took a map of the country and drew a partition line with a green pencil. That line closely parallels the cease-fire line following the 1974 Turkish invasion. So, both the line and the color seemed to have stuck." But Jim's long-winded explanation had lost his new bride already.

"Oh, look. What's that city out there on the plain?"

"That's the capital, Nicosia. You can't see it from here, but the old, walled city is a perfect circle, a circle with eleven arrow-shaped bastions. The wall was started by the Venetians in the 1570s to protect themselves from the Ottoman Turks, but the Turks showed up earlier than expected and easily breached the unfinished walls. The Green Line runs right through the city, separating the Turkish and Greek sectors. Nicosia is now the world's only divided capital—now that the Germans have unified Berlin."

"Look." Samantha interjected. "We seem to be going over some more hills now."

"Those aren't just 'hills,' honey. those are the foothills of the Troodos Mountains, the volcanic mountains that make up the entire southwest quadrant of the island. They are even higher than the Kyrenias—almost twice as high. If you were on the other side of the airplane, you could see them."

He probably should not have said that, for he was immediately crushed back into the seat as Samantha struggled over him and to the windows on the other side of the aircraft. He wasn't complaining, though, as in the scuffle, she had smothered his face with her well-rounded bum for what seemed like a glorious eternity. He wasn't sure whether he could endure the hour drive from the airport to their hotel on the eastern coast before he ravished her.

She was squealing with delight from the other windows. "Snow! There's snow on one of the mountains!"

"That would be Mt. Olympus—the highest peak on the island. The highest point on every Greek island is named Mt. Olympus—to designate it as the property of the gods. It's a bit late for snow to be on the mountain in April, but I've known that to happen. It makes a good contrast to being able to swim in the sea on the same day."

And then Samantha was back, as the stewardess was announcing that all should buckle their seatbelts for the swing over the mountains and to the east of Larnaca, out over the sea, and down on the runway parallel to the European-style, palm tree-lined seafront promenade of the old city that legend held was founded by the grandson of Noah.

This time Jim was ready for Samantha. As she flounced across him to regain her window seat, he pulled her down into his lap, one strong hand cupping a breast and the other, waiting, palm up, on his own lap to grasp and prod from below as he clasped her to him. He buried his face in the nape of her neck. God, she smelled good.

Samantha giggled and flapped at him with her hands, winning her way to her own seat just as the stewardess was passing by to check seat belts.

Round One was inconclusive. But a bare hour later, when he had firmly closed the hotel door behind the bellboy in the seaside Grecian Park Hotel, located midway between the tourist town of Paralimni and the rugged Cape Greco on the island's southeast tip, bells went off in Jim's brain and clothes being scattered everywhere. Round Two was no contest.

In the mid afternoon sun, while Jim was stretched out on the bed, attempting to regain his strength, Samantha was standing at the room's balcony. She was gazing off toward Cape Greco, which projected into the sea like a mini Gibraltar in the distance toward the southeast. Just below her was a large, inviting pool and terrace area, and immediately to the west, behind the sweep of the hotel complex, was a cliff drop-off to a secluded sandy beach cove below. She had been uncertain about traveling as far from home as Cyprus for their honeymoon, but now she was very happy that Jim had persuaded her to come. Brighton had been good enough for her mother's honeymoon, so she had always assumed it would be good enough for hers as well. Jim knew so much about the world and she knew so little. It was almost scary. But it was a nice scary.

She was already in her bikini, having donned it with the intent to sunbathe on the balcony. It was glorious to be able to sit out in the sun in April. And she had resolved to return to London with a tan she could be proud of. No wonder so many of her fellow countrymen went off to the Mediterranean at a drop of a hat.

But the pool and terrace looked so much more inviting than this isolated balcony. That's where she wanted to be.

As she passed her supposedly sleeping husband, both virile and vulnerable in naked repose, he reached out and tried to draw her in. But she wriggled away with a squeal of delight and tossed an "I'll be at the pool" over her shoulder as she raced out of the room.

When Samantha reached the pool area, she could see that the sun would be dropping behind the main, central section of the hotel and pulling the pool area into the shadows within an hour or two. She couldn't stay in the sun unless she parked herself well out on the fringe of the terrace toward the bushes that hid the lip of the steep slope going down to the small cove. So that's where she dragged her lounge bed.

The Grecian Park was a first-class hotel, so no sooner had she settled on her lounge than an attendant—a very handsome attendant—was there with two large beach towels and a menu. She was famished after her new husband's expert ravishing, so she ordered a tall drink and kebab—cubes of braised chicken and pork in a pocket of pita bread.

She was half way to the pool to cool off when the food arrived, so she only went in for a short dip. When she returned to her lounge chair, however, both the food and the towels were gone. When she brought this mystery to the attention of the attendant, he showed great concern—perhaps a bit greater concern, she thought, than was warranted by the circumstance. But she was enjoying the contact with the attendant. She had already noticed that Cypriot men were very attractive, and this one, with his black, wavy hair, his Apollo-like body, and his sweet, friendly smile, was particularly appealing. If she wasn't newly married and hadn't just had a very satisfying afternoon between the sheets with her own husband . . .

"No, I'm sorry, madam," the attendant was saying, "it *is* a bit more serious than it looks. We have been having small thefts like this around the hotel for several days. This is very disturbing. Cyprus is a very safe country. Almost nothing ever gets stolen here. I think perhaps you had better draw your lounge chair back closer to the rest of the bathers on the terrace. I will bring you replacement food and towels."

His eyes were so soft. He so much wanted her to believe the best of Cyprus. She felt herself being drawn into his eyes and his infectious smile. And she noticed, with an inner smile, that *his* eyes were not being held by *hers*, but were roaming to more southern climes.

But then Jim was there, himself looking strong and sexy—if not as well-muscled as his Cypriot competition—in his barest of swimming briefs. Her mood and desires intensified instantly. After the attendant had brought a couple of replacement towels and assured her a kebab was on its way and moved off toward the terrace, she moved close into Jim, hooked her fingers into the waistband of his swimming briefs, and whispered her desire to descend to the sandy cove and find a private spot at the water's edge beyond view from the hotel complex balconies.

Jim didn't require a second invitation. The bells for Round Three were tolling away. They skirted the rim of the cliff until they came to the pathway—actually a narrow dirt roadway—that had been carved into the wall of the cliff and that brought them down to the cove. It was still early in the season, so there were only a few bathers on the beach in the main part of the cove.

Arm in arm Jim and Samantha walked the tide line to the southeast, toward Cape Greco. Dark brown and gray rock outcroppings jutted above the beach. It was not long before they were beyond visual range from the hotel. They stopped at a narrow strand of beach, separated from the bathers in the main cove by several rock outcroppings. They were in a little bowl of sand, protected from the light wind by the face of the cliff.

As Jim was shaking the towels out on the sand near what appeared to be an entrance into a shallow cave in the base of the cliff, Samantha dashed out into the sea. Almost as soon as she had run out to where the water reached her chin, however, she turned and started to walk slowly back onto the beach. As she approached, Jim could see that she was holding both parts of her bikini in her hand. She was beautiful, with a voluptuousness that might turn to fat in the confines of a drab life in the London suburbs but that now brought to mind the legendary rising of the goddess Aphrodite—the goddess of sensual love and beauty—from the Mediterranean Sea onto the shores of Cyprus.

Jim could feel himself rising as well, and he took a few short steps toward the sea, to meet her in the water. But Samantha started to run. She hit him with the force of a steam engine, and the two tumbled onto the towels. Jim rolled over on top of his wife, who tugged at the sides of his swimsuit as he encased her with his elbows and buried his face between her breasts. As the honeymoon satisfactorily progressed, a moaning sound, which was increasing in pitch, wafted above the reclining couple. Jim was surprised. He had never known Samantha could be this intense and wild.

But Samantha had gone rigid. Jim looked up into her startled face. The moaning continued, but he could clearly see that it wasn't Samantha who was doing the moaning.

They remained frozen in position for a long moment, and then they both turned their heads toward the cliffside. The moaning was coming from the cave entrance. Jim rolled off Samantha and took up and tied one of the towels around his waist as he rose to his feet. Motioning his wife to stay behind him, he slowly and quietly moved to the cave entrance. Once there, he could see that the cave was not shallow at all. Just inside the entrance, still in the circle of light from the beach, Jim was brought up short. Someone—or something—had been living in this cave. And obviously had been living off the Grecian Park Hotel on the cliff top above, unless the logo of an ancient Grecian battle barge was used more widely in these parts than just in the five-star Grecian Park and Grecian Bay hotel chain. The cave floor was littered with broken hotel plates and tangled towels. One of the hotel's terrace chairs was also here, backed against the wall of the cave.

The moaning continued, resonating from the depths of the cave, farther back, in the darkness. Jim carefully moved toward the echoing sound. A shadow fell across the mouth of the cave. Samantha, now back in her bikini, was following her husband into the cave. He turned to motion her back, but at that instant the moaning changed dramatically into a terrifying yowl, and she was upon him, claws flashing and lashing, forcing him to the sandy floor of the cave.

Samantha let out a bloodcurdling scream.

Chapter Two

All of the five-star luxury hotels along the Amathus "golden mile" beach coast to the east of Cyprus' primary, south-central coast port city of Limassol were frantically gearing up for the most important event of the area's history. At the Le Meridien, they were bustling around closing off floors and attempting to find acceptable alternate accommodations for their wealthy regular clientele. At the Sheraton, they were refurbishing the marina and redecorating both the renowned Panorama conference hall, projected venue of the main events, and the penthouse floor, to meet the specifications of the entourage of one of the most important participants.

The Hawaii Beach and the Amathus Beach were still actively campaigning for the bookings of several of the auxiliary delegations. It was a closely held secret, but the Amathus Beach was also preparing its conference facilities to host the private meetings of the most important leaders who would be in attendance.

The Mediterranean Beach and Four Seasons were stringing countless miles of cabling through their conference facilities, as just these two huge hotels alone would soon be bulging with the various news agencies and newspaper reporters and magazine columnists who had blocked out the two central hotels as the command post for the press that was gathering to cover the historic event. The venerable Appolonia Beach and the glitzy Elias Beach were still suffering under the strain of an employees' strike that threatened to keep them out of the running for a slice of the conference action and, in addition, made it all that much more difficult for the other participating hotels to redirect their prebooked visitors, many of whom nearly rivaled in importance and financial clout of those who were displacing them.

It would be a gigantic feat to be able to accommodate this conference. The conference would begin at the height of the high season on Cyprus—that period in the mid spring when reliably hot, but not unbearably hot, weather had reached the beaches of the lower Mediterranean, while the colder weather in more northern climes had decidedly lost its charm. The conference had been called on very short notice. It would be a miracle if the Amathus coast would be ready to receive the vast number of delegates anticipated. But the Cypriot government—and the Cypriot Hoteliers Association itself—were pulling out all of the stops to see that the conference would be successfully held here.

To say that the coming event would be the historically preeminent happening along the island's Amathus coast was quite a serious claim. Amathus, one of the most ancient seaside city states of Cyprus, was no stranger to the grand events of history. Reputedly forged by a grandson of the god Hercules, the coast had been the venue of the last scene of the legend of Crete's Minotaur and the

Labyrinth; the kingdom of Androcles, who supported Alexander the Great in the siege of Tyre; a major Phoenician, Greek, Roman, and Egyptian trading port; the landing spot for King Richard the Lionhearted when he conquered the island to revenge the island's impolite reception of his intended, Berengaria; and the harbor from which stones quarried in Cyprus were shipped to build the Suez Canal. Now the Amathus seaside to the east of Limassol was currently the most glittery strand of resort-bedecked beach in the eastern Mediterranean.

It was almost outrageous to think that anything could top the history that the Amathus coast had already seen. But what was gearing up to happen there in less than two weeks would top all of its prior experience. If it came off, it undoubtedly would rival events on the level of the Paris treaties of Versailles and the signing of the United Nations Charter. For here—in the refurbished conference centers of the Sheraton, Le Meridien, and Amathus Beach hotels—designed for just such events—the major leaders of the Middle East nations, including Israel, and the representatives of all of the world's major powers would gather to put polish to negotiations and sign the final documents for the permanent implementation of a Middle East peace settlement—that is, if everything went as planned, which was not lightly assumed in any quarter.

The man who maintained much of the burden for ensuring that everything went as scheduled running up to the signing day was even then wandering around the Sheraton's octagonal-shaped Panorama conference room, named thusly because, in contrast to most conference facilities, its walls were devoted to large picture windows that overlooked the hotel's lawns and seaside marina on three sides. On this sunny mid-April morning, the meticulously observant official was scrutinizing the progress of the work, checking entrances and exits, and making notes for his staff to follow up.

He was not a Cypriot government employee, although he was a Cypriot. Neither had he determined that Cyprus would be the venue for this historic occasion. That was generally agreed to by the diverse participants themselves, because Cyprus had long existed as the Geneva of the Middle East, the one place within the region that enemies and occasional friends could meet on safe and neutral ground to negotiate their differences and, not incidentally, to plot against third parties.

This man would have been overseeing the security aspects of the setup for such a significant international conference even if it wasn't being held in Cyprus, however. That was his job. His name was Takis Koniotis, and he was the head of a relatively new international investigations unit for the United Nations—UNICIS, or the United Nations International Crime Investigations Service. This new UN office had been established within the previous two years as the world organization's concerted attempt to respond to international criminal and terrorist groups whose activities transcended national borders.

In an unusual move, Takis Koniotis had not been selected to form and head up this unit because he had been a successful, high-profile national leader or because he was the best compromise appointee who could be found. He had been chosen, rather, because he was a highly successful policeman who had founded such an investigative unit in his own country of Cyprus and had, over the previous three years, led that unit in smashing several highly publicized international crime and terrorist schemes.

Anyone who saw him today as he carefully examined the main conference premises before moving on to inspect the other conference facilities at the nearby Le Meridien, the private meeting rooms at the Amathus Beach, and the accommodations for the major Middle Eastern leaders at these and other hotels would not have guessed that such a man had risen to such an important post. He looked more like an international movie star in his thirties than an important international bureaucrat. This quality came not in any sign of aloofness or demeanor of self-importance on his part, but in his olive dark, handsome features and well-cut body, in the calm confidence with which he comported himself, and in the engaging smile and air of interest and attention he accorded to all of those he encountered.

In many respects, however, the ease with which he approached and dealt with problems—and sometimes massive, complex problems that involved life and death situations—was part of his professional skill. He often felt almost overwhelmed internally with the responsibilities and demands that his new job had brought to him.

Today was just such a day. He was as enthralled as was everyone else with the possibility that the age-old Middle Eastern conflict could be settled within a matter of days. He and other Cypriots were probably more taken up with this possibility than almost anyone else. This was so not only because the prestige of having been the venue for such a final settlement would bring the small island of Cyprus within the familiarity of most of the world's people—most of whom had no idea where or what the island paradise was—but also because a Middle East settlement could presage a settlement of Cyprus' own festering ethnic problems, which had kept the island in a perpetual limbo of partition for more than two decades.

Takis Koniotis couldn't permit himself to be taken too far up in the general euphoria over the signing of a final settlement by the national leaders of the Middle East region, however. The same experience that made him yearn for settlement also made him wary and cynical about the possibility. He had been down this road before—if never quite this far. As he knew all too well from the workings of his international investigations unit, getting rational national leaders, motivated by a sense of responsibility for the well-being and prosperity of their country's peoples, to agree to a political settlement that would genuinely benefit everyone in the region was a far cry from forging such an agreement among leaders who were less than rational or who fed upon and used the divisive forces in the world, whether based on race, ethnic background, economics, or politics, to undermine calls for rational national policies.

Koniotis was thrilled that the leaders of Egypt, Israel, Jordan, and Palestine could see the light of reason and regional and national development self-interest and bury their differences. And there was hope that the leaders of such countries as Saudi Arabia, Syria, and Lebanon would sign up to the conference before it began. But the other forces—the leaders of Iran, Iraq, and Libya, and the radical regional organizations and movements, the Hizballah, the Muslim Brotherhood, the radical Palestinian factions, the militant Zionists, and the violent Muslim Fundamentalists—had thus far remained ominously quiet on the movement toward final settlement in the region.

Much too quiet. The world's leaders had caught the forces of disunity off guard, Koniotis knew, by agreeing to and scheduling this event on such short notice. But everything Koniotis knew about these movements—and he had learned a considerable amount since establishing his UN office nearly two years previously—told him that they would not accept this settlement without a fight. It was his job to counter their activities if they tried to stop or to undermine the final settlement discussions.

And he shuddered at the thought—his worst nightmare—that two or more of these elements would combine to fight the final settlement process. They were dangerous enough as separate threats. If combined, they would become a truly many-headed monster in character. They had always been too particularized in their hatreds and unreliable and dishonorable in their actions to have combined forces effectively for very long before now. But the very aspects that made the signing of a final Mideast settlement so momentous an occasion were the same aspects that might forge and focus the hatred of the radical factions of the region.

* * * *

He himself had been in the military parade on that sad day in 1981—on October 6th, 1981, more than fifteen years ago, to be precise, although the members of his unit had already cleared the reviewing stands well before the tragedy had happened and thus didn't see it and were not permitted to go back afterward.

Now why did his thoughts keep returning to that day? He hadn't thought about it much since then, and this was a routine military parade just like the many thousands that had proceeded from that day to this. There had not been any changes in the customary arrangements for the national leaders either. But that had been just a routine military parade day as well; there had been no plans for a major presidential speech and the parade had not marked any significant national event.

The Egyptian vice president, General 'Abbas Sulayman, rose from his overstuffed chair and went to the refrigerator in the small kitchenette off the lounge in his private apartments to find another soft drink. He was known by all as a very religious and straight-laced man. He did not drink alcohol; he was neither married nor a womanizer (nor was he gay, although that had been mooted about as a possibility in his younger days, during which he had cut a striking figure in Alexandria society); he attended prayers dutifully; he was a political conservative, although he was somewhat closed-mouthed concerning his personal political convictions—he had risen to the vice presidency based on his success as a military general and his spotless reputation for integrity; and he lived simply and alone.

Today was an example of his lifestyle. National security dictated that the Egyptian president and vice president never appear in a public venue together. Thus, while the president was reviewing a military parade in the coastal city of Alexandria, Vice President Sulayman was here, alone, in his official, yet Spartan villa on the Corniche Al-Nil in central Cairo's Garden City district on the banks of the Nile.

Sulayman rose from his chair, turned on his radio, and walked over to the window. Across the waterway, on Al-Gazirah Island, he could see the Cairo Tower rising above the Al-Tahrir Gardens and the city's exhibition grounds. To the left of where he was standing, across Al-Zahra Street, was located the British embassy; the huge American embassy compound was located on the street behind his own residential complex. Below him, across the road and tied up to the banks of the Nile, was the *Isis*, one of the Hilton Hotel Corporation's tourist boats that normally steamed the mid-reaches of the Nile, between the ancient temple at Luxor—across the river from the Valley of the Kings, the burial ground for many of the pharaohs—and Aswan. Here, the gigantic Aswan Dam prevented the boats from sailing any farther up the Nile.

The floating luxury hotels rarely came down as far as Cairo anymore, because the jet age had arrived in Egypt. While a five-day meander up the Nile in Hilton and Sheraton splendor, with stops along the way to visit temples and tombs, was attractive to the well-heeled in search of exotic, yet comfortable, adventure, they rarely were prepared to devote more than five days to one activity. Thus, the wealthy tourists who visited Egypt usually toured the Cairo region—principally the pyramids of Giza, of course—by air-conditioned tourist taxi and saved "roughing" it in Upper Egypt for a separate trip.

The *Isis* was in Cairo because the president had engaged it to come down and to pick up the representatives of Jordan, Palestine, the United States, and the United Nations who had been working on the final wording of the settlement documents to be signed in Cyprus in less that two weeks. Their work now concluded and the draft documents having been sent off to all four corners of the globe, they were receiving a four-day vacation, steaming up the Nile and visiting various attractions en route, before they flew to Jerusalem for final double checking of the documents with the Israelis, who were the most problematical of the participants. The last of the representatives were boarding the boat as the vice president watched from his window, waiting for the radio coverage of the military parade in Alexandria to begin.

Maybe that was what was haunting him and bringing up the infamous day of the assassination of legendary Egyptian president Anwar Sadat. Sadat was killed both because of his far-reaching policies of participating in the earlier Middle East settlement agreements and for attempting to suppress the Muslim Fundamentalists in Egypt, when they opposed his policies with terrorist violence.

The current president was now concluding the process that Sadat had started and for which he had died—one clear morning in 1981 at an insignificant military parade. Sulayman thought the president was personally brave just as his predecessor had been personally brave, but he had never really made up his mind whether either of them had been right in trying to proceed to a settlement. He himself had been there—in the ranks—in the 1967 Sinai war. Several of his comrades had died in that short, humiliating conflict. If he were president, he felt, he would have to give the matter of trusting the Israelis to hold to a final settlement much deeper thought.

The radio began to crackle with the Egyptian national anthem. Sulayman turned from the window and settled in his chair. There was to be no presidential speech, but, by custom, all public appearances by the president had to be carried live by the national media. The television stations could usually apply sophisticated visual techniques to maintain an audience's interest, but this parade was too insignificant to rate television coverage. It was much more difficult for a radio announcer to provide exciting commentary for a military parade, where the listener could only hear faint music and the stamping of feet and clanking of military hardware in the background.

On this day, the radio commentator was fighting a losing battle in providing fresh insights into the endless passage of identically uniformed soldiers in front of a rostrum, where a frozen-smiled president—also a former army general—stood ramrod straight and stiffly saluted once every thirty seconds. In spite of himself and his loyal intention to remain alert to the description of the parade, the vice president sank into his chair and started to doze off.

However, on this day the radio commentator received an unwelcome boost to his commentary. In mid sentence during which he was identifying a new unit that was passing the reviewing stand, the announcer simply stopped speaking. All that could be heard in the background were a crackling sound, as if the radio reception was not good, and a hubbub of noise that was very uncharacteristic of a military review.

But, military man that he was, Sulayman immediately sat bolt upright. He knew that what he was hearing was not the result of poor radio reception, but was automatic weapons fire and a frantically screaming crowd. But the weapons carried in Egyptian military parades did not contain ammunition; soldiers had not gone on parade with loaded weapons for several decades. The weapons that had been carried in the parade during which President Sadat had been assassinated had not been loaded—or supposedly so. But, of course, some of them *had* been loaded.

"Oh, no. It has happened again," the vice president moaned. And he leaned over the side of his chair and retched onto the threadbare Oriental carpet.

But now the announcer was back on the air and was in control of his commentary once more. In a strained, but clear voice, the announcer was reporting that the radio transmission had experienced technical difficulties, that the parade had now concluded, and that the president was leaving the field. Martial music—canned music interposed from the radio studio—was playing in the background.

Sulayman, however, remained slumped in his chair, his face ashen, and his thoughts racing. Sulayman was not fooled. The parade had been scheduled to go on for at least twenty more minutes. And what the announcer had said—"The president has left the field"—was exactly what the announcer had said over the radio on the fateful day in 1981. President Anwar Sadat had, indeed, left the field on that day. But he had been carried from the field and he had over a dozen bullets in his lifeless body. Sadat's death had not been officially announced for more than eight hours, during which time the continued security of the nation and the effective transfer of power was being implemented. It was happening again.

Sulayman could already hear the running footsteps of his military guards coming up the stairs, and, in shock, he slowly rose from his chair and started for the door to let them in.

He got to the door more quickly than he expected. Luckily, he was already limp from the shock of the radio broadcast, for, as he neared the door, an explosion pushed in the large windows overlooking the Nile, hurling Sulayman's body to the base of the doorway and sending deadly shards of glass slicing into the overstuffed chair he had just vacated.

The guards pushed in the door and started a belated and ineffectual hunt around the suite. As two guards also hunted for evidence of an explosive device and another, the obvious leader of the squad, barked into a mobile phone concerning an assassination attempt on the vice president, the dignitary in question drifted over to the window and gazed down on the Nile.

He turned to the squad leader and said, "It wasn't for me."

The solider, in respect, pulled the phone away from his ear and responded, "Excuse me, Your Excellency, what did you say?" He wasn't really interested in hearing what this shell-shocked old man had to say, but he *was* the vice president and the soldier had been trained well in his duty toward authority figures.

Sulayman cleared his throat and spoke in a stronger voice: "I said the attempt was not on me. And you need to clear all channels on your mobile communications. You'll find soon enough that our attention will be needed elsewhere. We need to get over to the parliament building as soon as possible."

The soldier just stood there, looking confused.

"Come here," Sulayman commanded. The soldier obeyed.

"Look down there. That was the target here, not me."

The squad leader looked down at the Nile, but he saw nothing. This, of course, was the point. Where the luxury boat, the *Isis*, had floated just a few minutes ago, there now existed nothing but the usual accumulation of flotsam that could be seen at all times on the lower Nile.

The guard captain was still confused, but it was all quite clear to Sulayman. The president was dead, assassinated on the parade ground in Alexandria. And at almost the same precise moment the visiting peace process representatives had been blown up in the center of Cairo. Sulayman knew two things: one was that the final Middle East peace settlement was under active, coordinated attack, and the other was that he himself was now the president of Egypt. What he did not know at this precise moment was what this meant for the future of Egypt and for the possibility of genuine regional peace.

Chapter Three

It was amazing how well he had been able to assimilate into the local scene. it had probably been the choice of location that had saved him—that and his extraordinary expertise as a wood carver. Two years ago he had been Salem Qazzar, a Lebanese fighter of the Beirut-based, Tehran-controlled Hizballah terrorist organization. His unit, under the name of the Mouflon Brigade, had been training to conduct—and had been conducting—terrorist operations in the western quadrant of Cyprus, in the Troodos foothills to the north of the city of Paphos. Now he was Symeon Parikan, an artisan of mixed Cypriot and Lebanese parentage, who had returned to his father's homeland to ply his trade and to regain his national heritage.

It had been Qazzar's good fortune on that fateful day two years previously that he had become separated from his terrorist unit and had reached the planned rendezvous for being evacuated from Cyprus back to Beirut too late. Although he hadn't reached the rendezvous too late, the band that had gathered at the northwestern fishing and tourist village of Lachi had been cleared off a day earlier than scheduled because they had been hotly pursued by the Cypriot police forces. And those who had been evacuated as and where planned, but earlier than planned, had all perished, when their ship had been attacked off the coast of Cyprus.

It had been Qazzar's good fortune that he was sent off into the Troodos hills on a mission of his own before the Cypriot police set up their trap for his unit and that he arrived too late for the evacuation. He was in despair at the time, but he quickly appreciated that his life had actually been spared.

It was also Qazzar's good fortune that his mother—not his father, as he now claimed—had been Cypriot and that he was raised in London. Many London-raised Cypriots, who, like him initially, were not able to speak Greek, had moved back and forth between the UK and Cyprus. Such Cypriots by indirection are not fully accepted as totally "Hellenized"—Greek—in Cypriot society, but they are accepted as Cypriots. Qazzar certainly passed as Greek Cypriot in appearance. That is why he was sent on his solitary mission by his ill-fated terrorist brigade in the first place. Only he knew that it was his mother, not his father, who had been of Cypriot blood. His Londonized English speech also did not betray his dominant Lebanese origins.

When he recovered from the panic of having been irrevocably separated from his terrorist comrades, he had the presence of mind to ring through to a Hizballah contact in Beirut. He had, of course, telephoned for help to get away from the island and to return to Beirut. He had his falsified passport, but he didn't have the funds for an air ticket.

The Hizballah in Beirut had other ideas. Its leaders immediately recognized that Qazzar could still be of some use to them in Cyprus—more use probably than in Lebanon. He was a trained mountain fighter and assassin, but he was of no great standing in the movement, did not have any mentor who cared much about him, and had not been considered as a potential leader. In addition, they didn't want him to try to use his current forged passport to leave Cyprus. They suspected that the Cypriot police had gotten onto the terrorist band they had located in Cyprus through the passports. The police somehow had uncovered the alias identities those in the unit were using and had picked up a couple of the fighters when they tried to transit the airport in Larnaca. The Hizballah would rather have had Qazzar dead than in the hands of the Cypriot police interrogators.

To satisfy all requirements, the Hizballah contact gave Qazzar the telephone number for its most secret agent on Cyprus and a means by which Qazzar could verify that agent's credentials. The contact provided him with new documents, a new life, and a new home. Thus, for nearly two years now Salem Qazzar had been Symeon Parikan, a Greek Cypriot who had returned to his home country after many years of residence in London. Only in the past two weeks had Qazzar had any indication that his past might catch up with him. But he had taken care of that in a way that he was sure protected his identity and his location.

The choice for his new home had been extremely fortunate. The village of Fikardou was located in the eastern foothills of the Troodos Mountains some twenty-five miles to the southwest of the capital of Nicosia. It was thus almost in the very center of Cyprus. But it was now quite remote, even though it had once been in the center of the island's civilized world. Now all of the major thoroughfares on the island bypassed Fikardou by many miles—a good thing for someone trying to hide his past and to establish a new identity.

Fikardou was a delightful mountain village with a rich history, having once been considered the capital of the island and the center of its then-wealthiest city state, Tamassos. It, along with several other villages in the vicinity, had become known in recent years as a favorite retirement village for British citizens who were helping to reconstruct the buildings in the village and make it one of the most impressive restoration efforts on the island.

It was double good fortune for Symeon Parikan to have been resettled here. The villages of the valley were already being taken over by people who didn't have roots here that went back centuries, and Parikan was taken as just one more one-half British import who was helping the local economy even though he would never be accepted as a true villager. In fact, he was accepted by the villagers more fully than most of the Britishers who were moving into the valley—at least his father had been Greek Cypriot. Or so everyone thought.

The most fortunate aid to Parikan's quick assimilation, however, had been his great skill as a carpenter and a wood carver. The village was being brought to life—even if in an artistic folksy way that had never characterized it in the first place. People with Parikan's abilities were highly valued in the village, and his services were constantly sought, heavily booked, and richly rewarded. No one— British or Cypriot—had asked or was likely to ask many personal background questions about the quiet artisan who had such skills in a village under active restoration.

Parikan had settled quickly. It was only a short time before he was able to cut off all assistance from the unseen contact who had given him a new life. And within a year he had married, picking the most presentable Cypriot girl—and the one with the largest dowry—from the neighboring, larger village of Gurri. His choice in mates also had the desirable virtue of showing no curiosity in Parikan or his background beyond his ability to put groceries on the table and satisfy her in bed. She knew nothing of his wife and children in Lebanon. Salem Qazzar was no more; Symeon Parikan had a happy, prosperous new life.

Except for two nagging issues. First, not more than two weeks previously, when he drove into Politiko to buy some fruit for his wife, he ran across a woman who had been going around the village and asking people if they had seen the man in a photo she was showing. Imagine his shock when she put the photograph under his nose and he saw his own, clean-shaven face staring back at him. If he hadn't grown a beard, dyed his hair a darker color, and put on weight since he traded the rigors of mountain combatant life for village wine, she probably would have recognized him. But to her own misfortune she had not, and he had made sure she would not be nosing around his own village of Fikardou and finding someone who might see the resemblance. He was sure he had taken care of the problem, but he was left with the nagging question of who she was, how she had gotten his passport photo, and who might show up looking for her.

41

The other sword hanging over his head was that the Hizballah had his telephone number and had not relinquished claim to his life and to those services to which he had been trained other than carpentry. They could crush him in an instant, and he well knew the score. And here and now, in his Fikardou workshop on an early April afternoon, Parikan received the overseas telephone call that reactivated, after two years, his life as Salem Qazzar.

"Symeon Parikan?"

"Yes?" Parikan answered without any undue reserve, his mind on the grape design he was carving into the cedar wood to be used in the front eaves of a village house under restoration by a teacher at one of the English-language schools down in Nicosia.

"The harvest is ripe in the Al-Baqa' Valley."

Qazzar's heart leaped into his throat at the hearing of the nearly forgotten secret cipher, and his mind raced with the contrasting emotions of feared danger and remembered militancy.

"Speak. I'm alone."

"It has started. Do nothing, say nothing, but prepare for assignments and develop means of, and excuses for, within-country travel on short notice."

"Wait . . . ," Qazzar sputtered, as he tried to form the words of warning that he may already be in danger of detection.

But his response had not been quick enough. The telephone line had gone dead.

"What does it mean?" Qazzar wondered. "What has started?" He couldn't imagine what had happened to cause his activation. But his mind, as useful as it was for carpentry and for quietly and swiftly garroting an enemy of Islam in the dark of the night, didn't have an overdrive gear. Therefore, he stopped thinking about the overarching meaning of the Hizballah's activities and ideals and began devising plausible excuses that would permit him to take his old, beat-up Opel Kadet delivery coupe out of Fikardou upon demand.

Symeon's wife, Lenia, entered his shop from the door leading into the kitchen of their home, the home they had received as a traditional dowry present from her parents, who seemed quite proud to have a skilled wood carver in the family, even if he was a foreigner.

Without looking up at her, Symeon said, "That was a contractor in Nicosia. He has heard about my work and says he will employ me from time to time for good pay if I can leave on short notice to work on various jobs he has around Cyprus. The pay is good," he said. "It will be a good thing to get other jobs than here in the village. The work here will all be gone eventually." He spoke in halting, simple Greek. He was learning, if slowly, and his Greek was already better than Lenia's English was.

"Your mid-day meal is ready in the house. If you will be traveling much, we will need a new automobile. My brother can get us a BMW duty free. Maybe you will make enough for a new automobile." Lenia's statement had all the markings of a hopeful, often-raised topic.

"We'll see," answered Symeon, beating the dust off his trousers in preparation for his meal. After over a year of marriage, Lenia still showed no trace of curiosity about his activities or in the hours he kept outside the home. Beyond adding to their possessions, as possible, her interests seemed to be focused on having their first son—and on the activity that brought that about. Well, Symeon was doing everything he could to help in that department. Maybe he would work on that further after the meal, when he was supposed to be taking a siesta. Suddenly, he was no longer taking his new life and his future here for granted. Not after the telephone call from his Hizballah contact and the renewed nagging fear it had raised in just how well his true identity was concealed.

* * * *

Maria Solonos stood there staring at the blank wall of the Homicide Division, across the narrow courtyard. How often had she walked into this office and seen her predecessor and mentor, Takis Koniotis, standing at this same window, deep in thought? And how little thought had she given at these times to what this reflected in having to shoulder the great burdens of being chief of the Cypriot Police International Investigations Division?

It wasn't that she didn't feel up to the job. She had trained as the deputy to the best—to Takis Koniotis—and she had now held this position in her own right for two years. She thought she had done well. Crime by and against foreigners in Cyprus had not risen despite an influx of tourists and expatriate settlers, and Cyprus remained one of the safest countries in the world. What international-related crime there was here tended to only use Cyprus as a conduit and transit point rather than as a battleground. But international-related crime had not fallen in recent years, either. She knew she should be encouraged by the fact that Cyprus had more or less stayed the same while much of the rest of the world was sinking ever deeper in rising personal endangerment by crime, civil strife, and international terrorism.

But whatever police work there was in Cyprus that involved foreigners was her responsibility, and now Cyprus had been designated as the venue of the final Middle East peace settlement signing. The Cyprus government was euphoric. The Cyprus Tourist Organization was euphoric. The Cyprus Hoteliers Association was euphoric. Well they might be, but Maria could see the dark lining to this cloud. She had talked to Takis and he agreed that there were challenges—very serious challenges considering the small size of the Cypriot police force that could be put to her disposal. But even he had been more pleased than fearful that the conference was to be held here. Of course, he had to handle conference security wherever it was held, so his relative burden was totally different from hers.

Solonos sighed and turned from the window, picking up from her desk the list of names she was putting together of officers she would need to be reassigned to her during the conference. For this purpose she was sorry that Takis no longer was chief of police, the job he briefly went to after leaving the International Investigations Division and before having been appointed to head the United Nations' version of that unit. It would be very hard to convince the new police chief to reassign so many officers to her for the duration of the conference. However, the same police chief would hold her solely responsible for the well-being of all the important heads of state who would be on the Amathus coast in just two week's time.

She was saved from further worry on this topic by one of her senior investigators, Spyros Steliou, who popped his head into the door and tossed a folder onto the desk.

"The report on the mystery 'cave woman'?" Solonos queried.

45

"Yes. You needn't even bother opening the folder. She's still totally mute."

Solonos frowned and beckoned her investigator to a chair. "You'd just as well sit down while I read what's there. Maybe we can get a lead from what's not there." As Steliou sank into a chair opposite Solonos, the latter felt a stabbing pain in her solar plexus. She normally would be brainstorming this case with her deputy, Androulla Varnavidou. But Androulla had gone missing—in pursuit, her assistants said, of a case she was following quietly on her own. Everyone Solonos could spare was out looking for her colleague and friend. It wasn't peculiar for Androulla to be secretive about a lead she was following until it had developed, but it *was* peculiar for her to be out following a lead for this long without reporting in. Her talents were much needed now.

But Maria's concern for her deputy went much deeper than a need for her to be on duty. Solonos tried—not fully successfully—to put her worry about Androulla's whereabouts and welfare to the back of her mind by concentrating on the contents of the folder laying before her.

A very strange case. A woman had been found the previous evening living in a cave outside Paralimni on the southeast coast and below the posh Grecian Park Hotel. She had probably been there for more than a week, because she had been stealing food, towels, and lawn chairs from the hotel, which had been noting these small thefts for at least that long. There was no indication where she had come from or what she was doing in the cave.

The clothes she was wearing—now mostly in tatters—had once been very expensive and were finely sewn. The labels were from high-quality London fashion houses. She had yet to speak and she was not very responsive, but, following her original, inexplicable physical attack on the young couple that found her in the cave, she was quite placid and cooperative. Since no one in the area claimed knowing her, she was assumed to be a foreigner, and, thus, her case had landed in Maria Solonos's lap.

The mystery woman had been brought to Makarios Hospital here in Nicosia, where she was cleaned up as best as possible and photographed. It wasn't a good photo, however, because that was the only other point of agitated resistance the woman had shown so far after the initial attempt to maul the honeymooning couple from the Grecian Park. She obviously didn't want her picture taken—which made the case all that much more interesting for Maria.

Solonos picked up the photograph and walked over to the window to obtain better light. The woman was neither young nor old—possibly in her forties. Her visage showed signs of great beauty at least at one time, but who could tell from the combination of bad focus, bad positioning, and the bruises and swelling of her face. There was an air of familiarity about the face that tugged at the back of Mara's brain. But there was something else not quite right about the face. Solonos frowned and brought the photo closer to her own face for a more detailed inspection.

"Ah, I see you've noticed it," Spyros spoke up. "It's not an illusion. The right side of her face *has* fallen. The report is there in the file, the last document. And that may go far to explain the mystery."

Solonos returned to the desk and picked up the file. The report on the doctors' examination when the mystery woman had been brought into Makarios Hospital noted that she had suffered a slight stroke, probably very recently, and quite possibly just before or after she had taken up residence in the seaside cave. Her face probably would return to normal within a few days, and eventually there might not be any evidence of a stroke to be seen. But just as likely, she might have another stroke at any time, either slight or severe. Without knowing her medical history, the doctors disclaimed the ability—or responsibility—to predict much about how serious her condition was.

But if she had had a stroke—and here Solonos readily agreed with the doctors' hypothesis—that could mean she had temporarily lost her memory and her bearings and could go far in explaining her presence in the cave and her current behavior.

"Spyros, let's get this photograph into all of the papers. Someone must know who she is and is probably looking for her. She didn't just rise up out of the sea."

A logical hypothesis, of course, but, in fact, the woman *had* just risen up out of the sea.

* * * *

Qazzar's deeply hidden contact in Cyprus gently returned the telephone receiver to its cradle.

The caller in Lebanon couldn't say much on this line. It was to be taken for granted that the switchboard in this office was tapped and that all of the telephone calls were monitored. All information and instructions had to be conveyed in as innocuous a fashion as possible. But, by the same token, the information that everything had started had to be conveyed. They had to take the risk of making the telephone call to Nicosia.

The official sat back and contemplated the developments. It would be highly risky, of course, and the situation in the Middle East would never be the same again. But something had to be done. Moscow's default in the superpower cold war struggle had been bad enough. It had upset the balance, of course, but even worse than that it had entirely changed the nature of world politics. There had been a wild swing toward emphasis on domestic needs over foreign programs. This was bad for business. Very bad indeed. Now, if the Middle East situation, festering now for nearly the entire century, was also settled—or even was negotiated down to a minor irritant—this would be very, very bad for business.

No, the Amathus coast peace conference had to be undermined. It really must be stopped before it even started, and it was heartening to hear that the process had already successfully begun. But, if the leaders ever did reach Cyprus, they must be stopped here.

"Now, who was it who said they knew where the explosives that had been stolen from the abandoned asbestos mine up in the Troodos had been taken?" The official started to flip through the address book on the desk top.

"It's never too early to start making contingency plans."

* * * *

Takis Koniotis was greeted with very disturbing news when he returned to the newly constructed UNICIS headquarters building on the main UN peacekeeping forces base that straddled one of the ridges in the Makedonitissa suburb to the west of Nicosia. Although his

49

organization had heard rumors over the past week that the forces in the Middle East region whose interests would be threatened by a final peace settlement were beginning to coalesce and were even planning a summit conference of their own, it was only today that the plans for such a meeting were confirmed. The summit conference was programmed for the Mediterranean island nation of Malta, beginning tomorrow. That didn't give Koniotis and his unit much time to respond.

He called in one of his most experienced agents, Stefan Gunnerson, a Swedish criminologist who had come to the new unit following more than a decade working as the chief of UN security in Geneva. The two discussed the impending counter conference, and Koniotis put in a telephone call to the Maltese foreign minister, who was not at all inclined to stop the conference. In fact, he was more afraid of what the unwelcome guests who were forming up in his country would do to the small state of Malta if he tried to cancel the conference than he was of negative world public opinion for permitting the meeting to proceed.

"But no, of course the Maltese government would not object to a UN official such as you traveling to the island to monitor the proceedings." Koniotis wasn't surprised at the response; he knew the Maltese would be delighted to have the opportunity to push some of the responsibility for whatever happened off onto the world organization.

Koniotis and Gunnerson were making their plans to travel as soon as possible, when the bombshell telephone call was patched through to the UNICIS chief. The Egyptian president had been assassinated at a military parade. The deed was being credited to a known underground organization of Muslim fundamentalists that permeated the middle ranks of the Egyptian military and that opposed the president's role in the Middle East peacekeeping effort. In what was considered a related move—which connected the president's assassination with the Middle East peace conference—at nearly the precise time the president was shot, all of members of the internationally composed drafting committee for the peace pact had perished in the bombing of their boat in Cairo.

At nearly the same time he received this startling news, reports started coming in from elsewhere in the region. There was unusual activity across the board among the dissident movements throughout the Middle East. Koniotis realized that, under the circumstances, he could not, himself, go off to Malta. He had to stay to monitor this activity and try to devise countermoves.

But someone had to go to Malta, and Gunnerson was the only experienced agent that could be spared, although even Gunnerson could not easily be spared if the trend in activity in the Middle East accelerated. Gunnerson needed help.

Koniotis only chewed on this problem for a couple of minutes. He knew that Malta had been a British colony—just as Cyprus itself had been. This meant the British probably still had intelligence assets in Malta—just as they had them here—and would not be any more pleased than he was that the island was being used as a summit conference venue for all of the nefarious governments and terrorist organizations of the region.

He suddenly realized he knew what to do. He picked up the telephone and placed a call to the British high commission to his old friend Alec Stuart, who, not incidentally, was the chief of British Intelligence in Cyprus.

"Yes, I know about the convocation, Takis," Stuart quickly replied. "In fact, I'm shipping out for there this evening myself. I would be happy to have Gunnerson along and will ensure he receives every possible assistance of the British service in Malta."

Koniotis disengaged the conversation, relieved that he had managed to apply a bandage to the problem this time. But this had just emphasized how large his field of responsibility was and how few assets he could count on. Not for the first time that day, he wondered why he had ever taken this job.

Such was his concentration that he didn't see the look of raw hatred he was receiving through the glass partition that separated his office from the main operations room. The operations chief, the former American Federal Bureau of Investigations official, Thomas Jameson, had first watched Koniotis's discussion with the Swede with distress and then with barely disguised anger. Jameson thought that he himself was the best street agent in UNICIS. In fact, he had thought that he was so good that he would be in the chief's seat in short order. Why was Gunnerson receiving the call to go to Malta rather than him? He had been here for three months already, and Koniotis still had him tied down to routine desk work. Well, he'd show Koniotis. He'd show them all.

Jameson tugged at his billfold and removed a small folded sheet of paper. It was time to make that call. But not from here.

Jameson went over to the duty officer and signed out for the next hour. He'd best be far away from the reach of the UN base switchboard when he made this telephone call.

The feeling that someone's eyes were boring into him finally broke Koniotis's concentration. But he misjudged the source of the scrutiny. A guilty conscience had told him that his wife had divined—as was her special talent—that he was going to stand her up for dinner again.

"Oh, well," he reasoned as he picked up the telephone to call her with the bad news. "With what is happening now, I'll just be getting home late this evening. If I'd gone to Malta, I would be missing more than dinner at home."

Chapter Four

Takis Koniotis's feeling that his wife's eyes were boring into him as he sat by the window in his office on the UN base was right on the mark. She was, in fact, staring straight at him even though, at this distance, she couldn't actually see him. Caitlyn Spencer Koniotis, an American archaeologist and honey-blonde, but wholesome beauty who could be equally mistaken as a high-fashion model or a college professor, was sitting at the double window of the workroom she had established in the house she inherited two years previously. The house commanded the next ridge over toward the Makedonitissa Valley from the UN base in the buffer zone to the west of the capital of Nicosia. And the window of her workroom looked directly toward the new UNICIS headquarters building that had been built within sight of the new Koniotis home.

Caitlyn Koniotis had come to Cyprus a few years previously as a visiting scholar in archaeology to help with a Neolithic dig. Her specialty was carbon dating, and she had already gained an enviable reputation for her mastery in the field. On top of this, her talent was in channeling back to the past. Since arriving in Cyprus, she had also been responsible by means of a well-honed intuition—one that rivaled her husband's reputation for sharp intuition in his own field—for discovering three new, significant ancient sites in Cyprus.

Her original study grant had been sponsored by the Ledra Foundation, whose founder had been Eleni Piccard, a businesswoman who represented the Cypriot end of a larger family-owned French shipping empire and who owned first-class hotels and a handicraft exporting firm in her own right. Mrs. Piccard had taken Caitlyn under her wing, and, to Caitlyn's great surprise, had willed her this home on a mesa above the Makedonitissa Valley when she had been murdered at one of her mountain hotel restaurants.

When they were first married, Caitlyn and Takis lived in the house within the commercial district of greater Nicosia that he inherited from his parents, but they moved out here two years ago, at the same time Takis accepted the job as head of the newly forming UNICIS. The location of the organization's headquarters here in Cyprus was a condition Takis had set for having taken on the international position.

The setting of their new residence was ideal for Takis; his commute to work was less than ten minutes, including clearing the security gates at the UN base—a time that often was challenged by the worldwide crises he was called in to help quell. Once at work, he could keep an eye on his family from his office window on the opposite ridge. Caitlyn's commute to the Cyprus Museum near the Paphos Gate into the old walled city of Nicosia had been lengthened, however. This was not a big problem in and of itself. Caitlyn could still get to the museum in not much more than fifteen minutes. But a new wrinkle had been added to her life. A year and a half ago she had become a mother.

The Koniotis's solution to balancing a family and two demanding jobs was twofold. First, they succumbed to the desire of Takis's widowed aunt, Irene, to function as nanny and housekeeper. And second, Caitlyn arranged to be able to do much of her own archaeological research work at home.

The house had come with an attached double garage, one that inexplicably also had a double window with a breathtaking view— across the UN base buffer zone ridge to the northwestern end of the Kyrenia Mountain range—in its side wall. Caitlyn had the garage walled in and winterized, and—because Takis wouldn't hear of having his beloved old Jaguar saloon car sitting in the open—she had a covered carport built for the automobiles between the old garage and the street. She now had a perfectly serviceable and sunny workshop— far lighter than her basement office at the Cyprus Museum, if not quite as convenient to her research.

The only sticking point, as far as Takis had been concerned, was that Caitlyn was threatening to bring her work home in more ways than one—just as she had already done at their former residence. The original Koniotis home had been located immediately adjacent to an ancient, unexcavated acropolis—the hill upon which the major public buildings of a Greek city state were located. Shortly after Takis and Caitlyn were married and moved into the house, Caitlyn found a major royal tomb complex at the base of the acropolis that far predated the Greek period. As a result, the yard of their house and the open area

56

under its bedroom wing had been turned into the headquarters of an archaeological team and a storehouse for artifacts.

Shortly after moving into the Makedonitissa house, which was perched immediately above the ancient monastery that had given the valley its name, Caitlyn noticed that their hill had been fortified. The hilltop was laced with trenches, and a network of concrete pillboxes circled its rim. Remnants of a trench ran the length of the hilltop, which also was sprinkled with foxholes that, in the dry season, when all the spring foliage had burned off, made any part of the area that wasn't landscaped appear almost like a lunar surface.

Caitlyn had asked how far back the oldest fortifications could be dated, and Takis had made the mistake of saying he didn't know. The ridge the UN base was on had been a military encampment as far back as recorded time, he thought. It was a British base before the UN forces moved in and an Ottoman Turk base before that. It had once supported a Venetian fortress, and there was some evidence of Greek fortifications. All of the hills around this ridge were also fortified, most recently in 1974 when the Turkish army invaded up to the boundaries of the UN base in this sector and the Greek forces dug into the hills toward Makedonitissa in case the Turks overran the Un base as well.

Caitlyn had not been able to find any information on the history of the hill under her new house, so she had started walking around it on her own and poking here and there for signs of habitation that predated the 1974 fortifications. To Takis's chagrin, she had found something. On the slope facing the old monastery—not just below the house and opposite the monastery, which buffered the hill from the International Fair Grounds, but to the south, across the road

57

from the national sports complex—Caitlyn had found evidence of an ancient wall. She had wanted to call in the museum archaeology team—and still wanted to do so—but Takis put his foot down. He said he had had enough of the noise and inconvenience of having become the center for an archaeological dig at his family home. But he also told Caitlyn that if she let the archaeologist start digging at the base of this hill, her precious house might be undermined and end of sliding down into the monastery.

"Anywhere you poke a shovel in on Cyprus will come up with evidence of ancient history, Caitlyn," he'd said. "But Cyprus isn't a museum. We have to live here. Cyprus is for the living."

"But this is your past," Caitlyn had responded. "This is your connection back through the ages."

"And we honor it. We have excavated examples of it back through time and we preserve quite a bit of it. But our past is just too rich for us to be able to afford to rope off every sign of it we find and not develop our own, newer civilization. We have to choose. You have to choose, Caitlyn. Do you want to live in a museum case or in the home Eleni left to you?"

Caitlyn hadn't taken him seriously, but she did love the house and would never do anything to endanger it. She was enthralled with it—visibly delighted—from the first time Eleni Piccard brought her here. That was probably why Eleni, whose husband and son had predeceased her—reasoned to have been murdered in Kyrenia Castle during the chaos of the 1974 invasion, their bodies left undiscovered in one of the castle's remote dungeons for the past twenty years—had left the villa to Caitlyn.

The two-story residence was large, but it was also light and airy. The views from the hilltop were gorgeous. The rear terrace looked down into the wealthy residential area in the Makedonitissa Valley and across the older part of Nicosia and the central, Mesaoria plain to the Kyrenia range, running the length of the island from west to east. The front of the house looked directly down the Mesaoria across the UN base ridge toward Morphou Bay. This view was bracketed between the western end of the Kyrenia Mountains to the north and the distant Troodos Mountain range to the south.

Caitlyn had inherited the house furnished, and it had been decorated with the Cypriot folk motifs that had been authenticated through the work of the Ledra Foundation and manufactured by Eleni Piccard's own handicraft center.

The condition of the furnishings, which Caitlyn had once particularly admired, had been the one blemish on Caitlyn's fairytale inheritance. When the Koniotises took possession, they found that the house had been ransacked. It was true that it had sat vacant for more than six months while the will was being settled—and that the Koniotises had no idea they were inheriting until the will was made public—but it was very unusual for such a burglary to occur in Cyprus. Especially, in this case, because none of the electronic equipment, carved pine furniture, or valuable paintings by Cypriot artists had been taken.

Most of the furnishings themselves had been left intact, although turned on end. But all of Piccard's personal memorabilia had been broken or taken—or at least most of it had. While moving in, Caitlyn had found one box of family papers and photos behind some construction material that had been left in a storage closet in the loft area above the bathroom in the master bedroom suite. Caitlyn had briefly looked through the box but had left the carton where it was, saddened at the thought that there appeared to be no living relatives of Eleni's in Cyprus who would be interested in having it. When she had time, she planned to have some of the photographs framed for display in the house. She thought that something should be displayed here of the woman who had built and cherished this house.

While her gaze had gone from her work to the UNICIS building that could be seen on the next ridge, Caitlyn's thoughts had gone once again to the unfortunate Eleni Piccard, as they often did. The woman had possessed everything in life except for her family, and, in the end, everything else she possessed in large quantities had been meaningless to her.

But then battle sounds from the playroom across the hallway broke into Caitlyn's thoughts and brought her out of her reverie. She reached the room just as one twin, Eric, was about to bean the other twin, Ahmad, with a plastic airplane. The twins had supposed to have been girls. The medical tests had said so. Caitlyn's intuition had even said so. But that he had boys instead only told Caitlyn that life could not be pinned down—that it would always bring surprises. At least Takis had been pleased. Like any Cypriot man, he had assumed that sons would come first.

If her own mother could only see her now, she mused. Caitlyn's mother had been so sure that Caitlyn would never marry, let alone have children. Caitlyn's focus on her archaeology work had seemed to be so intense that there was no room for anything else in her life. Well, mother's aren't always right—as Caitlyn had learned in the gender of her children. While Caitlyn was doing all she could to maintain her exciting professional career, there was no doubt in her mind that her husband and her twins came first. So much had happened to her here in Cyprus over the past few years. Some of it had been life threatening. All of it had taught her that nothing was more important to her than Takis and her sons.

The telephone rang as soon as she had negotiated a tenuous peace between the active one-and-a-half-year-old boys and turned them back to Irene's care.

"That will be Takis, changing our plans for the evening," she thought as she headed back to her workroom. She wasn't psychic. She had been listening to the radio news for the previous hour's cast and had heard about the probability that the Egyptian president had been assassinated. There had been no official announcement of his death, as yet, but no one was fooled by the official silence—certainly not anyone outside of Egypt. This, of course, would mean that the family would not be seeing much of Takis for some time.

"He will have to answer one question for me before I'll let him go," Caitlyn thought with determination as she picked up the receiver.

It was, as she had surmised, her husband. Before she would let him disconnect, however, she asked him her question: "You haven't given Paul an answer yet, and we need to get back to him. Will you be his best man?"

"Yes, yes. The conference should be over by then and we should be able to get away for the wedding. It just slipped my mind."

"I wonder if it just slipped your mind," mused Caitlyn to herself when the conversation was over. Paul Conte, formerly political officer of the American embassy in Cyprus and now posted to Jordan, had been her first male friend—more than a friend, she admitted to herself—when Caitlyn had just arrived in Cyprus. She had known him before she had known Takis, and they had been close—even intimate on one occasion—when she first met Takis. Ever since Paul had asked Takis to be his best man and Takis had dragged his feet in replying, Caitlyn had been worried that Takis harbored some sort of resentment about the relationship that she had once had with Paul—a short relationship; it had barely started and then had abruptly ended when she realized that it was Takis she really wanted.

This was the first shadow that had been cast over their marriage, and it disturbed her deeply, as any possible first crack in a fairytale dream would. But now Paul was getting married, and to one of the Koniotises' best friends, Ellen Larkin. Ellen was a political officer with the Canadian high commission, although Caitlyn knew with a great deal of certainty that Ellen also was the Canadians' chief intelligence officer in Cyprus.

Surely Takis didn't bear a grudge about the past. But no one ever knew what would ruffle the feathers of a Greek man. Often when Caitlyn had assumed that her husband's American education would prompt an American response to an issue, he surprised her by being very Greek instead. If Takis resented Paul's past relationship with Caitlyn, he certainly had done nothing to reveal his feelings over the past few years, however. The fact that Paul had asked him to be his best man was proof of this.

"Ah, well," Caitlyn thought, as she went back to her dating of an amphora that had been recovered from Paphos harbor when it was being dredged to remove the ever-shifting silt, "Takis has every reason to know how much I love him."

She did not have time for further contemplation on that worrying topic. World War Two for the afternoon had broken out in the playroom, and it was almost time for Irene to be relieved of her guard duties for the evening so that she could start making supper.

"What would we do without Irene?" Caitlyn mused, as she carefully wrapped the delicate pottery she'd been working on and labeled the container. Hers was not the standard experience of motherhood, she fully realized.

* * * *

"What arrogance! What audacity!" Egyptian vice president 'Abbas Sulayman—no, now Egyptian president Sulayman—stormed around his private suite at the vice presidential residence in silent anger. Silent, because he had no idea who to trust or what he could do, or even what he wanted to do, for that matter.

He had been packing his necessities in a suitcase for delivery to the presidential palace, packing the bag himself in reflection of his self-imposed austere lifestyle, when his favorite captain of the guard force detailed to him entered the room and drained all of the self-confidence Sulayman had pumped up in anticipation of the announcement to be broadcast within an hour that the president had died and that he was now the president of Egypt.

The captain had been like a son to him, and there he stood, saying that he was a member of the Muslim fundamentalist military officer organization that had been responsible for the president's death and that he was proud to serve and represent that group. They wanted Sulayman to know in no uncertain terms that it had been they who had assassinated the president and that they had done so because they considered his cooperation in a final peace settlement with the Israelis to be an act of treason against Islam and against Egypt itself.

The young officer stood before Sulayman to claim his loyalty to the cause or to put him on notice that he himself would be eliminated if he followed in the traitorous steps of the deceased president, and that the president had died for following in the steps of his predecessor.

Sulayman had been noncommittal and had tried to stall, offering to discuss the issue with his protégé at greater length. But the young captain refused to discuss the issue and had departed, as silently as he had come. Sulayman knew he would never see the man again, although he would try his best to have him searched out and arrested. Regicide was not to go unpunished however justified the principles might be.

The Egyptian leader caught himself up short. And just what were his own views and convictions on regional peace and the Israelis? Up to now he had been the model military man. He had not allowed himself to question his president's strategic decisions; he had expended his energies in helping to provide the tactical support to realize those strategic goals. But now *he* was the president. Now *his* personal views and goals were important. But what *were* his personal views and goals?

Sulayman's head was spinning. He had not realized until now that he had not been a leader to this point. No matter how important he had been and how many troops and projects he had commanded, he himself had remained a follower.

He was suddenly frightened. The visit and disclosures of his subordinate had not frightened him half as much as this new challenge did. Would he be a leader? Could he be a leader?

* * * *

After departing the UNICIS headquarters building, Thomas Jameson stopped at the Samurai bar in the nightlife sector at the mouth of the Makedonitissa Valley, near where October 28 Street intersected with the main cross-town boulevard, Grivas Dhigenis. The former American FBI agent had trained well, and, although he was quite sure that no one in his office was the least bit suspicious of his activities, he was taking no chances. He quickly involved himself in the revolving darts game with a group of UN soldiers he recognized from the base. The game was on whenever the pub was open. He also lost—purposefully—and stood the bar to drinks before he slipped off to the wall telephone near the toilets and placed his call.

An hour and a half later, Jameson and his contact were sitting at the back of the Milano Café, an Italian eatery that almost never closed—a rarity in Cyprus, where it was difficult to find a restaurant open for lunch or an early dinner. The mostly foreign and largely men-seeking-men clientele in the Milano, located on Grivas Avenue several street lights farther toward central Nicosia from October 28 Street and within the shadow of the Israeli embassy, fluttered around the restaurant like bees around a hive, here more for the social contact than for a meal or a drink.

Jameson and his contact would be unobtrusive in all this confusion but, at the same time, could maintain a direct line of sight on all possible approaches to the restaurant.

It didn't take long for Jameson to pass on all that he knew.

"Well, it seems the action now is in Malta, wouldn't you say?"

"Yes, of course, but Koniotis wouldn't send me," Jameson spat out angrily.

A long pause, and then: "It's a shame. A man of your extraordinary abilities would be very useful there. Is there no way you could go anyway?"

"I do have my two days off starting tomorrow, but . . . I don't know."

"We'd like to help, and it would be very useful for us to have you there. There's something you could do for us there. What if we were to arrange it?"

And, with that, Thomas Jameson was off to Malta.

Chapter Five

Ayman Abu Hani, former Lebanese ambassador to Cyprus, patron of the Tehran-sponsored Hizballah terrorist movement, and a key powerbroker in the summit meeting of forces in opposition to the impending final Middle East settlement, laughed dryly and walked over to the window overlooking Mediterranean Street and the mouth of the Grand Harbor of Valetta, Malta. He paced back and forth between the fireplace and the window of the small lounge in the Mediterranean Conference Center, the former Sacra Infermeria Hospital that had been founded by the Order of the Knights of St. John in 1574. He had arranged for private use of the room in order to be able to gather some of his closest associates together before the next day's meeting. Later he planned a very private meeting here with an emissary coming in from Cyprus who was in a position to give him an update on how the coming hated Middle East peace accord signing was shaping up, which was another reason for the need for strict privacy.

Obtaining the room in this huge complex had not been difficult. The prime minister was scared stiff at the potential danger of having this counter summit in Malta, and he would do anything to keep Abu Hani happy and quiet—at least to his face. Abu Hani wasn't at all sure what the Maltese were up to behind his back, and he knew that they were as close as lips and teeth with their former colonial masters, the British—although Abu Hani didn't feel entirely vulnerable on that score. In return for the cooperation of the Maltese, therefore, Abu Hani had made only partial promises of good conduct for any of the groups he had called together.

Malta, composed of a small group of islands located in the center of the Mediterranean, just off the tip of Sicily but well within the embrace of the huge, militantly Islamic north African country of Libya to the south, felt itself to be quite vulnerable to the whims of the Middle Eastern states.

"What amuses you?" asked Abu Hani's closest associate, the controller of the Piccard's French shipping conglomerate and the arranger of transportation for the major terrorist organization of the region, as he sank his tall, thin, elderly, yet still-elegant frame into a comfortable chair and sipped at his martini.

"There—out there. I know The Colonel's yacht and his Libyan patrol craft are just beyond sight out there in the Mediterranean, preparing to host tomorrow's conference. And here sit the Maltese, too frightened to even call for help. What a change a couple of hundred years make. Here, in this very same harbor, the Knights of St. John held off a four-month siege by the entire might of the Ottoman Turk empire in the mid sixteenth century. On that occasion their obstinacy prevented the Turkish invasion of Europe through Italy and France. And now, just over four hundred years later, the forces of Islam can walk into the city at will, and the Maltese bow their heads in fear. That one mad Libyan colonel out there, with a navy of only three patrol boats, is more powerful than was the full might of the Ottoman Turkish empire."

"I don't think I'd call The Colonel mad, if I were you," Piccard responded with a smile. "At least not until this conference is over—and certainly not within his hearing."

"You never have been quite comfortable with the play fellows we have acquired, have you, my friend?"

The Frenchman answered with a sigh, as he rose to refresh his martini. "Business is business. I won't question the people who, as you say, we have to 'play' with to keep business healthy. But don't you think it is more than a little risky to bring all of these forces together in a meeting?"

"What do you mean?"

"Well, as you yourself indicate in referring to the esteemed chief of state of Libya, not all of these people are well balanced. In fact, most of them hate each other almost as much as they hate the idea of a Middle East Settlement. And our strategy until now has been to play one off against the other—at a comfortable distance from all."

"The operable word, of course, is 'almost'," Abu Hani interjected. "They are all fanatical; I'll grant you that. But that means that as long as they have to hang together to prevent a final Middle East peace, they will do so. No longer than that, I grant you. But that is enough for our purposes. All of those who show up here can be counted on to stick together as long as they have a shared enemy as prominent as Israel and the Mideast peacekeeping plans of the United States, Great Britain, and the United Nations."

"And the Syrians?"

"They will be here, although I'm not sure they will participate in the end. But, as they are one of the more rational and cautious—and cagey—elements in this, I don't think we need worry that they will disrupt the conference or sell us to the West."

"And your own government?"

"Those in power in Lebanon are hiding under their beds, as usual. They are so mesmerized by the possibility of renewing Beirut as the tourist-Mecca Paris of the Middle East that they will neither show up here nor give us any problems. I still control Beirut's policies on Middle East issues. As long as I control Lebanon's external affairs, my country will do my bidding—or, at worst, not oppose them

"I still worry about the Libyans. They are so unstable, and, here, you have put yourself under their control. Why can't we have the conference right here? Why do we have to meet out at sea under the control of The Colonel?"

"First and foremost, of course, is that The Colonel would not cooperate otherwise, Beyond that, if we take rationality into consideration, it's primarily because that was the bone I threw to the Maltese to keep them cooperative. I said that, although most of us would be accommodated on Malta, we would actually meet off shore, and the Libyan colonel would not himself be stepping foot on Malta and, technically, they can claim the conference isn't being held on Malta. Also, the ship will be more controlled. Here, I fear too many spies to keep in order. There, we will, of course, be in a veritable den of spies and of treachery. But it will be the spies we know. We'll at least know everyone we're dealing with. Besides, I have the question of safety under the mad colonel's wing under control."

"How so, if I might ask?"

"The Colonel may be mad, but he's not crazy. Also, in spite of what many think, he's not self-destructive. He has survived more attempts on his life—including by American bombers—than any other Middle Eastern leader. He might consider blowing the rest of us up on that yacht out there, but I don't think he would blow himself up in the process. And, as irrational as his demand for isolation and privacy seems to be, he can make a strong argument that it is what works for him. And, besides . . ." Abu Hani paused and looked up at Piccard, as if he was considering just how trustworthy this partner of his was.

"And . . . ?"

"And, I have someone who both helps serve the Libyan leader and is on the boat launch crew from the yacht. When we leave for the ship, he will assure me that The Colonel is actually on board. That being the case, we can risk going on out to the yacht. If my man doesn't appear as part of the launch crew, one of us will get deathly ill on the dock and our small group of associates will fail to appear on the yacht. It will be devastating, of course, if all of the representatives we have tried to assemble should die unexpectedly, but we have other contingency plans. Should the settlement conference actually get started in Cyprus, we have assets there as well."

"Speaking of planning, where are the others? And speaking of devastating, where is that beautiful, wicked wife of yours?"

71

"The others should be here shortly. Alas, my dear Suzanne outlived her usefulness to me. I had to have her put down. I found that she was using her feminine wiles to her own purposes."

"Pity," Piccard responded, trying to pick just the right intonation. He himself had indulged in Suzanne Abu Hani's feminine wiles, but he had also counted her as one of his most useful informants, even on her husband's activities. He thus didn't want to leave the impression that he was especially saddened at her demise.

"Yes, a pity," shot back Abu Hani, who knew precisely to the number of rendezvous and sexual positions—and amount of shared information—what Piccard's interest in and involvement with Suzanne had been. But this was not the place or time. "Ah, here's another one of our comrades now," he said, slightly irritated at the change of subject because he was rather enjoying the effect of Suzanne's death on Piccard, which the Frenchman was trying to conceal—but not convincingly so to Abu Hani.

However, the new arrival had brought disturbing news. The new investigations unit of the United Nations had managed to get an agent into Malta. Both the Maltese and the local British intelligence assets were pledged to cooperate with an investigation into the summit meeting. If the representatives of the various terrorist forces realized they would be identified and their activities in Malta might be scrutinized, they might scurry back under their rocks and not make their planned appearances.

"A small irritant, of course," Abu Hani said, brushing the news on the presence of a UNICIS agent aside almost as incidental, "but we do need to handle it before it gets out of control. And we need to handle it in such a way that the delegates will know we are in control and watching out for their well-being."

Abu Hani went back to the window and began to develop a plan.

In the end, the most recent arrival was sent off to take care of the matter.

"I do have a contact or two who can take care of the problem," Abu Hani said, "one of whom I've been informed is just arriving. Leave it to me. I'll handle it myself, if and as necessary."

And then Abu Hani and Piccard were alone once more.

"Now, my friend," Abu Hani said as he turned back to a visibly shaken Piccard. "Before the others arrive, what was it we were saying about Suzanne?"

"Nothing. Absolutely nothing," Piccard nervously responded, his face in his martini glass to hide his involuntary expression of slight consternation from his dangerous colleague.

* * * *

"Nope. Nope. Yep. Nope. Absolutely." American Embassy Amman political officer—really the U.S. Treasury Department's agent in Jordan—Paul Conte was going through the invitations on his desk. He usually wasn't this selective. The affable, somewhat cocky, but decidedly handsome American, built in the style of the movie version of a football quarterback, loved to eat, drink, and socialize, especially on someone else's budget. But the diplomat was closing out work at the Jordan embassy. He wouldn't miss the large, fortress-like structure that had been plopped down on a dusty hill in the Abdun sector to the southwest of the center of the seven-hilled city of Amman five years ago. But he would miss the assignment and the Jordanians, who he had found to be very friendly and personable.

Two weeks from now he and Ellen would be married here in Amman. She already was here. She was staying over at the Regency Palace Hotel, near the center of the city. And two weeks following that he would start working as an assistant professor of international economics at McGill University in Montreal. Not an ideal situation, because Ellen would be working in a government office in Ottawa, nearly 100 miles away, but they hoped to find somewhere to live that would split the difference in the mileage that each had to drive to work. At least they had eventually made the decision that both of their careers would be restarted.

Although they had met on Cyprus, where Conte had held down a job identical to this one at the American embassy there and Ellen Larkin was the relatively new political officer at the Canadian high commission, their jobs just didn't match unless they could perpetually find assignments in the same countries. This was an impossibility—on security grounds alone—because they worked for different governments, both in intelligence roles.

Ellen's job was highly classified, and Paul had to promise to apply for Canadian citizenship for her to be able to remain in her line of work at all. He kept telling her that she would never require greater evidence of his love for her than that he was willing to give up not only his own career, but his U.S. citizenship as well, to be able to marry her.

He had once never thought he would feel this way about anyone other than Caitlyn Spencer—now Caitlyn Koniotis. Their fling had been brief and had come in the context of Caitlyn's innocent involvement in and endangerment by an international drugs and arms smuggling case. The adrenalin let loose by the experience had been responsible for both throwing Caitlyn into his arms and pulling her away into the arms of another. The other was Takis Koniotis, who had been the investigating officer in the smuggling case.

As Paul swept the "nope" invitations off into the trashcan, he wondered for the umpteenth time whether Takis would accept his request to serve as his best man. He had thought it a simple, natural request. But, since Takis had not responded immediately, Paul was beginning to wonder if Takis held a grudge against him because he had had a prior relationship with Caitlyn. Greeks were strange that way. But, did he really invite Takis to be his best man because he wanted to see Takis again, or because he wanted to see Caitlyn again?

"Nah!" he exclaimed out loud as he tipped his top desk drawer over the trashcan. That was over. He had found Ellen. She was truly amazing. A petite, perky, sweet, next-door-neighbor type on the surface, but a very smart, highly competent intelligence agent underneath. Yes, he knew that she was the intelligence chief for the Canadians in Cyprus. That was the context in which he had met her in the first place. But she had also stolen his heart.

Ellen would not give up her profession, but she had been willing to give up her current posting. So, after their wedding, they would be settling in Canada and she would be working in Ottawa as an analyst.

Paul picked up the "absolutely" card. It was an invitation to the palace for a reception on the next evening. That would be his last official event in Amman. He could say no to all of the other invitations, but he could not say no to the Jordanian king, who he had grown to know personally during his year's tour here and who, along with his elegant, American-raised wife, had been very gracious to him. The king was even sponsoring a dinner for Ellen and him to mark their wedding. But that would be after Paul had given up his official duties here.

"We'll have time after the reception for dinner out at the Re Kan Zamen," Paul thought. This popular restaurant and shop complex was located about seven miles south of Amman. Before it was renovated into an entertainment complex, it had been a fortress and horse stables dating back to the nineteenth century. Its Arabic name translated to "once upon a time" in English. Ellen had heard about it and wanted to see it. So much to do and so little time to do it. Paul pulled out the other top drawer of his desk and turned it over the trashcan. Moving on to a new life had its difficulties and finalities.

* * * *

"Where's Jameson?" Takis Koniotis bellowed. He was beginning to be inundated with all of these reports on unrest in the Middle East underworld following the news of the assassination of the Egyptian president and members of the peace settlement team in Egypt and of the convocation on Malta of the forces opposing a final Middle East settlement. He needed help putting all of this information in order and he needed Jameson, one of his best section chiefs, to help him make order out of this chaos. He had really wanted to send Jameson to Malta with Gunnerson, or maybe instead of Gunnerson, but he couldn't spare his operations chief. He needed his very best people here at UNICIS headquarters as this complex challenge unfolded.

"Where's Jameson?" Koniotis repeated as he stood in his office doorway and surveyed the busy operations floor.

"He's gone for two days," came back the reply from the duty officer. "He said he needed some rest. He had two days scheduled off anyway. Said he would be out of touch during that time. Something about needing to recharge his batteries. That he was worn out. I didn't think to question him. He's a section chief."

"Yes, of course," Koniotis answered with resignation. It wasn't Jameson's fault that they were shorthanded and everything was falling apart. Maybe it was just as well. If Tom came back to work refreshed, he'd be just in time to take over for quite a few very tired people.

Koniotis turned to reenter his office and was followed in by two of his favorite people in the world, his deputy director, Safa Ziya, and his head of laboratory research, John Patterson. It was quite unusual that Safa Ziya would be one of his favorite people, because she was a Turkish Cypriot. But over the previous few years, the two Cypriots had learned to work with each other to fight crime island wide in Cyprus.

He and Ziya had trained at the same university in America— the University of Texas at Austin—although Ziya had come and gone from there several years before Koniotis attended the university's criminology school. She also made a much deeper impression on the school than Koniotis had, having received her doctorate under a Fulbright scholarship and having taught for a time before returning to northern Cyprus as one of the Turkish Cypriots' chief police investigators. After earning his masters at the university, Koniotis returned to the Greek side of Cyprus and rose in the investigation ranks.

Over the previous three years the two had combined forces to tackle a whole panoply of international crimes that transcended the buffer zone. Their willingness and ability to work together had helped considerably in reaching solutions of mutual problems quickly that benefited the island as a whole.

When Koniotis was named as head of the UN investigations office and was given free rein to choose his own staff, Safa Ziya had been his first appointee. Such was her reputation internationally, a reputation that went far beyond her work in northern Cyprus, that no one batted an eye at the appointment. The location of the new UNICIS headquarters in the buffer zone on Cyprus perfectly matched Ziya's circumstances. She could enter the zone directly from the Turkish side, and, as an appointed UN official, she was able to get to work directly with Koniotis on the base without hassle.

The appointment of John Patterson to head the lab *did* raise a few eyebrows. Patterson, a Britisher, was a well-known agronomist and had been teaching at a university near Famagusta in the northern zone. This in itself could hardly have been considered to qualify him for the laboratory head at the new UN unit. However, he had helped Koniotis in a major terrorism case—the kidnapping of a Russian diplomat's wife; of a UN official; and of Koniotis's own wife. Caitlyn—and he had thus proved his worth.

He was a specialist in analyzing and providing geographic placement for the sorts of fibers and soils that are picked up on a person's clothing. In doing so, he had developed a precise scientific methodology of research. It was this research talent and precision, and Patterson's amazing capacity to grasp problems and apply innovative scientific solutions that had prompted Koniotis to appoint the man as head of the UNICIS lab.

Koniotis would have made these two appointments to his senior staff even if Ziya and Patterson had not been living together. Indeed, he had received some criticism for appointing Patterson as well as Ziya precisely because they were living together. They had been an unlikely couple. Ziya was no spring chicken. She also was quite plump and frumpy and walked with a limp. Patterson was half her size. He was bald and near-sighted and very shy. But they had found each other—probably recognizing the quality of outstanding intellect in each other as well as the mutual need for companionship. And now they lived together—they weren't married, they just lived together—in Safa Ziya's small apartment in the Turkish zone of Nicosia.

The two were almost inseparable, and they entered his office together today.

"I know you are swamped, and I've come to help out," Ziya started in, "but I wondered if you'd like to hear what we have found out about the Piccard holdings."

"You know I'm always game to hear about the Piccard business," responded Koniotis. Even though his wife had been friendly with Eleni Piccard, Koniotis had been trying to track down the connection between the French shipping house and the movements of terrorists in the region for the past two years. Three years earlier Koniotis cracked a scheme in which a Cypriot travel agency was providing false documents and travel tickets and was laundering money for members of the radical Abu Nidal faction of the Palestinian Liberation Organization. At the same time, the then French ambassador to Cyprus, who just happened to be a Piccard—Jacques Piccard—the nephew of Eleni Piccard through her deceased husband, Guy Piccard—had been implicated in related illegalities, which included drugs and arms smuggling and murder. Jacques Piccard subsequently was returned to France for trial and incarceration.

More recently, Koniotis discovered that the documentation, ticketing, and money laundering services, plus the actual transportation of terrorists, had transferred over to subsidiary companies of the Piccard shipping empire. But these companies kept being closed out just before Koniotis's unit could document a linkage with the Piccards. The difficulty in getting to them before they closed down was maddening, and Koniotis's closest associates spent considerable effort trying to determine if the Piccard interests had inside information concerning the investigations.

"More subsidiaries uncovered?" Koniotis asked without a great deal of expectation.

"No. Much different than that, Takis," Ziya responded. "It's Jacques Piccard. The French are very protective of their citizens, even their criminals. By tapping into Interpol reports, we've discovered that Jacques Piccard has been on the loose for more than two years."

"On the loose?" Koniotis exclaimed, sitting bolt upright in his chair.

"Yes, his family is extremely influential in France—and he, himself was an ambassador."

"And a murderer," Koniotis exploded. "Here in Cyprus. I arrested him. I watched him murder a woman."

"And your government permitted him to be returned to France for trial," Ziya said softly. "He wasn't even imprisoned while he was awaiting his trial in Paris. Before the case went to trial, he jumped bail and has not been seen since that time. Do you suppose, Takis, that he might be the mastermind behind this transportation service for Mideast terrorists?"

"Yes, I do just suppose," Koniotis answered grimly. "Well, at least we have a specific name for our target. Let's get a report into the hands of the police departments of the member states, and I think I'll just make an unfriendly telephone call to Paris in my guise of a UN official."

* * * *

Stefan Gunnerson always enjoyed coming to Malta. He loved its Mediterranean climate, its Neolithic ruins, its sixteenth-century Spanish architecture, and the way its sturdy fortresses just rose up out of the water. He liked the compactness of the island, the breathtaking views from the coast, and even the gaily painted fishing boats. He was standing on the balcony of his room at the Phoenician Hotel, in the Floriana suburb just inland from the capital of Valetta, and was surveying the rooftops of the fortress-like city.

He and Alec Stuart had traveled on the same flight into Valetta but had kept their bookings and seats separate. And he had booked into the luxurious Phoenician hotel, while Stuart had, by

81

choice based on prior visits, picked a smaller, but more picturesque pension overlooking the yacht club basin in the small harbor of St. Julians, some ten miles to the north of the capital. Stuart had suggested that the two should remain apart but had promised to go right over to the British high commission and muster up an intelligence agent or two to contact Gunnerson directly at the Phoenician to coordinate on surveillance of those arriving to attend the summit conference of the nefarious Middle East forces the next day.

The maid had been cleaning the room when Gunnerson returned from a short walk around the hotel, and she must have left the door to the corridor open when she left, because when Gunnerson turned to enter the room from the balcony, he saw that he was not alone.

"Oh, it's you. I thought . . ."

Gunnerson had no time—or inclination—to finish his sentence, for in a blink of an eye, he was over the balcony and headed, face first, for the street below. The fall didn't kill him. He was already dead from the knife wound between his ribs before he ever reached the pavement.

Chapter Six

If the Israeli prime minister had had any sense of history, the meeting of the pro-settlement members of the Knesset—the Israeli parliament—would not have been held at the King David Hotel in Jerusalem. The meeting might have been held—just not in that venue. Her husband, of course, did know full well that this was where the Swedish Count Folke Bernadotte, the UN's first Middle East mediator, was assassinated forty-nine years earlier. Her husband remembered, because he had been at Bernadotte's assassination, although few others had ever known he was present. The question then, of course, was why he didn't warn his wife off the meeting. The truth of the matter, however, was that he had been trying to warn his wife off her focused move toward signing a final Middle East settlement for several months.

It was not supposed to turn out like this. Rachel Gilat was not supposed to have a mind of her own. She was supposed to have just been a front for her husband, Moshe. But it had not worked out that way.

Rachel had been a quiet, but determined woman all her life. None of her acquaintances would have guessed her life would turn out this way when she was a young girl teaching in a Minsk secondary school in the Belorussian Republic of the Soviet Union back in the 1950s. If she had done what everyone had expected of her at that time, however, she would have been married young, to another Minsk Jew, and she probably would have died young as well, as many of her faith in Minsk died in the pogroms unleashed by the regime of Joseph Stalin in the mid 1950s.

But young Rachel had foresight and she had courage and determination as well. When the pogroms started in Minsk, she was already well on her way to the new state of Israel that had been founded in the Palestinian region of the Holy Land. Rachel didn't go there because she was particularly religious but because she was tired of being treated as a member of the underclass. She had a full sense of her self-worth, and she was tired of being underrated by others—by her own family, by her own community of faith, and, most definitely, by the Soviet state.

When she reached Israel, Rachel found she was in the vanguard of those who were able to understand modern international economics, something the new state sorely needed in order to survive in the hostile environment in which it found itself. It was not long before Rachel found a teaching post at a national-level university, and, after that, she was never to be looked down on again.

She still, however, was not and never had been anyone's idea of a national politician. That was where her husband, Zionist and liberation war hero Moshe Gilat, figured in the equation. No one quite understood what the original attraction was between Rachel and Moshe. She reflected intellect, refinement, logic, and good humor. He was the opposite of all that—his was the world of action, rough manners, emotion, and fiery temper. What had brought them together, although neither probably ever was able to recognize it, was that the two saw in each other the personification of their own primary ideals—independence and perseverance in the face of adversity.

Rachel arrived after independence and was a member of the Russian immigrant subgroup that had attained acceptance and a power position in Israeli politics only in the last couple of years, with the influx of new immigrants following the break-up of the Soviet Union. In stark contrast, Moshe reflected tradition, and, more important, he reflected the Zionist liberation movement. He could trace his family line back to the time of King David. When the Jews of the area were taken off into Babylonian captivity, his ancestors had escaped the net and therefore had never been displaced from Palestine. When the Maccabees revolted and briefly introduced Jewish self-rule, Moshe's ancestors were there. When Zionism was founded by Theodor Herzl, Moshe's grandfather—and then his father—were there. When the struggle was on for the creation of an Israeli state, Moshe himself was there.

As a freedom fighter and a close associate of the nation's first prime minister, David Ben-Gurion, Moshe was, at the young age of twenty-five, present at the founding of the Jewish State. And what he had seen and what he had done in the Zionist underground to reach this day in history had hardened him far beyond the natural effect of his years.

In spite of their differences, the marriage between the Gilats had been a happy one. Moshe had worked in various government ministries and in party politics, while Rachel, on the surface quiet and domesticated as always, had successfully fit her economics teaching duties into her busy schedule and had managed, beyond that, to become an international authority in her field. The miracle had been that she had also been there when Moshe needed her, and he was too self-absorbed to realize that she had become an important national figure in her own right.

There had been no children, but the subject was never discussed and neither husband nor wife lamented the absence.

Rachel had been such a dutiful wife that, over time, Moshe had forgotten the iron will and independence in her that had attracted him in the first place. For that reason, the present state of affairs in the Jewish state, the possible accommodation—and to Moshe's mind, the inevitable assimilation and defeat of Israel into the Muslim-dominated Middle East, if accommodation was brought about—was really his fault.

Moshe really should have been prime minister now, and he and the leaders of the Likud Party had thought they had cleverly arranged it so he would be prime minister, if by indirection. It was Moshe Gilat's time for the post, and the Likud wanted to put him forward for the position. However, the powerful Jewish lobby in the United States counseled against it. Now was not the time, they said, for yet another renowned Zionist revolutionary to take over the reins of the Israeli State. The mood in the United States dictated a more moderate, forward-thinking prime minister, one with less historical baggage. And Israel needed American support now—now more than ever before.

Surprising enough to Moshe, his own wife's name was among those the American interests indicated would be an acceptable prime minister. All of these years Moshe had been so wrapped up in his own activities and his own importance that he had completely overlooked his wife's rise to international prominence. Well, there was more than one way to peel a lemon, he and his Likud party cohorts thought. So, they backed Rachel Gilat for prime minister, with the certainly that Moshe would be pulling the strings.

But there were no strings on Rachel, and she shocked and dismayed her husband and his conservative friends by forming coalitions of her own, coalitions that supported a final settlement in the Middle East and the opportunity for Israel to leap ahead in economic development.

And thus the scene had been set for the meeting of Rachel Gilat's primary supporters at the King David Hotel this mid-April morning in preparation for the signing conference in Cyprus next week. And thus, also, was explained Moshe's reticence in warning her off from meeting at the venue of the King David Hotel, with all of its peace-settlement related ghosts. Such a meeting was just too provocative for the Zionist right.

It wasn't that Moshe didn't love his wife deeply in spite of her radical political stances—and her maddening ability to make the policies seem so logical to the majority of the voting public. But her latest move had forced him into an angry silence. For, when the working delegates to the Cyprus conference had been blown up in

Cairo the previous day, Rachel Gilat had the gall to go on public television and declare that she would accept the wording of the settlement document they had established in Cairo and had been scheduled to bring her for scrutiny in Jerusalem and that such acts of terrorism would not affect in any way her own plans to be in Cyprus for the final signing.

This was just too much for Moshe. And, although he had accompanied his wife to the breakfast meeting in the King David, the situation must really have been upsetting to him, because just as they were all sitting down at the large, round table for the working breakfast, he had gotten sick and rushed out of the room. Rachel had risen to go with him, but he waved her off with the acerbic comment that she must not keep her fellow conspirators waiting. Moshe had acquired a habit of referring to Rachel's close associates as "the conspirators."

Dutiful wife that she instinctively had always been, however, Rachel did follow along behind her husband to tend to him. For that reason she was already in the hallway when the bomb under the table went off.

It was a very small bomb, and no one was killed. But several were maimed and quite effectively put out of action for some time. And the bomb had been located right at the position where Rachel had been seated.

As luck would have it, Rachel's personally selected chief of security, the Russian, Sergey Stepanov, was also in the hallway when the bomb went off and thus had not been hurt. He didn't trust Moshe

Gilat an inch, and wherever Rachel Gilat went while in public, there Stepanov was determined to be as well.

But on this occasion, Rachel had other ideas. After an initial sweep around the room to survey the damage and to offer personal, genuinely conveyed words of comfort to her closest associates, she left Stepanov in charge and went looking for her husband.

She knew she had been playing with fire when she hired Stepanov. He had been recommended to her by one of her old family friends in Minsk. The man undoubtedly had been KGB—the Soviet intelligence service—at one time, and he obviously was running from something. But that made him more dependent on her largess. She had been firm and open with him from the start. She knew enough of his background to know he had no place else to turn, and she also knew that he was good at his work. If he served her well, she would protect him and he would prosper. If she ever suspected even a hint of bad conduct on his part, she would throw him back to the various European intelligence services that seemed to be looking for him. Stepanov had readily agreed to her conditions and had been totally loyal ever since.

She had not relied on her own observations to verify Stepanov's loyalty either. Her own secret service, the MOSSAD, was continually vetting Stepanov's activities.

Both the appointment and the constant surveillance of Stepanov served to show that Rachel Gilat was one tough cookie. It also reflected the lengths to which she would go to remain independent of her husband's associates. She needed people around her she could implicitly trust. She no longer trusted her husband's politics, but she loved her husband and would not give him up or distance herself from him in spite of their differences. This morning for the first time, however, she was getting a glimmer of the price that had to be paid for her decisions.

Rachel found Moshe in the men's room. His face was ashen. He cast on her a look that could only be described as one of horror, turned, and was sick in the water basin. Then he fell into her arms and cried like a baby. She must have been completely mistaken in her slight suspicion, Rachel thought in despair as she silently asked for forgiveness for what she had thought her husband might have been capable of.

* * * *

Willie Hamilton, Major William Hamilton (retired) of the British Infantry in a former life, took a quick glance around the *Cyprus Mail* newsroom to see if anyone was looking and then opened the bottom drawer of his desk and took a swig from the always-nearby brandy bottle. He needn't have been so secretive; everyone in the newsroom—indeed almost everyone on the island—knew that he was a lush. However, they also knew he was one of the best political affairs reporters in Cyprus. He also was mellowing with age. He was still wiry and tenacious, but he was now less pugnacious than he had been in years past. He was no longer hailed very often by the nickname he had been saddled with in the office—the Bantam Rooster. He was still small and would fight for a story to the end, but he no longer blindly lashed out at his colleagues or crowed loudly whenever he felt he was being maligned. Everyone agreed that it must have to do with his improved domestic circumstances.

In fact, Willie was just then thinking about his home life and thanking his lucky stars, when one of the subeditors ran through the room and announced to one and all that "She has been identified."

The "she" in question was the mystery woman who had been found in a cave below the Grecian Park Hotel near Cape Greco two days previously. Her circumstances and her failure to speak or to be identified had been the talk of the island for the past day. Of course, it was a small island, and it had been a slow news day.

Willie had not himself even looked at the picture that had been carried in all of the papers at the request of the police. His own time was taken up with covering the impending Middle East summit on the Amathus hotel coast. But he took the opportunity of everyone gathering around the subeditor to take another swig, and, because in this process he had to take his mind off the peace conference, he listened in to what the subeditor had to say.

The subeditor said the woman had been identified by the couple who worked for her at her home in the hills above the southern port city of Limassol. She was an Italian businesswoman who owned an Italian name-brand kitchen equipment off-shore export company here on Cyprus. She had been away on business for several weeks and had not appeared home last week as her servants had expected. They hadn't reported her as missing, however, they said, because it wasn't unusual for her to change her travel plans or be gone for long periods. She was single and came and went as she pleased.

The couple could give no explanation of how the woman might have wound up on the east coast and in the state in which she had been found. They didn't seem too surprised, however, and it was clear from their statements that they thought their employer was decidedly strange, strange enough that she was capable of this bizarre behavior.

This sounded a bit too pat for Willie. It almost sounded as if the couple wanted the missing woman to be their employer—that maybe they didn't want too much dwelling on the woman they worked for and didn't particularly like having gone missing. On a premonition, he dug the day's edition of the *Mail* out of his in-basket.

"How could you say this was *anybody*?" Hamilton muttered derisively. The woman had been flaying around, obviously a good deal less than interested in having her picture taken. In addition, the photo was blurry and the woman's face was unnaturally puffy. One side of her face even looked like it had given up the attempt to stay on her cheekbone.

"What did you say her name was?" someone asked the subeditor.

"Sophie Mancini."

The name caught Hamilton in the process of lifting his bottle out of the open drawer and leaning over for another swig of brandy. He sat upright instead, almost flipping his chair on its back.

"Sophie Mancini? I know Sophie Mancini," Willie's mind screamed. "She's not strange. She's just Italian. She also doesn't look anything like this photograph."

But as Hamilton stared more closely at the photo, he began to think he *had* seen this woman before. His mind was racing. He couldn't make an identification, but he felt he knew, back in the deep recesses of his brain, who this woman was. And he knew that his

92

planned trip to Amathus to conduct background research on the Middle East conference was shot. He had a new story to work on now.

* * * *

Ever since the world's most famous Palestinian leader married his blonde secretary—his first marriage and one that came very late in life—and since he realized his dream of the creation of a Palestinian state over which he reigned, he seemed to have become very sloppy in his security. At one time he would not sleep in the same bed— sometimes not even the same country—for two nights in succession. He was not only a man without a country; he was also a man without a home, a man without even a bed of his own.

Now that he had actual Palestinian territory to govern and a wife to think about, he appeared to be settling down. He had his own house and his own bed. He had become predictable. He had always been a man who had kept one step ahead of the grim reaper—to the admiration of the few and the disgust of the many.

For decades, the scruffy international figure had tweaked the noses of a succession of leaders from the West who had been bent on reaching a settlement of the schism in the Middle East. Many of these leaders had schemed to have him murdered, and most of those leaders were now, themselves, dead. Thus, it was ironic that when the squad from the Abu Nidal radical faction of the Palestinian Liberation Organization gunned their way past the villa guards and into his bedroom and riddled his new bed and its two occupants with bullets, it was to keep him from going to Cyprus and signing away the Palestinians' right to more of the Holy Land, including Jerusalem—the land that was sacred to and had been fought over for centuries by Christian, Muslim, and Jew alike.

Again ironically, the once-pervasive religious aspects of the struggle for the area around Jerusalem were irrelevant to the Abu Nidal faction. The land was Palestine. It was their homeland. They had always lived here and they had a right to rule it—all of it, not just the bone that had been thrown to them and accepted by the mainline PLO leaders. A final settlement between the religious factions contesting the region couldn't be permitted to force the Palestinians to remain the underdogs in what was rightfully their own nation. In the end, it was the simple political aspects of the issue that served to bring deadly firepower to bear on the first permanent bed the PLO leader had ever owned.

* * * *

It had been a busy day for the forces opposed to a final Middle East peace settlement. Thomas Jameson smiled broadly as he listened to the strident news being broadcast in the departure lounge of Malta's Luqa Airport concerning assassinations and assassination attempts across the region. His smile broadened as the newscast was concluded with the announcement of the local murder of a visiting UN official, Stefan Gunnerson.

Jameson had already heard the news report as he was sitting in the Phoenician Hotel's bar. Malta was deceptively slow paced. Things actually happened very fast in Malta, and thus far they had happened his way.

Jameson had hurriedly redone his flight reservations, his work here having been satisfactorily concluded more quickly than he had

94

anticipated it would be. He would be in Paris briefly and then on to Larnaca. There was nothing left for him to do here.

"We'll just see how much Koniotis needs me now. His precious agent in Malta is dead, and the operations center at UNICIS must be clogged with emergency messages on all these assassinations. If he only knew. It's going to get a lot worse."

Jameson laughed wickedly as his flight was called and he stood and slung the strap of his overnight bag onto his shoulder.

Chapter Seven

Willie Hamilton couldn't get the picture of the mystery cave woman out of his mind. As he sat in the center of the stone-floored courtyard in a rush-seated and carved village chair, he was in deep contemplation. So deep were his thoughts that he was not aware that he was absentmindedly adding carving to the chair with a knife he had been using to pare the fruit from a basket of small mountain-grown apples on the rough wooden country table.

Willie was supposed to be proofing the lengthy article he had written for the Sunday edition of the *Cyprus Mail* while he took in the last rays of the sun in the courtyard of the Hamilton's Lefkara, Troodos mountains, retreat. The column concerned a "sting" operation in which the Cypriot police had participated in an Iraqi attempt to ship seven tons of nuclear-grade zirconium from the United States through Cyprus. Pretty heady stuff for a political columnist, and the story would run on the international news—*his* story if he did his usual thorough job of coverage. But the story was not quite heady enough on this unseasonably warm mid April Friday evening to sustain the sinewy little retired British Infantry major's attention.

Willie instinctively reached over and took a large swig from a nearby bottle of Anglias brandy.

"Quite a feat for the International Investigations Unit," he thought, his mind remaining at least half-way connected with the zirconium issue. "Maria Solonos's first major operation on her own. Good for her. She's a good police official. She shouldn't have to live forever under the shadow of Takis Koniotis's exploits while he was chief of that unit."

But these contemplations weren't enough to pull Willie back to his article, for the thought of Maria Solonos had, for some unknown reason, brought the picture of the mysterious cave woman stabbing back into his consciousness.

"Maria? Maria and this woman? There must be some connection. I know I've seen this woman before. Recognition is in my consciousness somewhere. And for some reason the thought of Maria has brought it closer to the surface."

Another swig of brandy, a return to the rhythmic jabbing at the chair arm with the fruit knife, a shielding of his eyes with his free hand, and an intentional drifting down into free-floating contemplation, with the hope that his prior connections with the unidentified woman of the Cape Greco cave would coalesce and rise into his consciousness.

In this state of mind, Willie was oblivious to the rustic beauty around him of the stone-encased village courtyard house, to the magnificence of the pink-blossomed oleander bush and deep magenta brackets of the early-coloring bougainvillea, to the millions of stars that began twinkling on in the clear sky above his head as late-afternoon sun turned into dusk and then into night, and even to the humming that was wafting from the balcony above his head.

Ginger Hamilton, a model-thin, extremely fair-complexioned, high-cheekboned woman in her late fifties, was standing in front of her dressing table in the master bedroom above the courtyard. She was tenuously brushing a loose strand of hair in place as she untied the flour-dusted apron she was wearing and prepared to join her husband in the courtyard.

Ginger had the look about her of former beauty, and, indeed, she had once been a celebrated and often-wed high-fashion model and had battled hard through her forties and mid fifties to preserve that beauty. But she had lost that battle, and ironically, when she had admitted that defeat and stopped fighting the onset of age, a new, less-strident and more-convincing and compelling beauty had emerged. As she had come to grips with the reality of her life, she mellowed in disposition and attained a comfort level that glowed and softened the aging lines on her face. Luckily, good genes had given her a thinness and good facial bone structure that she would never lose. The effect was that her natural beauty shone through and was enhanced by her obvious calm and contentment with her current life.

The most startling effect of Ginger Hamilton's new contract with life was on her marriage—her current marriage, as one of the primary marks of her restless years was that she had married often and had drifted in and out of short affairs and one-night stands even more often. She married William Hamilton on the rebound and as an escape to Cyprus and from a disastrous life in Brussels that she was trying to totally obliterate. Life as Willie's wife would have been trying for even a saint. His first wife had been such a long-suffering saint—and he therefore tended to think that any woman he married would be so— and that it was his due that she was so. But Ginger had been no saint. Their fights during the ensuing years had become part of the rich folklore of the island. They were both high-profile, distinctive personalities in a small, closed environment.

But now, with the redirection of Ginger's life, it was as if night had become day. Willie had not, in truth, changed. But Willie had always worshipped his wife, and his end of the marathon battling had been supported wholly by frustration and raw jealous rage. Now, the two had become a devoted couple. Not that they cooed and obliviously nuzzled each other in public. But now they were a solid family unit, complementing each others' strengths and hiding each others' weaknesses and providing mutual support, encouragement, refuge, and counsel.

It was in this vein that Ginger sighed, turned from the mirror of her dressing table, and descended to the courtyard below. She recognized the signs of the beginning of a Willie Hamilton binge, resulting from obsession with a snagged news lead. She did not want to intrude on her husband's struggle with his news story. She recognized and accepted Willie's investigative and writing brilliance for what it was. But she also knew the man was killing himself with his bouts with the brandy bottle, and she needed to do whatever she could to guide his creative patterns into less dangerous channels. She wasn't sure she could do this without destroying his talent, and she was resolved that she wouldn't interfere if there was no other way he could create. But she had to try.

The most significant result of the traumatic makeover Ginger had undergone in her own life was the realization that she desperately loved and needed her husband. She had almost lost him at a couple of points nearly two years ago when he had gotten too close to his stories and suffered nasty brushes with death. But she had miraculously received reprieves and had, within the context of having thought she had lost Willie, experienced a traumatic face-off with her own life. After a realistic appraisal of what she had become, she resolved that she would never do anything to lose her husband again. She entertained no delusions about their remaining time together at their ages, time being all too short. Time that was too precious to waste.

Descending the staircase from the bedroom level, which in typical Cypriot village fashion was an open-air staircase hugging one of the courtyard's inner walls, Ginger quietly slipped into the kitchen and returned to Willie's side. She was bearing the tray of pastries she'd just baked. She had been planning this approach for some time, ever since she discerned the early signs of one of Willie's contemplation-induced alcoholic binges. She could try to break through to him and help him surface his thoughts through conversation. But she would need the warm sticky buns that Willie couldn't resist to help soak up the brandy he had already consumed.

"Honey, what is it? Doesn't something fit with the article on the nuclear material seizure?"

As she slid into the chair beside him, she gently extracted the fruit knife from one of his hands and maneuvered a sticky bun into his other hand. The newspaperman didn't resist the introduction of the sticky bun, and his sudden concentration on this object gave Ginger opportunity to push the nearly empty brandy bottle out of reach and out of view.

Between gobbles, Willie told his wife about the woman who had been found in the cave below the Grecian Park Hotel and of how he had been haunted by her picture.

"It's maddening. I can almost recognize her. I know I have met her before. And for some strange reason the thought of the police official Maria Solonos in connection with the zirconium operation very nearly managed to surface the woman's identity in my mind."

"You've reported many cases that Maria investigated," Ginger murmured. Her structured mind started probing. "And we've seen Maria at many social events as well. Maybe your mind just pictures the two standing next to each other. It could be as tenuous a relationship as that. Have you tried systematically working your way back from recent events in which you and Maria were both present? Maybe the mystery woman would enter the picture this way."

"Yes, of course I've tried that," Willie groused. But of course he hadn't, and Ginger knew he hadn't, as she knew he had become preoccupied with his Anglias brandy bottle. But she didn't argue with him now as she would have leaped to do two years previously. She just smiled and handed him a second sticky bun.

As he munched, he began working his most recent meeting with Maria Solonos over in his mind, just as Ginger had suggested. After a while, this started to get to be a tedious, thirsty business, however, and he reached for the brandy bottle, and then, when nothing turned up within his reach, he quizzically and grouchily started looking around for the brandy.

In a panic that she did not permit to show on the surface, Ginger grasped for a new line of attack.

"Do you know where they've taken her?"

"Yes," Willie's attention was arrested by the new line in inquiry. "She's in Nicosia—at the Makarios Hospital. Why?"

Ginger inwardly trumpeted the victory. Willie was hooked, if only temporarily. He had stopped looking for the brandy bottle. She urged a third pastry on him and pressed home with the line of thought.

"Well, you said the photograph of the woman was dreadful. Perhaps if you visited her and could see her in person, you would be able to recognize her more readily."

The strategy was brilliant; Ginger had won the skirmish. The brandy bottle was vanquished, if only for the evening. Given the path to the possible exorcising of his obsession with the mystery cave woman, Willie was able to set aside action on this issue until he could return to Nicosia the next morning, and he turned his attention back to the proofing of his zirconium sting operation article.

But before he focused his attention on his work, he took an appreciative look around the courtyard of their quaint Lefkara village house and took his wife's hand in his and patted it with his other hand. Ginger was ecstatic, completely oblivious to the caramel syrup from the sticky buns that Willie was transferring to her elegant fingers. Looking up, he brought her attention to the night sky.

"See that shooting star? I just remembered that I moved to the courtyard because the paper said we would be treated to a display of shooting stars tonight. I had forgotten all about that. Isn't it strange how easily we can be distracted from the glorious aspects of our lives?"

"Yes, strange," Ginger agreed, "but then life is so much more vibrant and rewarding when the important things are rediscovered."

Willie squeezed his wife's hand, and the glow of pleasure she took on rivaled that of the panoply of stars in motion above her head.

* * * *

The no-longer-young, but still strikingly handsome and mesmerizing leader smiled his best Cheshire cat smile as he stood at the rail of his impressive yacht and watched the stars shoot out across the becalmed Mediterranean and the lights of the finger harbors of Valetta.

They called him mad and enigmatic, he thought grimly—but not without amusement and smugness. Mad, perhaps, but mad in the connotation of anger, a seething anger at the perpetual abuse his people and his nation's resources had been subjected to. And abuse that had not dissipated in the more than two decades since he had risen to power in a colonels' 1969 "September" coup in the northern African nation of Libya.

Libya was less a nation with distinct boundaries than three historic and important port cities—Tripoli, Benghazi, and Tobruk. These three ports were connected by dusty caravan trails and served as the mouths upon the Mediterranean for a huge hinterland of sand dunes that had been considered worthless until the Americans' ESSO

103

petroleum conglomerate arrived on the scene. In 1957 the Americans discovered that the sand was hiding a subterranean sea of high-grade oil—not as much oil as was being found elsewhere in the region, but quite enough to make the American industrialists salivate.

The oil companies—not just the Americans but British Petroleum as well—had only been the last, albeit most obnoxious, wave of foreign controllers, manipulators, and exploiters who had drained Libya of its possessions and enslaved its people back into the dim memory of early civilization. The Colonel had changed all of that when he and his weaker cohorts overthrew the puppet government that called itself a loose constitutional federation of three traditionally independent states but that was really just one of the smaller foreign divisions of a giant British and U.S. petroleum consortium.

Madman? Megalomaniac? Isolationist? Cultist? International pariah? Uncontrollable and unpredictable? Yes, he had been all of that. But not because he was crazy or out of control. When Libya had played the game on Western terms, it had been pillaged, raped, and impoverished. In the two and a half decades that Libya had played the game on The Colonel's terms, it had been empowered, enriched, and, if not loved, at least respected and never underestimated.

There was a nudge at his elbow, and one of his personal servants handed him a beaker of sheep's milk. The Colonel practiced the religious fanaticism that he preached; he never drank alcohol.

For the briefest of moments The Colonel's hard, steel-blue eyes held those of the servant's in thrall. No one disputed The Colonel's gifts as a clairvoyant. He had the power to instantaneously undress the soul with his eyes, and his abilities had reached legendary proportions that far outstripped the real extent of his power but that had helped him hold sway over his close associates. The servant managed to hold his burning, probing gaze for only a couple of seconds, but that was enough time.

"So, it's true," The Colonel thought with some bitterness. He had trusted this man and let him get close to his person. The Colonel was never fully immune to the grief of discovered treachery. He had given his life to the Libyan people. They would be nothing but ants under the heels of oily petroleum company executives if it had not been for his sacrifices. Why could they not return the loyalty and dedication that he had provided?

"Is your treachery here in this cup, Jemal?" The Colonel mused silently as the servant hurriedly withdrew. "No, you are not brave enough to be so direct, are you, worthless one? But what is your part in Abu Hani's plans? Oh, you didn't know I knew you were working for Abu Hani rather than serving me as loyally as I have served you by allowing you in my presence and being so generous with your family, you say in surprise? What do you take me for? It is written in your face. I can tell you the very day and hour that you made your compact with the Lebanese devil. Well, I don't know what you are up to just now, but I believe I will know before you can do any harm. And then you will die for your treachery. You, and your family to the third generation. Such is the judgment of our rich history."

He had reluctantly cooperated with Abu Hani's plan for a conference, but he no longer thought this was the way. He would do anything he had to do to prevent a final settlement of the Middle East dispute on terms that satisfied Israel or the West—or even the current

Egyptian and Jordanian regimes, for that matter. He had seen the greed for personal power and wealth in the soul of both the Lebanese diplomat and that French imperialist dog, Piccard. The Colonel spat into the Mediterranean at the mere thought of French industrialists— the very scum that had enslaved his people before the American petroleum executives arrived on the scene to take their turn. No, The Colonel had his own ideas on how to stop the peace settlement. And his ideas had never failed to have an impact.

The Colonel's eyes had blazed forth such that anyone standing near him would testify that it was he and his eyes that were shooting the stars out of the sky on this unusual night. He drained his cup, pitched it over the railing, and turned toward the cabin door, motioning to the guards who had been lingering in the shadows to follow him. The night's work was just beginning. The servant was safe for now, but a plan—a very satisfying plan was already forming in The Colonel's mind. And the servant would serve that plan well.

* * * *

Symeon Parikan restlessly tossed and turned in his Fikardou village bed, the occasional blaze of a star across the open bedroom window not helping in the least in his fight to induce mind-numbing sleep. As he rolled over, he came into contact with his sleeping wife, who encircled him in her arms without waking. She was open to him once more, but he had already tried to escape his thoughts through lovemaking once this night, and it had only resulted in the heightening of his concern.

As he was making love to his wife, visions of the other woman intruded. It was all he could do to bring himself to finish that first time. He knew that if he tried again, his wife would know something was wrong. And, although she had been the most uncurious person he had known about his activities to this point, he highly doubted there was a Greek village girl alive who would be indifferent to the sudden inability of her husband to perform in bed.

Parikan gently freed himself from his sleeping wife's arms and sat up on the edge of the bed, face in hands. He could not dispel the vision of that other woman, the woman who had been showing his photo around the village of Politiko and asking searching questions about his whereabouts. She could only be from the police—or worse, an agent of the Americans or of some other country who was unfriendly to the Hizballah movement. There were so many possibilities on that score.

He had no choice. He had to silence her. And it had not bothered him in the least to do so until he had received that telephone call to prepare for reactivation. That telephone call had brought him back to the world of his past and had, in one brief moment, reminded him how dangerous and precarious his life still was.

And once he had begun to think of the woman agent again, he had begun to worry about what he had done—not remorse for what he did but, rather, worry that he had not done it right and might have left loose strings that would lead back to him.

There was no way around it, he concluded, as he arose from the bed and started pulling on the clothes that had so easily been tossed aside when he and his wife had tumbled into the room several hours earlier. He had to check it out.

The night was moonless and he required a flashlight to see the way to his van. He was oblivious to the shooting stars above his head. His heart and mind were too heavy with concern. He drove out of Fikardou without headlights and only turned them on when he had passed the Machaeras Monastery.

Just past the monastery Parikan entered a one-lane dirt and pebble track that wound around the eastern foothills of the Troodos Mountains. A bare four miles past the monastery, the road broadened out at a secluded, abandoned quarry site. Parikan pulled the vehicle over into the shadows at the side of the roadway and got out.

Everything looked so different at night. But after a while, he thought he was able to identify the trees he had used to mark where he had entered the wooded area above the quarry. He took his flashlight and started climbing the rocks toward the trees. Still it didn't look quite right. When he had stopped here before, it had been in daylight, and he had approached from the direction of Politiko. He had also understandably been quite agitated at the time and had, afterward, intentionally tried to erase all memory of that day from his mind. Not that he had not done this before, but the sudden, out-of-the-blue brush with danger after so long a time successfully in hiding and constructing a new life for himself had been unnerving.

There, up ahead. That looked right for the rock formation he had used as a marker. And the field of wildflowers. The abundant and vibrant poppies, crown daisies, and French lavender. Afterward he had not been able to get the lushness of colors of that field of flowers out of his mind for days. It was mercifully dark now, so the colors didn't scream at him now, accusing him of introducing death in the midst of

108

so much life. But he could tell the field was where he had expected it to be. Parikan steeled himself as he approached the rocks. After all, it had been more than a week. It would not be a pretty sight.

But there was nothing to see. Parikan stood there numbly for more than a minute, unable to comprehend. Then he began to comprehend all too well and started to moan and scramble around the adjacent rocky ground in disbelief at what he had not seen. The body wasn't there. There could be no doubt about it; the body was gone.

Of course, that must be why his mind wouldn't let the killing rest. For some reason—it must have been the original shock of finding he was being searched for in such a remote area of the island—he had screwed up. He was so sure he had finished her off. But he must only have stunned her. No wonder his brain had been sending him warning signals. But where could she have gone? Did she get a good look at him? Was she alive, or did she just stumble off somewhere else in the quarry to die?

One thing he did know. He couldn't stay here any longer tonight. He couldn't see much of anything around him on such a dark night, and, if she *had* been found alive, then this was no place for him to be found.

Parikan stumbled blindly back toward his van. As he reached the lip of the quarry above where the vehicle was parked, his attention was caught by a particularly bright shooting star that seemed to be racing straight for him from out of the sky, almost begging to be taken as an omen of what was to come. Parikan cried out in fear, slipped, and painfully rolled the last several yards down to the van.

Chapter Eight

The news of Stefan Gunnerson's death in Malta nearly paralyzed the headquarters of the UN's International Crime Investigations Service in Nicosia. Alec Stuart telephoned the news to Takis Koniotis directly at home from the British high commission office in Valetta.

A British agent had arrived at the hotel to contact Gunnerson within moments of his plunge from the Phoenician Hotel balcony and had thus been one of the first officials on the scene. After having examined the body as closely as he could without actually touching anything, the agent went directly to Gunnerson's room and found the door to the corridor open. There was no sign of an intruder, however. He arrived back on the street just in time to pointedly note to the Valetta police that they could hardly write the death up as an accidental fall from a balcony if a knife handle was protruding from Gunnerson's side. The Maltese police were notoriously wary of bringing any public attention to the murder of visiting foreigners if this could be avoided.

Immediately after Alec's telephone call, Koniotis rushed over to the UNICIS office. The office had just received its own confirmation of the murder, which came as a debilitating double whammy to the office personnel. Just before receiving the report on Gunnerson's death, the operations center had monitored news reports on the assassination attack on the PLO Leader. The Palestinian State was remaining very tight-lipped about the assassination or about who now spoke for the PLO, but that was to be expected under the circumstances. There were dozens of splinter organizations—most notably the radical Abu Nidal faction—that would dearly love to take over control of the central PLO administration.

Although the operations center was fully staffed that Friday evening and with some of the organization's best people, it was swamped. It perhaps could have held its own with just the attacks on the leaders of Egypt, Israel, and the PLO along with a whole array of reports on unrest among the dissident organizations across the Middle East to contend with. But the grief that settled in with the shocking loss of Stefan Gunnerson was just too much to bear. And, of course the operation center's chief, Thomas Jameson, had not yet returned from his vacation.

After calling Safa Ziya via the office's single telephone line into the Turkish zone at her apartment in the Turkish sector of Nicosia, to tell her of Gunnerson's death and to ask her to wait to come to work until the morning, when she would be fresh enough to relieve him, Koniotis also turned his thoughts to Jameson.

"Where is Tom? I need him more than ever now. We just don't have enough help here yet. I hope he'll be back soon. If he was

111

somewhere that he could hear news reports, I'm sure he would have been on duty by now."

Koniotis's wish was soon to be granted. Jameson was, in fact, less than two miles away, having arrived from Malta via Paris two hours previously. He had planned to go directly to the office from the airport, and he had practiced the part of a grieving colleague during the flight from Paris to Larnaca. He had, however, telephoned the backer of his trip to Malta from the airport and had been asked to stop first at the Milano Café and report on his trip.

The contact was, of course, very pleased at the return on his investment and extended his contract with the UNICIS operations center chief.

It was an outwardly devastated coworker but an inwardly triumphant rival who left the Milano less than an hour later for the short drive to the buffer zone and the world of UNICIS.

* * * *

"Thanks for the vote of confidence, Lover," Ellen Larkin called through the half-closed door, "but I know you're lying to me. You just want to get on the road. I, for one, however, am not going to go anywhere where the queen is to be without taking every precaution I can think of. I don't know how she has managed to keep her fresh beauty. Scratch that, I *do* know. With the number of servants she has, she has no opportunity to earn a wrinkle. But, considering all the pampering she gets, I can't imagine how she has managed to remain as nice and down to earth as she has."

"Let's stop pontificating and get this show on the road," Paul Conte responded in mock—and exaggerated—irritation. "It's bad enough that you weren't ready when I got here. But they've changed the party to the Raghadan Palace, and the traffic in the city will be murder."

"The Raghadan Palace?" The question was accompanied by a questioning look, as Ellen popped her head around the door.

"Yes. I guess they are jittery about the attacks on the other leaders. The king is a prime target, and they probably thought they would spoil any already-devised attempt on his life just by changing the venue of the reception from the country residence to the rarely used city palace. If you ask me, they should have called the affair off altogether."

And then, as he focused in on her. "Hey, you look ravishing. You must be ready to go."

"Nice try, honey," Ellen retorted as she withdrew from the doorway. "I'll just be a minute—or two—more."

During the interminable "minute more" Paul's thoughts returned to the decision to hold the reception as planned that evening.

"The king certainly is brave," he mused. "Some, though, would say he was just downright stubborn and foolhardy. He's no fool, however. He seems to have figured that he can only stay on the throne by pointedly ignoring the ever-present threat to his life. And thus far he has been right—and has lived a charmed life. I do believe he's the longest still-reigning monarch in the world. Nosed out Britain's Elizabeth for that dubious honor by just a month or two."

Jordan's King Hussein, reigning head of the Hashemite dynasty since 1952, which claimed—with mixed acceptance—direct connection to the Prophet Mohammad and down through the grand

113

sharifs and amirs of Mecca as the hereditary custodians of the Muslim's holy shrines, was no stranger to danger and adversity.

As one of the Allies in World War II, Hussein's grandfather, Abdullah, had sought at war's end to reunify the Middle East, centered around Syria, under the rule of the Hashemite dynasty. The best he had been able to do, however, was to forge together a desert area with a population of fewer than 500,000 people—and most of those were Arab Palestinian refugees fleeing the formation of the Zionist State of Israel and refusing to relinquish Palestine as their home country.

Centering on the area then known as the Transjordan, Abdullah carved out the Hashemite Kingdom of Jordan in 1948, with the once-great city of Amman—the historical Philadelphia—as its capital, and proclaimed himself king and protector of the Palestinian people and cause. In truth, however, his real interests were in reestablishing the family's hereditary claims in the direction of Syria and the Arabian Peninsula.

From that time forward, the relationship between the Hashemites and the Palestinians was to be one of the most dangerous symbiotic partnerships in world politics. The Jordanian dynasty trumpeted the Palestinian cause and harbored the Palestinian people and leaders, with the greatest influx of refugees occurring first as the Zionist State was being forged and then again in 1967, when the State of Israel seized the West Bank region.

At the same time, however, the relationship was marked by classest hatred and distrust. Abdullah himself ruled his newly formed country for a bare three years. In July of 1951, he was assassinated on the porch of the Al Aqsa Mosque on the Temple Mount in Jerusalem as he was going into Friday prayers. He was assassinated by a disgruntled Palestinian. A bullet from the assassin's gun had also unsuccessfully tried to seek out Abdullah's sixteen-year-old grandson, Hussein, who was at the old man's side.

Barely a year later Hussein was on the throne of Jordan. And for the succeeding four and a half decades he had continuously put on one of the world's most astonishing juggling acts. With a nation that had virtually no geographically defensible boundaries and few marketable resources, with nothing more than a proud heritage that claimed to trace back to the Prophet, Hussein had managed to remain on his throne and as a major power broker in the Middle East, while continually juggling friends and enemies among the world's superpowers, the Middle Eastern nations, and the region's ethnic and political factions.

Paul Conte admired and respected the king. He had always found him interesting and his defensive game fascinating, if a little irritating from the American political point of view. But now that Paul had met the king and worked with his associates, he had been completely sold on the monarch's beneficial linchpin role in the move toward a Middle East settlement.

There was no other reason Conte would be attending this reception. Well, yes, the fact that Ellen had said she wouldn't miss the event for anything probably was a deciding factor in its own right, he admitted. But this near the end of an exhausting tour in the country, which thrived on diplomatic and business functions, only the king's personal magnetism sufficed to pull Conte into the evening traffic of Amman's inner city once he had been informed that the venue of the reception had been changed to the historic palace area adjacent to the city's ancient citadel. Even Hussein's magnetism was being countered with Paul's gut feeling that the recent events in Egypt, Israel, and Palestine should automatically close down any public access to Hussein until the Cyprus treaty signing had been completed.

As it was, the city traffic almost did defeat Paul and Ellen's attendance at the reception. Although it was less than a four-mile crawl from the Regency Palace to the Raghadan Palace, both of which were well within the city's limits, Paul was sure that they had seen all of the more than thirteen legendary hills of the city before the ordeal was over. He had only been about to maintain his composure by acknowledging that the traffic of Amman didn't hold a candle to that of Cairo.

He had plenty of road time, however to reflect that the village that King Abdullah had first occupied in the 1920s and that could count only 30,000 inhabitants when he chose it as the center of his kingdom was a far smaller place then than the metropolis of Amman was today.

Night had fallen and the party was well past its prime before Paul and Ellen arrived and made their way through the many layers of security—security that was quite welcome as far as Paul was concerned. He had noticed that, as a couple, they were treated with a good deal more care and deference than he himself was usually accorded in his position as an American embassy political officer. He credited that to the probability that the Jordanian security forces knew that Ellen was a senior Canadian intelligence official.

"Funny how quickly the intelligence folks latch onto their counterparts," Paul thought. Be he wasn't complaining. The fast-line service probably got them into the reception hall a good half hour earlier than they would have arrived otherwise.

This was actually to prove to be an unfortunate occurrence.

When they were finally released into the first reception hall, in which the king and his beautiful, significantly younger queen were standing in a receiving line, Paul pleaded an insistent call of nature and headed off in search of a men's room. Ellen drifted toward one of the many beverage bars placed strategically around the rooms. However, the couple had apparently been seen entering the room by the king, and Ellen quickly found a handsome, fully bemedaled and bedecked aide-de-camp at her elbow, guiding her toward the now mercifully short receiving line.

The king and queen, all smiles and charm, spent a good five minutes talking with Ellen and congratulating her on her impending nuptials and outlining the small wedding reception they were to hold in the couple's honor before the two left Amman. Ellen tried her best to hold her end of an unexpectedly chatty conversation without becoming tongue tied or letting her jaw drop to the floor. Her most panicked moment came when she had to explain why Paul wasn't at her side, but the king was all-knowing—and a little earthy—in response, which cut the tension considerably and left her all aglow when she departed the reception line and literally bumped into a very interesting—and distinguished-looking older man.

After trading apologies and mutual concerns of liquid spills, the suave gentleman in the elegant brown silk pinstripe suite and bold,

117

colorful tie and pocket handkerchief made the comment that he had not seen Ellen in Jordan before but that she certainly seemed to be on familiar terms with the royal couple. He spoke with a polished and disarming Continental accent and must, Ellen thought, be either a French aristocrat or a yacht salesman. She was close on both accounts.

Ellen explained that she was a Canadian diplomat assigned to Cyprus and had just come over to meet her fiancé, who worked in the U.S. embassy here. Ellen didn't miss the slight twitch about the Frenchman's eyes when she mentioned Cyprus. He, in turn, murmured his own name in introduction, but did so in such a low tone that Ellen was sure he didn't want her to actually pick it up. But she was a trained intelligence officer, and the name didn't elude her. However, trained intelligence officer or not, the name came as such an unexpected shock that she, in turn, was unable to hide her surprise.

Piccard? Could he have possibly said Jacques Piccard? She hadn't heard the first name, but the Piccard came across clearly enough—and she was well acquainted with the name Jacques Piccard. Paul had told her all about the former French ambassador to Cyprus—one of the heirs to a French shipping empire—who had been implicated in an exchange of arms for drugs deal and murder in Cyprus, and who had been sent back to France to stand trial. He had made the unforgivable mistake of shipping his drugs to Marseilles, which the French authorities didn't appreciate, fine old French family or not.

This might be an important intelligence find, Ellen instinctively thought, now all business. She was sure that Jacques Piccard, if that was who this was, should not be on the loose and roaming around the Middle East. But she had to be sure she had heard correctly, and there was only one way to do that.

"Oh, there's a Piccard shipping company and hotel chain in Cyprus. Are you one of those Piccards? If so, maybe you know my fiancé, Paul Conte, who was assigned to the American embassy in Cyprus a couple of—"

But she found that now she was talking to herself. Piccard had vanished, and now she was sure that she had heard his name correctly. But, actually, she was not speaking to herself. She found that Piccard had instantaneously been replaced by a waiter with a tray of canapés, and this gave her her second jolt in quick succession—but, alas, not her last—for the evening.

The waiter had also vanished almost as quickly as he had appeared, but Ellen had registered an immediate sign of recognition— and one that had a deeply negative impact on her. She couldn't identify the sense of recognition any further at the moment, but she knew that if she worried the idea, it would come to her. And something inside her told her she should worry the idea—she associated the picture she saw with mug shots of known terrorists on the loose that she had reviewed just a few days previously.

But then, just as if she was in a shooting gallery, a mischievously smiling Paul Conte popped up right where the waiter— and Jacques Piccard immediately before him—had appeared just moments previously.

"Well, now I know that Hussein's natural loyalties are with the United States," Paul pronounced coyly.

"Paul, just a moment ago, I had two strange encounters," Ellen countered.

"No, me first," Paul insisted, and he repeated, "Well, now I know that Hussein's natural loyalties are with the United States."

Ellen started to repeat her concern, "Paul I . . ."

"Come on. Play the game. Ask me how I know that."

"All right," Ellen surrendered. "How do you know that?"

"Because he uses American bathroom fixtures. American Standard; beige, as a matter of fact. Can't get more basic than that in your loyalties."

Ellen just gaped.

"That's the sort of thing *our* foreign services train us to observe," Paul said with a laugh.

Ellen was saved from telling her zany fiancé that he was a total idiot by the return of the aide-de-camp, who this time had been sent to summon Paul to "The Presence."

"Ta, ta, love. Catch you later. Royalty calls," Paul said breezily through a grin as he was led off to his fate.

"I'll be out on the balcony," Ellen called after him. "I've got to clear my head and do a mind search."

When she reached the balcony, Ellen's attention was caught by the most amazing display of shooting stars that she had ever seen. She turned back and called Paul's name, wanting him to follow her out onto the terrace as soon as he could.

But her eyes didn't focus first on Paul They focused on the gun, on the gun that had appeared from under the cloth-covered tray of canapés the waiter she had encountered just moments before was carrying—the waiter with the face that she clearly connected now with the mug shot she'd viewed of a Hizballah terrorist.

She screamed a warning, pitched her beaded handbag toward the waiter's outstretched hand, and launched her body after the bag. But the waiter was just too far across the room. Paul heard Ellen's scream at the same instant he saw the raised gun barrel. And, without thought, he did the only thing his training as a U.S. Treasury agent had drilled into him must be done under such circumstances.

* * * *

In disgust the UN's undersecretary for political affairs shoved the stack of papers that was in front of her across the desk and rotated her chair until she was facing lower Manhattan. The view of night descending on New York that greeted her through the expansive plate-glass windows of her vantage point near the clouds from the UN Secretariat building on Turtle Bay was, as always, breathtaking. But, alas, it was not compensation on this particular night for the stack of reports that littered Ingrid Bittmann's desk.

The statuesque, not fat, but large-boned Austrian, who was in her mid fifties, stood up, straightened her well-tailored, but severely square-cut suit jacket, and marched across to her drinks cabinet. After pouring herself a strong scotch, she returned to the desk and shifted through the reports.

Bloody attacks on national leaders in Egypt, Israel, Palestine, and Jordan. The working-level national negotiators lost in a boat bombing on the Nile. Fundamentalist Muslims and devotees of sundry terrorist organizations in the streets of Damascus, Beirut, Baghdad, Tehran—and even Istanbul, Paris, and Kuala Lumpur. Even New

York City itself. Zionist counterdemonstrations in Tel Aviv and Washington. Clashes of both factions in Jerusalem and London. Synagogue and mosque bombings worldwide. The first hijacking of a commercial airplane in more than a year—in Jakarta, of all places, which would only be surprising to those who don't realize that Indonesia has the largest population of Muslims of any country in the world. Diplomatic protests flying left and right—all of them crossing her desk.

Bittmann picked up the top-most report. This was the most troublesome of all. Not just that a UN international investigations official had been murdered in Valetta, but that he had been there because Malta was permitting the holding in its territory of a convocation of forces opposing the final signing of a Middle East peace treaty. This was perhaps the key to all of the other events of the past two days. The forces of evil were finally getting together to oppose the UN's efforts—*her* efforts—to settle the problems of the Middle East for all time.

The UN official swore coarsely in German and swept several of the reports onto the floor with one vicious sweep. This had been a brilliant plan. One that was meant to catapult her into the secretary general's chair. Not that she wasn't being groomed for the post anyway. But the organization's program was moving entirely too slow.

A career UN officer, Ingrid Bittmann languished for many years within the confines of the UN High Commission for Refugees. But sometime earlier in this decade, the powers that be in the United Nations decided it was time to join the modern world—which meant that the UN should endure at least one female UN secretary general of record, if only for a short time to have one token portrait of a woman in the Hall of Honor.

Bittmann had been one of several women pushed ahead as a possible candidate, and then her star had suddenly started to rise at a startling speed in the past two years. She had been assigned to Cyprus as the UN coordinator in that long-lived peacekeeping force mandate. A senior UN mediator, Eric Isaksen, had been kidnapped on Cyprus, and Bittmann had been credited with orchestrating his safe recovery. In the process, she had been acclaimed as having been instrumental in the formation of a new United Nations office to fight international crime and terrorism—what was eventually to become Takis Koniotis's Nicosia-headquartered UNICIS organization. There had been many who had grumbled that it had been Koniotis himself who had orchestrated the recovery of Isaksen from the hands of a Hizballah terrorist band and Isaksen who had conceived and sold the idea of a UN crime-fighting organization. But it was Bittmann who was being groomed for greater things, and so the credit went to her.

But she had now tied her star directly to the success of the Middle East peace treaty signing in Cyprus. It had been a great risk, but it was that last, brilliant maneuver required to put her in the secretary general's seat. And there could be no turning back. The Cyprus conference had to succeed—or, more precisely, the conference had to come off as scheduled; it didn't really have to accomplish anything. If they could just get all of the leaders in the same conference room espousing an interest in a settlement, that was farther down the road than anyone else had gotten them. She would just have to throw more resources at the UNICIS organization. Eric Isaksen was still the UN's roving mediator on international terrorism and crime. He'd just have to do something to make the conference succeed in opening.

And, speaking of Isaksen, as Bittmann sank into her chair once more with a tired sigh, the distinguished international diplomat, former Danish foreign minister, and former chairman of the United Nations Development Program, was buzzed into the wood-paneled office by Bittmann's private secretary.

He could see at once the tension that had built up in Bittmann. He took one half-critical, half-amused look at the papers that had been swept onto the floor and picked them up and placed them back on the desk. Bittmann said nothing. She just sat hunched in her chair and looking peeved. Walking behind her, Isaksen began to knead her shoulders with his strong fingers. She straightened up and started to rotate her head, the tension draining from her body. Isaksen buried his face in the crook of her neck and applied wet kisses behind her ear. As he moved his mouth to her earlobe, Bittmann emitted a low moan.

At the sound of the buzzer, Isaksen leaped away from the chair and turned to the window. Bittmann's secretary entered, handed two more reports to her, and discretely withdrew.

"Damn! Another report from Malta," Bittmann spat out. "The conference has been convened on the Libyan's yacht. Damn. I wish we had someone in place there to tell us what is being discussed."

"And the other report?" Isaksen asked wearily, as he dropped into the chair across from his lover's desk.

"From Cairo. Double Damn! The new Egyptian president is waffling on going to Cyprus. We have to do something and fast, Eric. What are we doing to do? The secretary general is off in Timbuktu gain—literally Timbuktu—and it's up to me to react to all of this. He's punting, of course. He always goes on the road to someplace remote like Timbuktu when the situation becomes serious."

Isaksen laughed. "That's how he's remained secretary general for as long as he has, Ingrid, love. When you are in the position, you will do the same thing, I'm sure."

Bittmann's only response was a low "Humph."

Isaksen, having seen the reports as they came in to headquarters, had, of course, planned what Bittmann's response to the situation would be before he entered the office. "First, I suggest you call a meeting of the UN representatives of the Middle East settlement participants for 9:00 AM tomorrow, to be followed by a closed session with the Permanent Five representatives at 2:00 PM. After the second meeting, I'll go and see what can be done with Sulayman in Cairo. I think you need to send Koniotis on a quick round of the key countries—concentrating on their security services and trying to get them to cooperate better. He probably should start with Egypt. I think you should call Malta directly to put pressure on them to make the counter conference go away. Here, I've outlined my views—in the form of directives, released in your name, of course," he said, as he pulled several sheets of paper out of his inner jacket pocket.

"And, oh," he began to wind down. "I took the liberty of drawing up a list of people who can be enlisted and sent to Cyprus to augment the UNICIS office there at least until the Amathus coast conference is over. I think the two of us need to get to Cyprus as soon as our schedules permit, as well. Same hotel but separate rooms— hopefully not too separate, however."

"Agreed," Ingrid murmured coyly, as she took the sheaves of paper and buzzed for the secretary. "Here, Benjamin," she said when the secretary arrived, "please have these directives I've drawn up released immediately. And get the Maltese foreign minister on the telephone. I have a bone to pick with that son of a bitch."

Chapter Nine

Jacques Piccard had managed to book at the last minute on the night flight from Amman to Zurich, but he was still highly agitated when he reached Switzerland. His heart was palpitating wildly, and his doctor had told him he should avoid any stress. As if he could avoid stress considering the businesses his family was in and the fact that he was a fugitive from the justice systems of both France and Cyprus. It had not helped that the only seat he could get on the flight had been in tourist class, and he had been trapped in a window seat by a very well-fed German businessman, who was taking a stuffed lamb back to his granddaughter as a souvenir from Jordan.

He had no trouble at Kloten Airport immigration and he hadn't anticipated any. The Swiss asked few questions, and he was well-documented as a member of the famous industrialist family, the Piccards, even if he no longer was specifically documented as Jacques Piccard, former French diplomat, illegal arms peddler, drug dealer, and murderer. He nearly ran from the airport, heart beating ever faster, and sped his Mercedes-Benz SL convertible out of the car park and southwesterly onto the autobahn toward Interlaken, in the Swiss lake district.

He only began to calm down as he was on the open road and almost to Lucerne. As he drove along, he began to assess his situation. True, he had encountered someone in Amman the night before who could link him with Cyprus, but, upon reflection, the danger of that was pretty slight. The pert young blonde he had been talking to didn't actually know him; she was only the girlfriend of someone who had known him. He had purposelessly mumbled his name. She probably hadn't even heard him. And she was just some blonde bimbo. Probably wouldn't have remembered his name even if she had heard it—not with all the commotion that went on after that. Thank god he'd been the only Piccard she encountered at the reception.

He had not stayed around after his encounter with the girl and what so unexpectedly followed after that. As he was withdrawing from the woman's side, a waiter had moved up to help block him from her sight. In an instant he had recognized the waiter as one of Abu Hani's trained Hizballah assassins. Piccard had not known Abu Hani planned an attack on the king that evening. Otherwise he, himself, would not have turned up for the reception. Now that he thought about it, he'd been obliquely warned not to, having heard Abu Hani declare that he hoped to see no Frenchmen there. Under the circumstances, he left the palace as rapidly as he could and didn't stop running until he reached the car park at Zurich's Kloten Airport. There were a few moments at Amman's Queen Alia International Airport when the security forces moved in to close down the airport following the attack on the king, but, luckily, they had permitted the flight to Zurich to leave before shutting down. Piccard had made it to the airport in record time and had invoked his family's considerable clout in the transportation business to quietly obtain a last-minute booking.

The flight itself had only managed to get off the ground because the airport manager had pleaded with the security forces that the timing of the departure of the Zurich flight was such that no one on that flight could possibly have had anything to do with attack at Raghadan Palace. A telephone call to the palace confirmed that the Jordanian government didn't want to irritate any of the European bankers and businessmen on the Zurich flight, and so Piccard was able to slip out of the country.

So, on review, what was the danger? He had whispered his name toward a dizzy blonde who surely had forgotten it in the excitement that followed, and this was the first time since he had fled France to avoid trial that anyone had come anywhere close to connecting him with his Cyprus activities of more than two years previously.

Still, the encounter had scared him. He didn't fancy being returned to either France or Cyprus for trial and incarceration—or worse. When his uncle had brought him back in on the Piccard connection with Abu Hani and the travel and money-laundering support for the Middle East terrorist organizations, Jacques had balked precisely on the basis that it was too dangerous for him to return to the region around the eastern end of the Mediterranean. It was best that he remain at the family castle in the mountains around the Jungfrau peak and above Interlaken, he had argued. And that, he now determined, was where he was going to go and where he was going to stay for a good long time.

The Interlaken castle had provided refuge for the Piccards for several centuries. He was not the first Piccard to get into trouble and to withdraw there, and he was not the first Piccard to have been hidden there and to have been presumed to have dropped off the face of the earth. The Swiss were protective and closed mouthed, especially where a great deal of money was involved. The mountains around the Jungfrau were remote, even though they were in the center of Europe. The castle itself was almost impregnable, and even within the castle's confines, there were countless hidden rooms and courtyards, where a person could live without detection in relative comfort and ease and with a minimum of support.

"Yes," Piccard thought smugly, as he cleared the last suburbs of Lucerne and pulled off the autobahn and onto a more rural road near the town of Sarnen, "my uncle is not one to talk about sticking one's neck out for the family and traveling into danger. He's done more than his own share of shady dealing and hiding. I'll just stay in Switzerland for several more years before I venture out again. There certainly are much worse punishments than being confined to Switzerland."

"Death by chocolate," Piccard whispered with a giggle. He was beginning to become playful. The Mercedes picked up speed. He enjoyed the way it hugged corners as he took them at high speed.

Already his heartbeat was returning to normal and his disposition was improving with every mile he drove into the interior of the lake district. He crossed a river at Sarnen, after which a string of lakes on his right would lead him down to Interlaken, from which he would start ascending the Jungfrau heights from the peak's northern slope. He could already see the snow-clad Jungfrau and its adjacent subordinate peaks straight ahead and above the windshield.

If Jacques Piccard had been paying attention to the road rather than looking up at the Jungfrau, he might have been able to avoid the beer truck approaching from around the next bend. Maybe Piccard could have stayed on the road and not hit the truck. But just maybe. The Mercedes was cornering at extraordinary speed, Jacques was not as good and attentive a driver as he thought he was, and the beer truck was wide and was moving at a pretty fast clip itself.

In any event, Jacques Piccard's hiding days were over.

* * * *

That Saturday morning the air was crisp and cool in the narrow, stone streets of the village of Lefkara in the Troodos foothills as Willie and Ginger Hamilton drove down to the Nicosia-Limassol highway in their baby blue BMW convertible. The heat and dust content of the air had risen considerably as the couple approached the Cypriot capital of Nicosia on the island's central plain.

Before entering the outskirts of the city, Willie turned left as the superhighway merged into Makarios Avenue and drove west to the couple's city apartment in the square of the old village of Strovolos. Once an independent town in its own right, Strovolos and its main feature, the presidential palace, had been swallowed up by the spreading Nicosia suburbs.

Willie Hamilton and his first wife had lived nearly twenty quietly happy, uneventful years in the five-room Strovolos apartment in the traditional-style building across the square from the Greek Orthodox church until his wife had the gall to die—as quietly and unobtrusively as she had lived—and Ginger had strutted into his life. Willie's and Ginger's own memories of the subsequent half decade in the apartment had not been nearly as soothing, and now the couple spent as much time in their Lefkara retreat, nearly an hour's drive to the south, as they could. Willie himself, however, did have to spend considerable time in Nicosia, as that was where his desk at the *Cyprus Mail* was.

On this morning, after he let Ginger off at the apartment, where she chatted amiably with the neighbors while he lugged groceries and baggage up the stairs, Willie drove over to Makarios Hospital, which was nearby, adjacent to the English School complex. He made one stop at a florist on his way, picking out the most vibrant and fragrant blossoms he could find. Hamilton was well known at the hospital, Nicosia's most modern medical facility, because he organized a charity collection annually through the pages of the *Cyprus Mail* to buy new equipment for the hospital.

Upon asking to speak with the notorious cave woman who had been found near Cape Greco a few days previously, Willie was informed that she hadn't spoken any words as yet. She had not, in fact, reacted to conversation at all. She had been thoroughly examined, C.A.T. scan and all, but nothing neurologically wrong had been found. She wasn't resistant; she just was totally docile. She even had to be fed, although once food and drink were placed in her mouth, she did chew and swallow normally.

Willie asked to be able to see her anyway, noting that there was a slight possibility he would recognize who she was. The doctors agreed on a meeting on this basis, but only on the condition that Willie not try to photograph or interview her for the newspapers.

"I think she's had enough exposure to the press for now," one of the doctors pronounced sternly. "Her most hostile response have been to reporters shoving their cameras and faces into her face. Too much contact with the press may cause her to regress rather than get better."

"I understand completely," Willie answered benignly. "This is probably more for my benefit than hers. Her face keeps haunting me. I probably never have seen her before, but the thought that I might have known her is eating at me. I have to put it to rest."

Hamilton was led to a private lounge area, where a picture window overlooked the English School sports field. Two teams of school students were dedicating their Saturday morning to practicing European-style football. As the youths ran up and down the field, Hamilton became absorbed in their play. He had been a good footballer himself back in the UK. So many years ago. So much time had gone by and so much had happened to him in the ensuing years. As he watched the boys, tears come to his eyes. He had always thought—and hoped—that he would have sons of his own. But that had not been in the cards. His first wife had not been able to have children. By the time he married for a second time, both he and his new wife were too old for that sort of thing. And Ginger—at least the Ginger he had known up to nearly two years ago—certainly would not have tolerated any thought that she should endanger her figure or to be tied down by having a child of her own.

It was just a moment of weakness. It no longer happened very often. Hamilton wiped the tear from his eye and turned. And there she was. She had been brought into the room in a wheelchair. The nurse still stood, protectively, behind the chair, holding both handles. The woman was small. The mystery patient looked more like a child, swallowed up as she was by the wheelchair. She sat hunched up and listing toward her left. Her right hand was in her lap. She was wearing a cotton hospital gown, and her left arm dangled listlessly over the arm of the chair. She was bent forward and was looking down at her right hand, not up at Hamilton or around her to take in her temporarily changed environment. She was turning her hand this way and that and kept following its movements with her eyes as if she had never before seen how a hand worked. Her long dark hair, probably luxurious and shiny in the best of circumstances, now was straggled, with strands hanging in her face. It was clean, however. The hospital had made every effort to tidy the woman up and to give her such dignity as they could provide. But she didn't show any effort to maintain that dignity on her own.

Hamilton walked slowly over toward the chair. When he was a few yards away, he introduced himself in a soft, reassuring voice. "Hello, I am William Hamilton. I thought I would come visit you today."

Although the woman's head had jerked up slightly at the mention of his name, it just as quickly dropped back. Willie still had not been able to get a look at her face.

134

He tried again. "It's such a beautiful day out. I thought you might like to see some of the spring flowers. Here, I brought you a bouquet of them."

He moved the flowers so that some of the blossoms intruded between eyes and hand in the woman's game of examining her own right hand.

Afterward, none of the doctors could be sure whether it was the bright blooms of the blossoms or their sharp fragrance that caught her attention, but the flowers arrested the woman's gaze, and she followed them up toward Hamilton's face as he raised the bouquet to just below his jaw.

She was looking up, across the bouquet, and into his face now, although her head was jerking in a slight rhythm that was causing the stroke-affected fallen right side of her face to move in fluid, disconcerting motion. Hamilton gently took her chin in his free hand, holding her face still and raising it a bit more so that he could get a closer look. He was receiving no more sign of recognition from a clear look at her in real life than he had from the fuzzy photograph. The woman was not resisting, but she remained in a dull, trance-like state.

Willie made one more effort. "I will leave you the flowers. Do you remember me? I am Willie Hamilton."

At the repeating of his name, the woman lifted her eyes so briefly from the flowers and to Hamilton's face. For that brief moment the eyes lost their dull sheen.

Hamilton exclaimed and dropped the bouquet of flowers. It was the sudden light that went on in the velvet eyes. The eyes were the giveaway. The effects of the stroke and her state of disrepair had masked her beauty. The smooth, olive-colored skin was familiar but hardly distinctive in this region of the world. But the velvety, violet eyes, with their diamond-hard sparkle—if only seen for a second— were enough of a clue. It had to be; there was no other like her.

"Suzanne," Hamilton stuttered. His gaze went up to the nurse and on to the approaching doctor. "It's Suzanne Abu Hani. It's the wife of the former Lebanese ambassador."

Hamilton's eyes dropped back to Suzanne's. Her eyes, now ablaze as in her former existence, latched onto his and they drank of mutual recognition. The muscles of her face tightened before his very eyes, and her features exploded back into distinct vestiges of her former beauty.

Her hands rose to her face, which dropped to join them, and she began to sob. Hamilton fell back into a chair, as the nurse and doctor enveloped their patient in a protective shell.

The shock wore off quickly, at least for Hamilton. A triumphant gleam in his eye, he rose, picked up the bouquet of flowers, and placed them in the wheelchair next to Suzanne. As he passed the doctor, he asked for a private conference. The two walked off a couple of paces and Hamilton murmured, "You'd best call in the police again. Mrs. Abu Hani is a fugitive from a terrorist activities charge here in Cyprus." Then he strode with bouncy and strong steps toward the car park.

Willie Hamilton was on his way to chalk up yet another exclusive story for the *Cyprus Mail.*

* * * *

The atmosphere in the New York UN headquarters building conference room was so heavy with tension that Ingrid Bittmann felt like she was on the interminable chug of a roller coaster car up to the top of the trestle just before the car plunged over the brink.

It was half past 10:00 AM already, and the Palestinian representative hadn't yet arrived for this most significant meeting on salvaging the Middle East peace effort. By a miracle, most of the other key players, including the representatives of Israel, Jordan, and Egypt—albeit somewhat dazed at the events of the previous two days, had arrived by the appointed hour of 9:00 AM. The Egyptian was quite noticeably avoiding the Israeli and the Jordanian, but he was here. Eric would just have to work on the Egyptian directly following the meeting, Bittmann thought stonily.

The Syrian delegate also hadn't arrived. The Iraqi delegate, who tried to crash the meeting, had been turned away and had lingered, belligerently, in the hallway. When the Syrian had approached, the Iraqi had given him a challenging look, and the Syrian had disappeared into an elevator. Eric Isaksen had saved that particular day by privately talking to the Iraqi in soothing tones, so that he eventually left, and then by tracking down the Syrian representative and guiding him back to the conference room.

Once all those expected, but the Palestinian, had assembled. Isaksen continued saving the day—and Ingrid let him do it. He was the experienced negotiator for the Middle East, and he was doing a great job of unruffling feathers and pointing out that nothing had changed over the last few days between the governments of the region and the goals they were striving for. What was happening was the natural attempt by the forces of opposition to undermine the agreement from the outside. It was the controlling and extirpation of just these forces that had been a major goal of the move toward a peace settlement by the region's legitimate governments.

While Isaksen was working his magic, Bittmann went to a telephone and started trying to track down and snare the Palestinian representative. The two had been friends for many years. A prominent woman doctor in the Arab sector of Jerusalem, the Palestinian UN representative's calm demeanor, moderate language, and sharp logic had brought her to the forefront as the PLO's official spokesperson during its recent successful bid for the establishment of a Palestinian state on at least some of the territory the Palestinians had long claimed was rightfully theirs. Her success in that venue had led to her appointment to the UN seat, where she had continued to function as a voice of reason for the Palestinian cause. Ingrid could not imagine why the woman would boycott this meeting, even in the face—especially in the face—of the assassination of the legendary PLO leader. The Palestinian UN representative was a brave person; she had asserted her intelligence in far more confusing and dangerous situations than this.

When Bittmann reached the Palestinian representative, the woman was apologetic but very mysterious.

"Yes, the Palestinians will be represented in your meeting. Our representative will arrive at the conference room at any moment. No, I won't be attending the meeting. But there's something you need to know, Ingrid—"

But the warning came too late. The "something" was already standing in the doorway of the conference room. It—or, rather, he—

had been accompanied down the hallway by a loud hubbub that had distracted Bittmann from her telephone conversation and had silenced and attracted the attention of all of the representatives in the conference room.

This was quite possibly the most dramatic entrance that had ever been made during a long and eventful career by the apparently resurrected legendary PLO chief.

"Ingrid? Ingrid?" The Palestinian doctor was calling insistently on the other end of the line.

"Ingrid, I must warn you that the PLO chief isn't dead. His wife was indeed gunned down in their Palestinian home yesterday morning. But it wasn't the PLO chief who was in bed with her. He was here in the United States for private talks in Washington. He's decided to attend your meeting himself. He's fighting mad and wants to bolster the support for the peace conference in person. Ingrid? Ingrid?"

Chapter Ten

Caitlyn and Takis Koniotis stood, arm in arm, in the rosy glow of the twilight, each lost in their own separate memories and melancholia. This was usually their favorite time of the day. And it was their favorite place in which to sip a predinner drink; discuss their separate challenges, victories, and defeats of the day; and watch their twin boys explore the small grassy plot—grass still being a high-premium landscaping form in the semiarid Cyprus—as night fell on the whitewashed walls, red-tile roofs, and exotic Mediterranean plantings in the Makedonitissa Valley floor below the terrace of their hilltop home.

On this evening, however, although both were looking down into the valley, neither drank in the view with quite the same delight as on previous evenings. The boys were not with them. They had been marched off by the family's nanny, Irene, in preparation for bed. Their happy chatter echoed from the bath above their parents' heads. That they were oblivious to the situation was seen as both a blessing and a painful stab to the heart by Caitlyn. She didn't want them to be touched by the burden of grief at this time in their lives, but their approach to this evening—as if nothing in the family's life had changed—added to their mother's depression.

Boys taken care of, Irene and her helper were fluttering about the kitchen behind where Caitlyn and Takis stood. The kitchen area extended out onto the terrace in a three-sided glass enclosure, and the bright light from this area encased the couple like a picture frame. The two were being as quiet as possible, but one can only be so quiet while preparing a full meal for eight.

Takis had suggested that they just cancel the dinner, but they had just invited close friends, and Caitlyn and Irene had already prepared most of the food the previous day—before the blow had been struck. This was supposed to have been the last relaxing evening most of those present were to have until after the peace conference on the Amathus coast had concluded. Now it would be more of a wake. All of those attending the dinner had known Paul Conte and Ellen Larkin well. Caitlyn had reasoned, therefore, that there was every reason for them to go ahead with the evening. It would still be the last time in a long while all could take the time to reflect and share , the shocking events of the last few days, now closer than before.

Caitlyn gave a sudden shudder and leaned into her husband, who wrapped a comforting arm around her.

"Why, Takis? They were so happy and so close to starting a new life together, far away from all of this hatred throughout the region and the terrorist activity."

141

"It doesn't make any sense, of course," responded Takis gently. "But that's all the more reason for us to continue to try to resolve these issues."

"Why should you care about the Middle East problems?" Caitlyn asked almost defiantly. "It's not your problem. You have your own problems to solve here in Cyprus. Takis, I'm scared. Suddenly scared. I always thought I was so brave, but now I want to just withdraw into our own life here, our own island, and let the Middle East just stew in its hatreds."

"Now, Caitlyn," answered her husband, as he wrapped both arms around her and stared down into the valley over her shoulder. "I know you are grieving, and you have every reason to grieve. You also have every reason to be scared. But you know better—better than most—than to suggest that you are ready to fold. You're probably the bravest person I know. You've proved your strength to be far greater than mine over the past three years. You've got to hang in there on this."

"Besides," he continued as he changed tactics by pulling her around to face him and smiling wanly down into her eyes, "you must not give up the ground you have gained in developing my sense of objectivity over these past three years. The Middle East peace settlement matters to me precisely because of what it might mean for a settlement of the division of Cyprus. I must believe that if the broader and deeper regional situation can be resolved, then there is hope for us Cypriots. Try to consider how far you—you and perhaps Safa Ziya— have brought me these past three years. Three years ago I would have been one of the first to declare that no settlement of either situation—

the Middle East or the Cyprus problem—was possible, and that no understanding on my own part was required. Now I know there are multiple rights and wrongs and justified hurts on all sides of issues such as these. Paul was working for this settlement too, remember. We mustn't take that away from him. Beyond his own very brave sacrifice, his own hard work for peace in itself justified his life."

"What will she do now, Takis? And I never did learn where she was. Was she at his side? Did she have to watch it?"

"I don't know what she'll do. No, mercifully, she probably didn't actually see Paul and the king's aide die as they threw themselves over the king and the queen. But she must have been nearby. She was the one who wrestled the assailant to the floor, I'm told. Couldn't keep him from turning his gun on himself, but undoubtedly kept him from making a follow-up attempt on the king."

"Ellen to the rescue again," Caitlyn whispered in bittersweet tones through a veil of tears. "She's so deceptive. Small and delicate. But such strength and lightning-fast reflexes. She saved me once under similar circumstances. I'm sure that if anyone could have saved Paul last night it would have been Ellen. I wish I were there with her. She's not so strong that she should have to face this alone."

"Would you be willing to leave the boys with Irene for a week or so?" Takis asked in a quiet voice.

"What do you mean?"

"You voice my thoughts exactly about Ellen. I have to go to Egypt on Monday, and I'm supposed to go to Jordan by Tuesday evening. Go with me. There will be a memorial service for Paul. The king is pulling out all the stops—as well he should for the man who saved his wife's life. As you say, Ellen needs someone—and the two of you are fast friends. And I also know that Paul meant a great deal to you—and no, not as a former lover. I knew that that stopped before it even really began. I knew he was a very good friend to you. He was a good friend of mine as well. He was a great support to me when you and Eric Isaksen were kidnapped by those terrorists. I don't think you'll ever be able to fully come to grips with this unless you go to Amman, can be with Ellen during some of her worst hours of need, and attend that memorial service."

Caitlyn didn't respond for the longest moment. Takis wrapped his arms around her and whispered once again into her hair, "Go with me."

And then after a bit longer, Caitlyn responded. "Yes, you're right. I'll go with you, but. . . ."

"But what?" queried Takis when his wife was slow to complete her thought.

"But first, let's please go up to Kakopetria tomorrow," gushed forth.

This took Takis completely by surprise, and he dropped his hold on his wife. But Caitlyn continued before he could ask any questions.

"I know that sounds strange. But increasingly over the past several days, thoughts of Eleni Piccard have been intruding on my mind. Even now, when I should only be thinking about Paul, Eleni keeps breaking in. You know my pattern of intuitions. They've led me to many an archaeology find. Something similar is happening with Eleni now. I walk through her house here, and she starts to obsess me.

144

I always wind up in the loft, looking through that one carton of her private papers and mementos that remained after this house was ransacked before we inherited it.

"I can't quite figure out why this happens to me; I just know that she's trying to tell me something—or if that is too much spiritualism for you, it seems like the inner reaches of my mind have connected something to do with her with something important happening in our lives. And now, in my mind, she's becoming intertwined with Paul. Even before you came over from the office to tell me he was dead, he and Eleni were intertwining in my thoughts. I feel I must go up to Kakopetria—perhaps to visit the grave sites there of Eleni and her husband and son. And maybe even to go over to her Old Mill restaurant and hotel, to visit her apartment above the restaurant. Maybe more will unfold for me there, or maybe it will all just unwind and leave me alone."

Caitlyn's face was starting to flush, and her speech had gained speed and intensity as she spoke.

"Of course," Takis answered. His tone was one of consolation and deep concern. "Safa is coming in tomorrow, and Tom Jameson has returned to work. I planned to take some time tomorrow to gather my thoughts for the Middle East round of visits I've been asked to make. I can do that as we drive up into the Troodos. But, I'm not sure—"

He was not to finish his sentence, as Irene was motioning from the kitchen that the first of the guests had arrived, and he and Caitlyn composed themselves and walked into the house, heads held high, and arm in arm, a unified defense against despair.

* * * *

Ayman Abu Hani, the convener of the conference and the delegate of the Hizballah, and a few of his "friends," among them a nervous secret representative of the Syrian government and a dejected delegate from the radical Abu Nidal faction of the Palestinian movement, stood quietly at the yacht basin dock of St. Julian's, a small, popular Maltese resort harbor to the north of Valetta. Other representatives had already gone out to the Libyan leader's vessel and more would be going later, all from different points on Malta's western coast, so as to be as inconspicuous as possible. Abu Hani was keeping the Syrian as close to his side as possible, though. Cooperation from the Syrians—open cooperation rather than the fence-sitting half-hearted help they had been mealy mouthing of late—would be a real plum for Abu Hani's efforts. With that in mind, he would be paying as much attention to the Syrian as possible.

Piccard wasn't with him now. He had left Malta to perform other vital services elsewhere. Early in the morning Abu Hani would return to Beirut briefly himself to bolster the strength of his own backing in Lebanon and within the Hizballah forces. He never could be gone from his power base too long these days. Just maybe he would fit in a trip to Damascus as well.

As they waited for the skiff that would take them out to The Colonel's yacht, Abu Hani reviewed the events of the last couple of days. One out of four on an initial assault wasn't too bad, especially since they had come close on the rest. Close enough so that the leaders of all four countries were surely terrified. In addition, the mass death of the national delegates in Cairo who had been working on the peace agreement for months would be a real setback for the Amathus conference—or at least Abu Hani fervently hoped it would be—and all the little brush fires that had been started worldwide had been particularly effective. The death of the Egyptian president was a big boost, and his replacement was very shaky. The loss of Egypt alone would be enough to bring the whole peace settlement process to a halt. The withdrawal of any of the four countries would do the trick, as a matter of fact.

It was a pity about the PLO chief—and the Abu Nidal representative standing beside him had every right to be embarrassed and frightened. He would not be treated lightly during this evening's meeting for having misjudged the whereabouts of the PLO leader and having killed his wife's hairdresser instead. They hadn't even known what country the PLO leader had been in. These people had always been so cocky about their intelligence network. There would be some well-deserved ridicule to pass on tonight.

In some ways, this was a good development for Abu Hani and the Hizballah, as it would keep the Abu Nidal faction from trying to take control of the opposition movement. But Abu Hani knew he couldn't let criticism of these people get out of hand. They still needed the Abu Nidal faction, and just as soon as the various groups started falling out among themselves, the benefit of their tenuous new-found unity would dissolve.

They had come close on the Israeli bitch. But they had managed to rough up a good many of her supporters, so that action had not been a total loss. And if they really needed to take her out of the picture, they could do so. She couldn't brush her teeth in safety.

Strange thing that they had managed to get even the rightist Zionists here for this "counter" conference. They wouldn't go out to The Colonel's ship, of course. But Abu Hani's own meeting with them a couple of hours previously had been very enlightening, and they offered up a surprising asset. If the peace conference actually opened in Cyprus or if he needed to know more about the conference's security plan, that asset should prove to be quite valuable. Of course, he had a couple of assets of his own to activate if operations on Cyprus proved necessary.

The attack on the Jordanian king had actually gone just as planned. They hadn't wanted to kill him—only to put him on notice. He was still needed to hold the core of Palestine together. When the situation was ripe, *then* they would kill him, and the whole fruit would fall into their laps—into Ayman Abu Hani's lap, if he played his hand cleverly.

The skiff was pulling up to the dock, Abu Hani could see. He could now see the faces of the deck hands on the boat. His eyes rapidly moved from face to face for the sign. Ah, yes, there he was. The slight nod of the head. The Colonel was on the ship and everything was in order. Abu Hani did not need to feign illness. It was safe for him to attend the meeting. Of course, he missed Piccard. He always felt safer and more assured when the suave French shipping magnate was by his side for such meetings. The two of them understood each other. Everyone else they had to deal with was just crude rabble.

Abu Hani's man in The Colonel's entourage helped him into the boat. As he did so, he gave the agreed nod once again, wanting to make sure Abu Hani had gotten the signal. Abu Hani nervously looked around at the other boatmen. He thought The Colonel was far too self-possessed and falsely confident to suspect that Abu Hani would have managed—or even considered—suborning one of his trusted servants. But they had to be very careful anyway.

Abu Hani's visual check of the rest of the crew was reassuring. None of these had seen the signal.

None of them had needed to see the second signal. The man who had been assigned to watch Jemal like a hawk had seen the first signal and had appreciated it for what it meant. When the time came, they could find out from Jemal exactly what message that nod conveyed to Abu Hani—that is before they killed the traitor, or maybe both Jemal and Abu Hani.

This was not the day that Ayman Abu Hani would come under the sway of The Colonel, however. Just as he was ready to climb down into the skiff, a man rushed down the dock, calling his name. The two men stood aside at the dock, and the more the man said to Abu Hani, the more agitated the Lebanese diplomat became.

"She's where?" the men in the skiff could hear him say. "That's done it, then. She'll have to go. I was supposed to already be done with her," after the man had whispered to him in agitated tones.

After a pause in which Abu Hani seemed to be in deep thought, the other man said something no one could hear, to which Abu Hani replied, not attempting to shield his voice. "I'll catch the next plane back. But phone ahead and tell them to take care of it—call our contact on the island."

And then the two men turned and strode away from the skiff and back toward dry land, leaving Jemal trying not to look dismayed and the men watching Jemal trying not make it too obvious they were watching him.

* * * *

The dinner party at the Koniotis villa did not start off as a disaster; the evening didn't disintegrate until later and even then went out with more of a double pop than a single loud bang. Dinner never actually got served, however.

Koniotis's former colleague and the current head of the Cypriot International Investigations Unit, Maria Solonos, had, along with her now live-in boyfriend, the *Simerini* political columnist Demetris Mattas, been the first to arrive. They had been out on a long drive in the countryside all day and looked physically tired as well as emotionally drained over the death of Conte and over the other international events during the previous few days.

Next the British high commission intelligence chief Alec Stuart had arrived alone. Caitlyn and Irene, who was making up the eighth guest for dinner, entertained Maria and Demetris while Takis and Alec withdrew to the back terrace for a few moments of private conversation.

"Entertained" wasn't quite the right word for the discussion in the main lounge, however. Maria and Demetris had also known Paul Conte well when he was a political officer at the American embassy in Nicosia, and they were almost as shell-shocked by his death in Amman the previous evening as Caitlyn was. It was left to Takis's aunt, Irene, to fill in most of the tense silences. The discussion wasn't all silences, however. Caitlyn and Maria, in particular, were sharing grief and were constructively engaged in a healing process, a process that would have to continue for some time, however, before Caitlyn, especially, was whole again.

Meanwhile, on the terrace, Takis and Alec had possibly the rougher task of not only coming to grips with the death of Paul, with whom Alec had shared many a beer and many a dangerous adventure, but they also had to work through the death in Malta of Takis's UNICIS subordinate and colleague, Stefan Gunnerson. Both exhibited evidence of deep feelings of personal guilt over Gunnerson's death. Takis had sent the man to Malta to check up on the counter conference of the Middle East dissident forces—an acknowledged high-risk assignment. And Alec had accompanied Gunnerson to Malta and had promised to look out for him.

Both now, in the dark gloom of the back terrace on the hill in Makedonitissa, expressed words of self-reproach and regret. Both knew the risks of this business, however, and more time was spent on Alec providing a fuller report of what had transpired with Gunnerson and what was transpiring with the conference being hosted on the Libyan leader's yacht than he had managed to convey earlier in the international-connection telephone call.

The review of what little the high commission in Malta had been able to glean thus far on the counter conference was just drawing to a close, when the evening started to disintegrated in earnest.

The Hamiltons, the *Cyprus Mail* political reporter Willie and his wife, Ginger, the other couple that had been invited this evening, had arrived. The Hamiltons were, of course, famous for arriving late and for making such a scene that events were hopelessly disrupted. Most of that, however, was a thing of the past. They still habitually arrived late, but, since their relationship had mellowed and solidified, they had stopped being party spoilers. For other reasons, however, on this evening they lived up to their old reputation.

Upon being greeted at the door by Irene, Willie fairly rushed into the lounge and looked like he was about to burst with a revelation. Ginger overrode him, however, and went straight to Caitlyn to offer words of consolation over the death of Paul. This discussion went for several minutes, with Willie expanding like an overfull balloon throughout. Not being about to hold himself any longer, he burst—just as Takis and Alec entered from the terrace behind where Willie was standing.

"I'm sorry, this is just too important to hold in any longer," he exclaimed. "You'll never guess what I found out this morning. An exclusive. Only I got it. We're late because I had to stay at the *Mail* until it was put to bed."

Demetris Mattas, Willie's friend, but also Willie's fierce competitor for political news, rose to the edge of his seat.

"Not now, honey," admonished Ginger as she looked over Willie's shoulder and started to gesture. "We need to talk about Paul now. You should wait to—"

But Willie couldn't wait and he completely missed Ginger's signals. "The cave woman. I went to the hospital today and I identified her. They've moved her to the central prison. You would never guess. The cave woman is Suzanne. Suzanne Abu Hani."

A glass crashed to the terrazzo floor behind Willie. Alec, in a strangled voice, said, "Suzanne? Here? Suzanne!" And the ugliest expression anyone had seen from the ruddy, carefree Englishman came across his face.

"Yes, Suzanne."

Suzanne Abu Hani, who was the wife of the former Lebanese ambassador to Cyprus Ayman Abu Hani. The ambassador had escaped the island nearly two years previously under well-documented suspicion of having supported terrorism, spying, kidnapping, and murder. His wife, Suzanne, had disappeared at the same time, implicated in the same crimes. Alec Stuart, her lover at the time—but only one of her many lovers—had also been one of her dupes. She had stolen secrets from him and she had tried to murder him. He had loved her and he had hated her. And at hearing that she was alive and back in Cyprus, he was out the front door of the Koniotis residence and gone—the first explosion of the evening for the ill-fated dinner party.

At Stuart's exclamation, Hamilton turned, but not quickly enough to see who had spoken before the figure had left the house.

"Who—?"

"Alec Stuart," Ginger answered quietly—in years past she would have used a cutting remark at this point that would have drawn blood from someone in the room.

Demetris Mattas, however, launched into an interrogation of Willie on the identification of Suzanne Abu Hani that more-or-less nullified the effect of Stuart's dramatic departure, if only for the moment. Takis, Caitlyn, and Maria were also fully drawn into the explanation, because they had all been deeply affected by Suzanne Abu Hani's duplicity and activities.

After having heard the basics, Mattas headed for the door. He might not have gotten the exclusive, but he still had time to get something into his own paper for tomorrow, which would still put him a step ahead of everyone but Willie. And, truth be known, he was only slightly less affected by the news than Alec had been, as he had been one of Suzanne's lovers of the past himself.

Mattas didn't begrudge Willie his exclusive. He clearly had earned it.

Maria had been biting at the bit to leave even before Demetris was ready to go. Since Suzanne was a high-profile foreigner, this investigation now was squarely on Maria's desk, and she should have been informed and on the job hours ago. No matter what the explanation was for Suzanne's return to the island, she was involved in several unresolved criminal investigations.

If Mattas and Solonos had stayed around for another ten minutes, however, Mattas would have been able to avoid letting Willie score a second news scoop for the day—because that is when the second bombshell hit.

The telephone rang and Takis picked up the extension in the lounge. It was his office. The news bulletin had just come in from Switzerland. A man carrying false documents but identified by Interpol as the fugitive former French ambassador to Cyprus, Jacques Piccard, had been killed earlier that day in an automobile accident in the lake district near Lucerne.

Jacques Piccard, who also was the nephew of the long-missing husband of Caitlyn's friend and benefactor, Eleni Piccard, had been the mastermind of the illegal arms shipment made in trade for illegal drugs case that brought Caitlyn and Takis together for the first time just a few years previously. He also had been implicated in the presumed deaths during the chaos of the 1974 Turkish invasion of Cyprus of Eleni's husband and young son, whose bones had been identified almost exactly twenty years later in a remote section of the Kyrenia harbor castle on the island's northern coast.

When Takis related what he had been told over the telephone, Willie Hamilton announced that, under the circumstances, he and Ginger, of course, would have to leave. He expressed his apologies for having upset Alec Stuart and for having to depart early, but he would have to return to the *Cyprus Mail* to get this new story verified, written, and into the next day's edition.

As Takis was seeing the Hamiltons to the door, Irene also left for the kitchen to do what she could to preserve the dinner that was getting cold through neglect.

When Takis turned back to the lounge, he found Caitlyn sitting where he had left her. She was as white as a sheet and almost in a state of trance.

"I knew something was trying to break through on the Piccards. I felt Eleni trying to reach me. Something isn't right. Something important is very wrong," she was saying in a weak voice. "Takis," she then said in a stronger voice, her eyes fully open. "I'm sure I'm right. I'm more sure now than ever that we need to go up to Kakopetria tomorrow."

"Certainly, whatever you want," Takis responded with concern. "But you're exhausted tonight, I can tell. Let's go on up to bed now. Irene will be happy to clean up for us. I think we've been visited by entirely too many ghosts from the past already this evening."

If he could have strangled these words in his throat before he uttered them, he would have done so. Even as they involuntarily bubbled out, he looked over at his wife in horror. But she wasn't listening to him. She was lost in her own thoughts.

Later, in the wee hours of the morning, when some slight sound woke Takis, he found Caitlyn in the loft above the bedroom, flashlight in hand, sifting once more through Eleni Piccard's pitiful, small carton of memorabilia.

Chapter Eleven

When the short-staff Sunday dayshift of the Cypriot Police International Investigations Unit started showing up for work at the Nicosia departmental headquarters the next morning, they were surprised to see their chief, Maria Solonos, in her office and hard at work. When she emerged into the central squad room a short time after 8:00 AM, they wouldn't have guessed that she had been in the office and laying plans all night from the energy with which she set forth assignments and dispatched investigative teams. By 9:00 AM they realized that there were not enough special police officers on duty in the whole Nicosia District this morning to handle her investigation schedule, and she called in extra help. Sunday or no Sunday, they couldn't sit on the disappearance of the unit's deputy chief any longer.

Maria and Demetris nearly hadn't even attempted to go to the Koniotises' house for dinner the previous evening. If anyone else had invited them and if Maria hadn't needed to give support to—and receive support from—Caitlyn over the death of Paul Conte, they would have begged off. They had spent the entire day driving around

157

villages in the foothills of the Troodos range to the immediate north of Limassol in search of leads to the now seriously disturbing disappearance of Androulla Varnavidou more than a week previously.

Through his newspaper connections, Demetris had found out on Friday morning that over the most recent two months Androulla had been seen in several villages on the slopes of the Troodos range in all directions and had apparently been checking out identities from a series of photos. When Maria was told this, she suddenly experienced a sinking feeling in the pit of her stomach.

Two years previously a Hizballah terrorist band that had been on secret training maneuvers and had been running kidnapping operations on Cyprus had been tracked down by the international crimes unit, then under the direction of Takis Koniotis. Takis's own wife, Caitlyn; a UN official, Erick Isaksen; and the wife of a Russian diplomat had been kidnapped. The chief of the band had escaped the island but had been killed while he was en route to London. The second in command, a woman, and one of the other members of the band had been seized while attempting to fly out of the country. The squad member had been murdered while in police custody, but the second in command had been kept alive, had been prosecuted and sentenced here in Cyprus, and was still in the central prison in Nicosia. All of the rest of the known terrorist force members had been presumed killed in a ship explosion as they tried to escape by sea from the island's western coast. The bodies from that explosion had been brought back to land, and the second in command of the terrorist brigade had identified them. It was this terrorist operation that both the former Lebanese ambassador, Ayman Abu Hani, and his wife,

Suzanne, had been found to have masterminded. They had both escaped, although not together.

Maria's sinking feeling had come because two months ago she had received word that the terrorist deputy commander, who until now had revealed very little information on the background of the terrorist operation, had told her jailers that she was ready to tell all in exchange for better prison conditions—that she had some significant knowledge she hadn't revealed before. This had surfaced at the same time that the Cypriots had learned that a major Middle East peace conference was set for the southern Cyprus coast, and Maria had instantaneously been swamped with the need to lay plans to ensure that the conference would be free from foreign threat. She had thus asked Androulla to interview the imprisoned terrorist and to follow up that investigation. And then Maria had promptly forgotten this case in the face of pressing and increasing issues in connection with the Amathus coast conference.

Maria now knew, by checking around the office on Friday afternoon and reviewing the files in Androulla's office, that the woman terrorist had given Androulla some possibly useful information that could cause the terrorist case—known as the Mouflon Brigade case, because the terrorists had named themselves after the endangered species of wild sheep that were found only in the Troodos Mountains—to be reactivated. On Friday evening Maria interviewed the prisoner herself and learned two disturbing things. First, although the woman had deserted the band before they boarded the ship that eventually exploded, the prisoner now said she thought that not all of the terrorists had been accounted for.

She had been forced to identify the bodies from the shipwreck and, at the time, had lied and declared that all of the terrorists except the leader of the unit were accounted for. In fact, however, she was now saying that three other members of the unit were not among the dead. Apparently she had thought for a long time that the unit leader and up to three of the others had gone into the hills of Cyprus rather than on the boat and were still on the island. She hadn't revealed the information earlier either through loyalty to her comrades or because she was afraid they would get to her and kill her if she revealed what she knew. She had not been told at the time that the unit leader had been killed on a flight to London, but she somehow had found this out since her trial.

The most disturbing fragment of information the prisoner revealed was that one of the terrorists she couldn't account for had been half Cypriot, and there had always been a plan for him to remain behind as a spy in place when the rest of the band returned to Lebanon. His name had been Salem Qazzar.

That was not the only result of the interview that had disturbed Maria. The prisoner had also said that, although the information had not been shared with her, she was sure that there had been someone other than the Lebanese ambassador and his wife who had been in place in Cyprus and was powerful enough to provide the Hizballah with information and help.

In checking around the office, Maria had found that Androulla had obtained the photographs of the three possible terrorist brigade fighters who possibly could still be on the island and had been showing these around in rural areas herself to see if she could establish identities. And she had been doing all of this by herself and without discussing it with Maria. Maria was now very upset with herself, because she knew Androulla had not called on any of the resources of the unit to support this investigation from the knowledge that Maria needed all the help she could get to set up for the Amathus coast conference. Androulla had even been so busy with this part of the job herself that Maria never suspected her deputy was conducting a separate investigation.

And if what the prisoner had revealed had any validity, Maria had now realized, Androulla's investigation was not separate from the protection of the Middle East conference proceedings. If there was one or more Hizballah operatives still in place in Cyprus, this, in itself, was a threat to the conference.

By half past 9:00 AM, Solonos had sent teams out with pictures of the three terrorists who had not been accounted for and of Androulla to blanket the country in search of information on her deputy. She was beginning to despair that Androulla was alive. But if she wasn't alive, then that quite possibly meant that her investigation had, indeed, flushed out a hidden Hizballah agent.

After the teams left, Maria set out for the hospital wing of the central prison. She would take up the initial interview with Suzanne Abu Hani herself. This was also connected with the case Androulla was working on. It was very peculiar that this terrorist band case, considered closed for more than a year, was suddenly coming to life again—and on more than one front.

* * * *

At the same moment, high above the Mediterranean, as the island of Cyprus disappeared under the left wing of the aircraft, Ayman Abu Hani—although currently traveling in style under an assumed identity and impressive but false Lebanese diplomatic documents—was also being hit squarely and unexpectedly in the face with the Mouflon Brigade case, the operation that he indeed had masterminded. He wasn't any happier than Maria Solonos had been to discover that the case had resurfaced. In fact, he was apoplectic over the finding and had spilled a whole glass of Remy Martin down his silk shirtfront to emphasize his displeasure.

For some time Abu Hani hadn't tempted fate by transferring flights through Cyprus, where he was on a stop list under his true name and with his "before Mouflon Brigade" physical features, but the situation with the case had been so quiet for over a year that he no longer avoided transiting Larnaca Airport. Cyprus was still one of the primary hubs through which one reached Beirut.

The Lebanese death merchant had flown from Malta to Paris and then down to Cyprus, where he stopped over for a couple of hours in the business class lounge to catch the flight into Beirut. He had not bothered to pick up a copy of the *Cyprus Mail* in the lounge— he had contented himself with the *Cyprus Weekly*, which had been published two days previously, for the quick check he required on what was happening on the island. But once he got back in the air, a freshly released copy of the *Cyprus Mail* was dropped in his lap, and his wife quite unexpectedly dropped back into his life.

There Suzanne was, in the form of a three-column front-page file photo of the then-ravishingly beautiful wife of the then-Lebanese ambassador to Cyprus. As controlled and unflappable as Ayman Abu Hani was, he could hardly have been blamed for spilling his Cognac when coming face to face with a woman he sent off from Tripoli, Lebanon, two weeks previously to be murdered and dumped at sea. When he had at least partially recovered his poise, he poured over the article on the mysterious surfacing of Suzanne on the Cyprus coast that had been written by William Hamilton, and then he began to seethe and scheme.

Luckily for Abu Hani's heart and for the dispositions of his fellow first-class passengers, the flight from Larnaca to Beirut was very short. When the sometimes diplomat disembarked—and all of the other passengers were held in the airplane's aisles until Abu Hani had descended the metal stairs—he walked right by the entourage strung across the tarmac to greet him, reached through the window of his waiting limousine, grabbed the cellular telephone, and began viciously punching in numbers.

* * * *

Maria Solonos's visit with Suzanne Abu Hani had not been very revealing, but it had been a start. It was evident that Suzanne had, indeed, lost touch with reality and with who she was as a by-product of the slight stroke she had suffered. She did not pretend not to know Maria or not to know that she was a fugitive from a whole list of international crimes charges in Cyprus. In fact, she was now enough in touch with her past to have declared that, as an ambassador's wife, she held diplomatic immunity from prosecution in Cyprus at the time of the crimes for which she had been charged. However, Maria was convinced that the woman was telling the truth when she said she didn't snap back into reality until William Hamilton visited her on the previous day.

That given, Maria was not sure how much of what had happened in recent weeks Suzanne genuinely didn't now remember and how much she was hiding on the pretense of not remembering. Maria was sure, however, that Suzanne was not being fully forthcoming about recent events, because when Maria said they would let the Lebanese government know of her presence here so they could inform her husband, Suzanne went white as a sheet and asked that her identity remain a secret. When Maria then showed her the front of the *Cyprus Mail* and declared that it was entirely too late for Suzanne to remain anonymous to the world, Suzanne withdrew into herself both physically and emotionally, and the interview was abruptly over.

But Maria wasn't finished with Suzanne, and she would be back every day until she had gotten what she needed. Not only would Suzanne eventually begin to remember the events of the last several weeks, but she also would not be able to hold back on information on the in-place support mechanisms, other than she and her husband, that had existed for the benefit of the Hizballah brigade that had terrorized Cyprus two years previously. Suzanne had led a pampered life. Once she was fully herself, she would fold under the threat of deprivation. Suzanne was a strong person, but Maria was ready for the challenge.

As she left the prison's hospital unit, Maria took the time to ensure that the full allotment of guards had been assigned to that section.

* * * *

Symeon Parikan replaced the telephone receiver. He had seen the article on Suzanne Abu Hani's mysterious reappearance in Cyprus in the Sunday morning edition of *Simerini* and, after sending his wife over to see her parents in the neighboring village, he had remained next to the telephone in his Fikardou home for the remainder of the morning and into the afternoon. He originally had planned to conduct a day search of the quarry area just in case he had overreacted on Friday night, but, upon seeing the *Simerini* article he knew he would be called. And he was, but not by who he had expected. However, the instructions themselves were no different than he had expected.

He was directed in no uncertain terms to find Suzanne Abu Hani as quickly as possible and to kill her as quickly as possible. He even was told how to find her. He was told to follow the *Cyprus Mail* reporter William Hamilton and that Hamilton should eventually lead him to Abu Hani. He was told that Hamilton was expendable as well, although he shouldn't risk his own life if getting Hamilton was a problem. After the Abu Hani action, he would still be needed to help ensure a Middle East conference was aborted if it actually was able to open in Cyprus.

Just after his local-call connection had disconnected, he received the telephone call he had expected, the one from Lebanon. As expected, this caller also instructed him to take care of Suzanne Abu Hani. Parikan didn't mention the earlier call; there would be no difficulty in fulfilling both requests, as they both centered on the death of Mrs. Abu Hani. He did wonder, however, why he was receiving the same instructions from both his international and his local contacts— and whether each knew the other had issued the same directive.

Parikan left a note for his wife, saying he had been called away to work in Paphos by the contractor he had told her about and that he would telephone or return when he could. He then took his hunting rifle and an assortment of knives out of the closet, walked out to his van, and started down the mountain toward the Strovolos address he had been provided by his local contact.

* * * *

Caitlyn and Takis maintained a silence as they took the late Sunday morning drive up to Kakopetria. It wasn't a case that they were upset with each other or that they normally didn't chat as they drove. But Caitlyn had promised Takis that he could use the travel time to think about what he had to do on their foreign trip that was to begin the next morning, and Caitlyn was lost in thoughts of her own.

The mountain village of Kakopetria and the river valley that led up to it from the floor of the central Mesaoria plain sat heavily in Caitlyn's memory. For thousands of years, the Solea Valley, with one of the few streams that flowed down from the Troodos Mountains year round, had served as the passage from the copper-rich mountains and from the island's highest peak, Mt. Olympus, down to Morphou Bay on the island's west coast. The valley had gotten its current name from the Greek city state of Soli that had commanded the port that had served as the Troodos Mountain area's mouth to the Mediterranean.

It had been in the small village of Kaliana in the lower reaches of the valley that Caitlyn had been introduced to Cyprus three years previously and had made her first mark on the island as a gifted archaeologist. She was brought to Cyprus on a Fulbright grant to help with a Bronze Age dig in that village on the western slope of the valley. The dig itself was financed by Eleni Piccard's Ledra Foundation. Although Caitlyn helped with the dig in Kaliana, she found an even older, Neolithic site just across from Kaliana on the eastern slope of the valley. This find had established Caitlyn's reputation internationally.

As they traveled up into the mountains and past Kaliana, Caitlyn and Takis could see both of these sites, where work was still progressing. And they already could see the lower reaches of the village of Galata, which now merged into the higher Kakopetria and also see up to the still snow-clad Mt. Olympus.

Kakopetria, once a Roman temple site and more recently a Cypriot health resort, held a special significance for Caitlyn as well. Although she married into a wealthy French family, Eleni Piccard had been a native of the village of Kakopetria. Her ancestors had lived here for untold centuries and had owned and operated a mill and flour processing and storage business at the confluence of two small rivers in the village's center. Eleni had proven to be an excellent businesswoman in her own right and had, after the disappearance of her husband and son, expanded the holdings of the Piccard family in Cyprus to include hotels, restaurants, and a handicraft manufacturing center and export house.

The family mill, with its multistoried stone and wood storage building that rose from the riverbed up the western side of the valley wall, had been imaginatively and lovingly transformed by Eleni Piccard into an exclusive hotel with a restaurant above that looked over the village rooftops and both down the valley toward Morphou Bay and up the slope to Mt. Olympus. On the top floor of the structure, Eleni had placed her own village retreat, an apartment furnished with all the family objects that had been in use when her husband and son had disappeared in 1974.

Caitlyn had visited this village with Eleni, who had become the younger woman's mentor in Cyprus. And it had been here that Caitlyn and Takis came in dramatic contact and the smuggling case of Eleni's nephew, Jacques Piccard, and the tragic fate of her husband and son had been revealed. And it had also been here a few months later that Eleni herself had been brutally murdered in the small elevator that rose from the riverside car park to the treetop Old Mill restaurant.

And it was here on this sunny April Sunday afternoon that Caitlyn hoped to come to grips with the subliminal messages of danger and foreboding that were coming to her with thoughts of Eleni.

Caitlyn and Takis went straight to the new church Eleni had funded, which was located on a high point between the villages of Galata and Kakopetria. Eleni had been buried in this churchyard. She had been laid to rest beside the graves of her husband and son, whose bones had been interred here twenty years after their deaths. Caitlyn spent considerable time at the grave sites, but the visit accorded her no peace and it didn't surface any revelations on why she was being hounded by thoughts of Eleni.

They had a luncheon date with Safa Ziya down at the UNICIS office in Nicosia, so after Caitlyn sat by the graves almost in a trance-like state for a while, Takis suggested it was time for them to return to the city. However, not quite knowing why she did so, Caitlyn said that she thought they should go on up to the Old Mill restaurant for lunch instead. She said that she was sure Safa would be understanding at their failure to show up in Nicosia. This surprised Takis greatly, as his wife wasn't at all fickle or cavalier about her appointments. But he didn't argue with her.

Although Kakopetria was crowded with weekend tourists visiting from the beach hotels in search of a variety of experiences on Cyprus, a prime outside balcony table miraculously became available just as the Koniotises reached the top of the stairs. Caitlyn had always refused to use the small elevator, which she had considered to be unreasonably claustrophobic and unreliable and since her friend Eleni had been murdered in the elevator, Caitlyn wouldn't even go close to that end of the restaurant building.

The long-time manager of the restaurant and hotel, who had inherited the business—although not the structure itself or the apartment at the top—from Eleni, was effusive in his welcome of the Koniotises. They had not visited his restaurant, famous throughout the island for its butter-grilled trout, in more than a year. Despite the busy lunchtime crowd, the manager sat down and chatted with the couple as the trout they had ordered was being prepared.

"Would it be possible for us to visit the apartment upstairs?" Caitlyn asked. "I'm sure that Eleni would have been pleased for Takis to see it."

"But certainly," the restaurant owner said. "We have tried to keep it just as she left it, but . . . now, where are the keys to the flat? I'll have to do a little rummaging, I'm afraid."

"I suppose the apartment has been closed these two years," Caitlyn said. "It must be covered with dust. The Makedonitissa house we inherited from her was. Of course, as you may not know, it had also been ransacked before we moved in."

"It's interesting you say that," the restaurateur responded with a serious expression. "I almost telephoned you last fall about something strange that happened here last July and August when my family and I were holidaying in the UK."

"While we were gone," the restaurant owner continued, "one of the French Piccards came here and stayed in the flat for three weeks. The substitute manager said the man had a proper passport and even had the key to the flat, so he didn't see any reason not to let him stay. The man apparently spent nearly the entire time in the flat. The replacement manager did think that it was strange, because few people come up to Kakopetria just to stay indoors, even though the views from the flat are magnificent. Well, when we came back, I went up there and everything had been rearranged. And then I had occasion to call down to the Piccard company's Cyprus headquarters in Limassol, and they claimed that there had been no Piccard staying in Kakopetria at all. Now, doesn't that sound strange?"

A concern was forming in Caitlyn's mind. "If the things had just been rearranged, why did you try to find the man?"

"I found that some things had been taken as well. Not the valuable things, strangely enough, but the—"

"—family pictures," Caitlyn filled in the sentence.

"Yes, but how did you know?"

"I didn't know," Caitlyn answered bleakly, "but the thought just popped into my mind. Obviously, it's an important piece to some puzzle. And I think perhaps this was what I was supposed to come up here to find out—in fact, for some reason I know it is."

* * * *

Ayman Abu Hani watched the extraction of information and the follow-up execution from the terrace of his Tripoli villa. In the end, the man who had been directed to take Suzanne out to sea had admitted that she had tried to work her charms on him and had begged him to take her to Cyprus, where she had friends who would hide her rather than killing her as her husband had directed. She had given him a convincing sample of her charms at the outset, promising to provide him with pleasure he had never before experienced when they reached Limassol. She had also assured him that Abu Hani would never learn that she had survived.

He claimed he didn't plan to let her leave the boat alive, but that he had indeed sailed for Cyprus to prolong his enjoyment of her talents. When they got near to Cyprus, he planned to take her one more time by force—he had been told that he could do what he wanted with her as long as she didn't come back alive—and then to kill her and dump her over the side. He hadn't thought there would be any difference whether her body sank in Lebanese or in Cypriot waters.

But Suzanne had attacked first. As soon as they could see the lights of the island off Cape Greco, she attacked him with a knife she found in the galley. He, in turn, punched her up so well that he was sure she was near death when she collapsed and slipped over the side and into the water on her own. He said he ran to the rail but wasn't able to see her in the water. After sailing around in circles for some time, looking for some assurance that she had drowned, without success, he came back to Lebanon. He didn't say anything about not seeing her dead because he had been sure he had done what had been asked of him.

Unfortunately, Abu Hani demanded work of higher standards and more closely in accord with instructions. The only thing that was important to him was that Suzanne had survived. She had always been a strong swimmer and her survival instincts obviously hadn't been dulled by age or the attentions of her appointed executioner.

Just to make the point that he demanded the highest quality of work, Abu Hani walked down to the pier from the terrace to ensure that this execution had been fully performed.

Perhaps, he thought, he should have taken care of Suzanne himself. It was so hard to find competent help these days.

Chapter Twelve

Suzanne Abu Hani was pacing up and down the prison interview room floor from wooden door to barred window. Nearly all vestiges of her recent, temporary life as a bedraggled "cave" woman had now been dispelled. She once more was the confident, controlled, calculating panther, sleekly gliding, hips sensually swaying, from one end of the room to the other. Her hair was now shining, her eyes flashing, and the still-partially paralyzed right side of her face no longer offered itself as a focus for attention. Only a woman like Suzanne could wear a simple cotton shift as if she was a model on a high-fashion catwalk. She was puffing on a cigarette as she moved.

As Suzanne paced back and forth, Maria Solonos sat primly at the small table in the center of the room, her eyes glued to her folded hands. Anyone passing by the door and glancing in the room undoubtedly would have assumed that Suzanne was the interrogator and Maria the one being questioned.

But she wasn't, and Maria was very experienced in questioning prisoners. On the other hand, Suzanne was very intelligent and didn't underestimate the head of the International Investigations Unit, so, although she seemed to have regained her famous poise, she remained guarded in her answers and either still suffered blank areas in her recollections of the recent past or was intent on pretending that she did.

"Once again, Mrs. Abu Hani, could you tell me how you came to be on the beach near Cape Greco?"

"I'm a good swimmer—and let's just drop the 'Mrs. Abu Hani' routine, Maria," Suzanne Abu Hani suddenly snapped. "We've known each other by first names for years. I know this is a formal interview, but I'm just Suzanne." And then more calmly, "Please."

"Fine, Suzanne. But is there some reason you don't want to be called Mrs. Abu Hani?"

Suzanne had reached the window. She tensed and stared at the view of the dusty courtyard with its single olive tree. She didn't respond.

"Well, we'll need to notify your husband," Maria picked up the conversation again. "Can you tell us where—?"

But Suzanne exploded with a loud "No," pushed off from the window wall with both hands, marched to the door, and proceeded to stare into the dusty, dimly lit hallway with the same intensity she had been devoting to the olive tree.

"No, you don't want us to notify your husband, or, no, you don't know where we can contact the ambassador?" Maria kept her voice at a calm, well-modulated, almost disinterested level.

"Yes, exactly," Suzanne shot back at the hallway.

Maria sighed deeply. "You say you swam to the Grecian Park Hotel beach. Did you swim from a boat or from the Lebanese coast or from London? The last we knew, two years ago, when we wanted to question you about certain terrorist activities, you had flown to London."

Suzanne flashed a look over her shoulder at Maria that registered both irritation and surprise—and maybe, for the first time today, a hint of fear.

"If you don't want to talk about—or you don't remember—how you got to Cyprus or why, perhaps we should start by talking about the last time you left the island. Did you know that the chief of a Hizballah terrorist squad that had been operating here in Cyprus was murdered on a flight from Paphos to London—a flight on which was also traveling a beautiful, olive-skinned woman who the stewardesses identified as you from a photo?"

"There was a boat," Suzanne sputtered as she sat in the chair across the table from Maria. "Now I remember. I was in a boat. And then I was in the water. And then I was on the beach. I was cold and wet and frightened and my whole right side was numb."

"A boat," Maria stated, as if half the battle had been won. She scribbled on a pad of paper in front of her and then continued. "And how did you get from the boat into the water? Did you fall? Were you pushed? Did you dive in on your own?"

"I don't remember," Suzanne said wearily, although she was gaining strength from having guided the detective away from her murderous flight to London. "I just remember that at some point I had to choose between being in the boat and being in the water, and I chose the water. I wasn't pushed."

"And were you alone in the boat?"

Suzanne lit another cigarette, rose from her chair, and returned to the window. "No."

"Who else was in the boat? Was there just one person or more than one person? Men? Women?"

Suzanne exhaled a lungful of smoke and ran the fingers of the hand holding the cigarette up and down one of the bars in the window. The window itself was open, and a slight breeze made her brunette hair sway back and forth. "Just one. A man."

"The ambassador?" Maria asked.

"No, not him!" Suzanne rounded angrily on the inspector.

Maria gave the prisoner a long, penetrating look, and Suzanne, not being able to hold the gaze, returned her eyes to the courtyard below.

Maria's voice took on a hardness. "You know, Suzanne, we aren't going to play your games for very long. You are a fugitive from justice here, and we have no requirement to release you before a trial can be organized. In addition, we think you have some information on your husband and the Hizballah that we very much need to know before the Middle East peace conference opens outside Limassol next week."

"You can't hold me," Suzanne rose to her full height, her voice edged with the authority and confidence she had long exercised as an ambassador's wife. "I had diplomatic immunity when I left Cyprus."

176

"Well, perhaps you're right. Perhaps we should let you out on the street."

Suzanne was taken off guard by that remark and looked startled. The cigarette dropped from her fingers and fell, burning and unnoticed, on the stone floor at her feet.

Maria honed in. "I just remembered. One of the people the terrorist band kidnapped was a UN official. The Lebanese government very quickly waved diplomatic immunity for both you and your husband." And then, before Suzanne could respond, "Did you know that at least one of the terrorists from the Mouflon Brigade remained in Cyprus, hidden these past two years?"

Suzanne didn't flinch. In fact, she regained her bearings a bit. Obviously she did know, but she didn't respond.

"Well, I guess that answers that," Maria state simply. "We'll get back to that in a bit. But what can you tell me about another one of your husband's helpers then located on the island—and possibly still on the island? Not someone directly connected to the terrorist band; someone well placed in the corridors of power; someone working secretly and separately for your husband who could make things happen?"

Suzanne turned from the window and looked into Maria's eyes. Her expression blank and questioning. For the longest moment, Maria thought she had drawn a blank on this line of inquiry—the most important information she had hoped to extract from Suzanne Abu Hani.

But then, as Maria was starting to formulate a question that would return the interview to the possible identity of the Hizballah fighter, or fighters, who had been left in place, Suzanne's eyes—which had never disengaged from Maria's—began to smolder, and her facial expression turned from wonder to enlightenment and fear. She groped for the wooden chair and sat down, her face going into her hands.

"Suzanne?" Maria asked after a few brief moments of silence.

Suzanne sat up and leaned back in her chair. She reached for the pack of cigarettes that had been on the table, but it was empty. She strangled the pack in her hand and looked back at Maria.

"I want to talk to Willie Hamilton. I'll talk to you, but only if I can do an interview with Willie Hamilton first."

"Willie's not here," Maria countered.

"Look, Maria. I don't ever have to answer *any* of your questions. You know me better than that. I said I'd talk to you further, but only if I can give a private interview to Hamilton first. You said you didn't have much time. Well, neither do I. You know me, and you know I will have what I want."

Maria gave the other woman a hard look. "As I said, Willie isn't here. But other reporters are here. They've been camping out here all night to interview you. They are just down the hall. Why Willie? I can get *Simerini's* Demetris Mattas in here in—"

A look of fright such as Maria had never seen before from the ambassador's wife flashed across Suzanne's face. She rose with such force that her chair fell over behind her and flounced to the window. Through clinched teeth, Suzanne forced out, "Willie Hamilton. I will first talk to Willie Hamilton, and then I will talk with you."

"You will tell me what you know about your husband's secret contacts in Cyprus?"

178

"Yes," still through clinched teeth and directed at the olive tree below.

"All right. If we can get this over quickly. I have to go back to the office briefly. I will have Hamilton brought here for an interview. But then we talk. I want to know whatever you tell Hamilton before he can publish. Otherwise, no deal. Agreed?"

"Agreed," Suzanne answered calmly, her composure returned. And then in a soft voice, meant for the ears only of the olive tree in the courtyard but picked up by the trained hearing of the departing chief inspector, "So, that's it. That's what the boat was all about."

* * * *

Symeon Parikan—Salem Qazzar once again if only for a brief time, was sitting in his van behind the blue BMW convertible when he heard the telephone ring in the building of apartments above him on the Strovolos church square. Qazzar had been winding the length of piano wire into a small loop, which was how he had often spent his nervous time before an operation and before his new life had turned him to a different, more benign trade.

Moments after the telephone rang, the front door to the stairwell running to the apartments opened and the *Cyprus Mail* reporter, Willie Hamilton, emerged. As he reached the street, he looked up and waved to a thin woman who had come out on one of the balconies above.

Qazzar experienced a brief moment of panic when Hamilton walked toward him, bypassing both the BMW and Qazzar's van. But then the reactivated terrorist saw that Hamilton was getting into another vehicle, a beat-up old Morris Mini, which he drove past

Qazzar and toward the center of Nicosia. Qazzar stuffed the length of piano wire back into his jacket pocket and pulled the van out into the street. In spite of himself, he found that he was smiling. He was exhilarated. He had thought he had put his previous life behind him and that nothing could mean as much to him as his new wife, his new job, and his new security. He had been wrong.

* * * *

Takis Koniotis had never fought so hard for a principle and for a recommitment in his life. He had had no idea before he entered the small reception room in the Abdin Palace in central Cairo that he so fervently believed in his own mind in the vital importance of a Middle East peace settlement or that he could so forcefully and—thankfully, in the end—persuasively bring home his points.

He and Caitlyn had flown into the Egyptian capital earlier that morning. After a harrowing ride through the stuffed and noisy streets in an official limousine that had been driven as much by horn and swearing and gamesmanship as a taxicab would have been, they had thrown their luggage into their Nile Hilton suite, overlooking the historic river itself and the Al-Gazira Island park, and Takis had been hustled off to see President Sulayman in what had been the presidential palace but that now was mostly a national museum. Sulayman had been moving about on a varied scheduled and had been working and meeting visitors in an assortment of venues in and around Cairo since it had become obvious to him that the opposition forces could reach his side without great difficulty.

While Takis was having his all-important "bucking up" meeting with Sulayman—to be followed by even more forceful visits from the UN officials Ingrid Bittmann and Eric Isaksen, Caitlyn was off for a tour of the King Tut collection at the Egyptian Museum, which was located on the river and adjacent to the Nile Hilton. She had been to Cairo previously to see the exhibition, of course. As an archaeology doctoral student, she could not have avoided examining one of the world's greatest collections of antiquities. But her original visit to the museum had been a bit disappointing. The collection had looked somewhat mundane the first time she had visited Cairo. It wasn't until the collection made its famous trip to the major museums of the United States that Caitlyn realized its full beauty.

She had come to learn that the difference had been a matter of lighting—and proper dusting. When she first visited Cairo, the lighting in the Egyptian Museum had been woefully inadequate and the artifacts had been permitted to gather thick layers of dull dust. The illumination plan in the American museums and the careful cleaning applied brought out the best in the beauty of the artifacts. Caitlyn was to find on her current visit to the Egyptian Museum that the lighting problem had been addressed and that here, in its natural environment, the collection was now even more fabulously displayed than it had been on the U.S. tour.

Caitlyn was thus in heaven, and she could have reveled in the museum for days without a single worry concerning Takis's vital primary mission meeting a bare ten city blocks away. In fact, she was so engrossed in her research that she didn't notice the young man with a military bearing and a determined gleam in his eye who was following her around the exhibit.

181

At the palace, across town, Takis was finding the new Egyptian president to be a man of deep integrity and honor but with unresolved suspicions of both Israel and the Western powers and genuine mixed feelings of what was really right and wrong in the Middle East peace agreement documents. The president himself brought up the pressures that were being brought to bear on him to abandon the peace process by the religious fundamentalists and the military rightists but soundly dispelled these pressures and the personal threats that accompanied these pressures as determinants in what he would do.

Upon discussion, Takis determined that the simple general had just been bombarded by too many advisers pushing and pulling him simultaneously. At the Cypriot's suggestion, everyone but the chief of the Egyptian secret service had been cleared from the reception room, and the three men who remained stepped carefully through the objectives and options before the Egyptians, just as if they were preparing for battle the next morning—which, indeed, they were. Takis was careful not to provide his own opinions or solutions. When Sulayman didn't readily have information at his disposal, he turned to his secret service chief, who either provided the information or left the room briefly in search of the information.

After three hours, the Egyptian president had reached the conclusions that Takis had intuitively been able to see from the outset and that he had known were the only avenues to regional peace and development. But Sulayman had reached these conclusions on his own, by methods he understood and respected, and thus his resolve was solidified.

An unknown surprise was that the secret service chief, who had privately opposed and had, in fact, been working against cooperation in the settlement, had also been convinced by this marathon session. And in the process he had gained a respect for and commitment to Takis Koniotis and the new UN International Crimes Investigations Service that would prove to be decisive in locking the Egyptians into active support for the peace process and extended UN security operations.

As they were wrapping the session up, Takis turned to Sulayman and the secret service chief with a look of concern.

"I am, of course, very relieved that you have decided as you have, but I am concerned that this decision inevitably increases the risk to your own person. We can't lose you at this juncture no matter what you ultimately decide to do about the specific peace agreement signing. You represent stability, rationality, and order in Egypt. No one will win if the country turns to chaos."

"I am not afraid, and I will not hide. In fact, if I were to show such a concern for my well-being, I could not go much longer roaming around the city as I have been doing. The people can smell any sign of fear, and Egyptians will not follow cowards."

"This is understood, certainly, Mr. President," the secret service chief interjected. "But, at the same time, Mr. Koniotis is quite right. May I suggest at least that you move to the base where we have our secret service academy? You won't be the first president to set up residence there for a while, and I assure you you will be quite safe."

"Yes, I suppose that will be satisfactory, Butrus," the president responded almost reluctantly. "I do know I can always rely on you and the service."

This statement didn't mean much to Takis when spoken, but it would have been driven convincingly home to him if he had been gazing down through the skylights of the Egyptian Museum at that very moment. If he had been able to see the jewelry room of the King Tut collection as he was packing his papers together for the ride back to the Nile Hilton, he would have seen that more was flashing just then than gold necklaces. As Caitlyn leaned over to examine the intricate enamelware on a particularly distinctive conical headgear in a display case, she didn't notice that the young man with the military bearing was moving around behind the column that was immediately behind her. She also didn't notice that he had pulled a sharp metallic object from his pocket that flashed in the newly improved lighting from overhead. Nor did she notice the figure that followed the movement of the young man around the column, pulled him back, redirected the thrust of the knife, and completely muffled the resulting mortal scream.

Yes, the Egyptian secret service was very effective—and Caitlyn never noticed.

* * * *

Cypriot prisons, even the central prison in Nicosia near the buffer zone as it exited the western end of the old city, could not be considered maximum security structures by any stretch of the imagination. Incarceration was simply not a well-understood concept in Cypriot society. This was primarily because capital crime had never been much of a problem in Cypriot society. Or at least it hadn't been much of a problem until the modern outside world, with its acquisitiveness and its strain of violence that had been enhanced by the themes of popular adventure movies and of television had reached Cyprus.

For many centuries, although rising dominant external civilization after declining dominant external civilization had washed over the strategically located Mediterranean island, each undeniably leaving an indelible mark, none of the occupiers had worked their own concepts significantly into the fabric of Cypriot society. The island essentially remained an intertwined, closely knit extended family.

Under these circumstances, there had never been much of any serious crime to speak of within the Cypriot context. To be sure there were crimes of passion—spouse murdering spouse or cousin murdering cousin—but these were usually inflicted in the heat of anger and were considered to be the result of temporary madness. In such cases the perpetrator might also perish in a follow-up fit of madness or might be locked in a back room for the rest of his or her life as a lunatic—or sent to the extended family in London. But an arrest, a trial, sentencing, and incarceration were alien concepts to the Cypriots. These procedures had been introduced by external occupiers.

Of course, as these external forces and influences introduced other forms of crime—crimes such as thievery, which Cypriots would rarely have succumbed to themselves, as every Cypriot was related by family connection to every other Cypriot to some degree—the Cypriot system did come to encompass courts and prisons. But their basic understanding of how these alien concepts should work never quite jelled. Thus, even today, although people were imprisoned for serious crimes, they often were free on grants of leniency within short periods of time, and they rarely were held completely behind bars even for the time they spent in prison.

For these reasons, although Suzanne Abu Hani was being held in the maximum security wing of the Nicosia Central Prison, she was discovered to be walking around in the central courtyard, under the olive tree, when Willie Hamilton arrived for the interview for which he had been called from his afternoon siesta in his Strovolos Square apartment. Although the separate buildings of the prison complex enclosed the courtyard, there were pathways at each corner that opened straight into the residential area surrounding the prison.

Since she was considered to be a very important prisoner, one who both had to be watched closely and had to be protected from unspecified external threats, Suzanne rated three guards to monitor her solitary period of exercise in the central courtyard. When Willie arrived, one of the guards had gone into the building to relieve himself and the other two were standing together on one of the shaded pathways that led directly out to the busy public street running across the front of the prison complex. Both guards were earning their pay, however, as they were both standing, faces glued to the courtyard, and staring intently at Suzanne's every move. The fact that Suzanne's every move was quite sensual probably had something to do with their attentiveness.

The two guards were scrutinizing their charge so well that they didn't even notice Willie Hamilton's approach from the street, through the shaded passageway, between them, until he'd reached

186

Suzanne's side on the bench under the olive tree. He was expected, though, so he didn't cause them to heighten their attention, and their eyes remained captured by the figure of Suzanne.

Hamilton found Suzanne in a highly agitated state, although that didn't prevent her from flirting with him in a very brazen manner. The *Cyprus Mail* reporter had certainly wondered what it was that Suzanne would only talk to him about, and he had his suspicions concerning what she was up to, but she completely bowled him over when she stated that she could deliver the name of more than one person whose disclosure would blow the schemes of the Middle East peace process opposition campaign to smithereens and that she would give him the exclusive story—but only if he first helped her to escape the prison.

Hamilton had been scribbling on his pad of paper and had, at hearing Suzanne's demands, snapped his head up, his face transformed by a look of utter shock and surprise. As his eyes met hers, he saw that the expression on her face matched his. But, upon closer inspection, he saw that Suzanne wasn't looking into his eyes, but over his shoulder, toward the front of the prison.

It had been no serious problem that the two guards hadn't noticed the approach of Hamilton until he had passed them or that they hadn't challenged his entry into the courtyard; he was well known to them and had been expected. The fact that the two permitted Salem Qazzar to come up right behind them without noticing his presence, however, was, at the minimum, very bad procedure. Both probably would have merited disciplinary action and retraining—if either had survived the breach of procedure.

As the two guards went down, Suzanne screamed in recognition of the assailant and in instant understanding of the danger she, herself, was in. She rose swiftly off the bench and ran toward one of the corner passageways exiting the courtyard at the rear of the prison complex.

It might have seemed that Hamilton was slow to react, but he was motionless initially only because he was calculating the best means to cover Suzanne's retreat and to intercept the assailant, who was now running across the courtyard in pursuit of Suzanne.

Hamilton slipped between Suzanne and the attacker just as she reached and entered the corner passageway. Although the other man was quite a bit bigger and younger, and certainly more powerful, than Hamilton, the wiry little retired infantryman was doing a marvelous bit of standoff, giving Suzanne several precious moments to widen her lead to freedom.

While wrestling with Hamilton, Qazzar managed to get behind the former major and wrap his length of piano wire twice around the old man's neck. This maneuver brought both men around to face the front of the courtyard in time to see Alec Stuart saunter into the courtyard to where he, first, saw the bodies of the guards and then the struggle going on across the courtyard. Stuart broke into a run, with Hamilton praying with all his might that he could keep his loosening grip on the biting wire around his throat long enough for help to arrive.

Just as Stuart reached the wrestlers, Qazzar thrust the gagging Hamilton into the British spy's arms and sprinted after Suzanne.

He could see the woman in the distance, some two blocks away, running back toward the commercial area of the city. He was gaining fast and he was sure that she wouldn't be able to reach any congested shopping area before he could catch and dispatch her. He had lost the length of piano wire, but he was also carrying a knife, which is what he'd used to neutralize her two guards. As he huffed along, he began to regret that he hadn't brought a pistol. From here he could have dropped her easily. He hadn't realized how easily he could become winded since he gave up mountaineering for the cushy village life.

Just one more block and he would have her. Unfortunately for Qazzar, they were approaching a relatively heavily populated and higher class neighborhood. But if she tried to go to one of these houses to escape him, he would come right in after her. If other people had to die in this process, it would be her fault, not his.

There. Just as he had surmised. She was turning into a gate and running up to the door to a large house. Qazzar redoubled his speed in an effort to be through the gate and upon the woman before she could even get through the door. But there was someone at the gate, a uniformed guard, and Qazzar was brought up so short and in so much surprise that he rocked back on his heels and sat down hard on the asphalt of the street.

She had won. For now, if not for long. He obviously couldn't follow her into there. Instead, he turned and ran in a direction that would take him away from both the prison and that house as quickly as possible.

If Qazzar had stayed a moment longer, he would have been greatly perplexed upon seeing that the woman who answered the door to Suzannne's knock took one look at the wife of the former Lebanese ambassador to Cyprus and rushed at her, fists flailing. Suzanne stood her ground and gave as well as she received for a few moments. As the older woman tired, however, Suzanne thrust her aside and strode through the building's double-doored entry. Throughout this unusual display of dubious welcome, the lone, uniformed figure standing inside the gate to the street looked on meekly, neither helping either woman or moving to separate them.

Chapter Thirteen

Perhaps if Maria Solonos had remained at the central prison for Suzanne Abu Hani's interview with Willie Hamilton she might have been able to prevent the carnage in the courtyard and the escape of the prisoner. Maria most certainly would have seen to it that the interview was conducted in a prison office rather than in the nearly open courtyard, and the guards surely would have been more attentive in the presence of a police unit chief. But perhaps the outcome had been inevitable and Maria and the people of Cyprus were just fortunate that she had not, herself, been in harm's way.

Maria had left the prison because she needed to check on the now one-day-old intensive search for her missing deputy, Androulla Varnavidou. She was in a foul mood when she reached police headquarters, located in the former colonial British administrative district of the city about a mile and a half closer toward the old city walls than the central prison complex. Demetris Mattas, her "significant other," who had been waiting at the prison for a possible interview with Suzanne Abu Hani, one of his own previous "significant others," for his "Under the Grapevine" political chat column for the *Simerini* daily, had driven Maria to the central prison. She thus had taken it for granted that he would take her back to police headquarters. However, he had insisted that he wanted to wait in the press room at the prison for a chance to interview Suzanne, or at least to wheedle what she wanted to tell his *Cyprus Mail* colleague, Willie Hamilton, out of him after their exclusive interview had been concluded.

Maria had been forced to have a taxi called to take her back to police headquarters. Demetris's decision to stay with the story rather than be her driver was not in itself the irritant. She could well understand that a good investigative reporter had to aggressively pursue his job, just as she, an investigative police official, had to pursue hers. But the whole affair had once again pointed out that she had permitted herself to become deeply involved in a conflict of interest.

The police were not supposed to be in bed with the press— particularly in a way that showed favoritism. And here she was, quite literally in bed with a member of the press—and one whose job it was to pursue exactly the same cases she was responsible for managing. The mere fact that she had permitted Demetris to accompany her to the prison, let alone driving her there in his own vehicle, reflected just how far she had let this situation get out of hand.

But at the core, this was not what had really put her in a foul mood. She was a talented professional and she was comfortable enough with her standing with Demetris that she knew she could get back on track by setting and carefully following a new set of ground rules. No, what really ticked her off was that, while Demetris was staunchly defending his intent to stay at the prison to see Suzanne, Maria suddenly remembered that Demetris and Suzanne had been heavily rumored some three years previously to have been lovers. Suzanne, of course, had been rumored to have been engaged in a love affair with any man—or woman—of great influence in Cyprus she could get into bed. But the sudden remembrance of the look in Suzanne's eyes when Maria had suggested to her that Demetris, who was present at the prison, be given the exclusive interview rather than Hamilton, who was not present, had been all Maria needed to validate both the fact and the intensity of this previous love affair.

When Maria entered police headquarters, therefore, she was suffering from a simple case of intense jealousy. The fact that she fully realized this was the reason for her foul mood didn't help her disposition. It did, however, make her launch herself into spearheading the search for Androulla with such focus and ferocity that the dreaded results came quickly.

In a little under two hours, and at the precise moment Salem Qazzar had managed to double his piano wire around Willie Hamilton's neck in the central prison courtyard, Maria Solonos was being informed by one of her senior investigators that they had just discovered an earlier example of Qazzar's handiwork in a rocky meadow above the old stone quarry between the village of Politiko and the Macheras Monastery in the Troodos foothills to the southeast of Nicosia.

After negotiating the delicate preliminaries in verifying what none of them wanted to verify, the detective Costas filled in the details.

"We got a break in Politiko," Costas explained. "We found people in the villages throughout that area just to the north of Politiko—Aredhiou, Espiskopio, Analionas, and Pera—who had remembered a police investigator meeting Androulla's description showing photographs around and asking if anyone had seen any of the men depicted. We were receiving negative reports from villages farther south, such as Kambia, Kapedhes, and Klirou on Androulla's activities. So, we concentrated our search in Politiko and were lucky enough to find someone who saw Androulla get into a van being driven by a man. The old woman who saw this happen remembered it because the policewoman had shown her the photos earlier and she had noticed that this man was looking on from a distance at that time. Sometime later, the village woman had noticed the man walk up to Androulla, look at the photos himself, and point to the mountains. Right after this, the two had gotten into a small van and taken the road toward the Macheras Monastery."

"We didn't find anyone in Kambia, the next village on the road between Politiko and the monastery, who remembered either Androulla or the van," Costas continued, "but near the even smaller village of Kapedhes we found a shepherd who had remembered the van traveling toward Politiko from Macheras earlier in the day and then back toward Macheras. There is very little traffic on this road, so the shepherd could remember having seen individual vehicles. He particularly noticed this one, though, he said, because there had been just the driver and he hadn't seemed to be in a hurry when the van first passed. However, when the van returned, there was a passenger and it was being driven quickly and somewhat erratically. The shepherd said he had to move some of his sheep off the side of the road when the van passed, and he particularly remembered the incident, because he thought the passenger in the van must have been sick. Says she was hunched over toward the passenger door and had her face pressed to the window despite the bumps the van must have been taking from the rough road surface. The shepherd said it took several seconds for the van to pass him while he herded his sheep off the road and that the passenger had not moved the whole time. Said he distinctly remembered the incident because her look haunted him for days. He said she watched him with a fixed, distant stare. I'm sorry, Maria. It sounds to me like Androulla was already dead at this point."

"Yes, of course, I agree," Maria responded, swallowing hard. "That might have been a mercy. Please continue. Where did you find her?"

"Just a short way farther toward the monastery. We found tracks going off the side of the road next to an abandoned stone quarry. We found double tracks, incidentally. We haven't quite figured out what the second track means, but our men think both sets were made by the same tires. One set looked fresher, though, quite recent. Those working in from the Gourri, Fikardou, and Macheras Monastery end of the road were coming up blank on sightings of either Androulla or the van, so we called them into the quarry site and we all fanned out over the area in search of evidence. I'm sorry, Maria, we found her between two large boulders in a meadow of wild flowers above the quarry."

"How did she die?" Maria asked, struggling for some sense of professional detachment.

"It looks like she was strangled—with a thin wire. It's been a couple of weeks, so they won't allow themselves to be pinned down on the cause of death until after an examination can be done down in Nicosia. But I'm afraid there's little doubt it's Androulla."

"Was the old woman in Politiko able to describe the man or the van?" asked Maria.

"Said he was in his thirties. Probably Cypriot, but he didn't have any resemblance to the families in the Politiko area. She said he was dressed like a laborer, but his clothes were too clean for someone working in the fields. Although she didn't notice the registration number on the van, she was able to describe it well enough that if it had any registration other than Cypriot, she surely would have noticed the license being a different color from those issued to the Cypriots."

"So, he's probably not foreign," Maria reason aloud. "We have two choices. Either she was picked up by someone who wanted to rape her or she was coming too close to success in trying to track down hidden Hizballah terrorists. Although we won't discount the former possibility, we'll concentrate on the latter. Rape is less likely as a motive in an isolated village and when Cypriots are involved. And, since she was clearly identifying herself as a police official, a rapist would also have to be lunatic to choose her over a village girl or a foreign tourist."

Both sides of the conversation were silent for a long moment while Maria's highly organized and creative mind made its calculations. At length she broke the silence. "Costas, your people seem to have pretty much accounted for the leading edge of Androulla's line of inquiry that day. She had a very methodical approach to her work, and we should be able to take up where she left off. Chances are good that the murderer is either one of the Hizballah brigade members or a close associate and that he was been living in the general area where Androulla was looking. He probably doesn't live in Politiko, though, or the people you talked to there would know who he is. It's unlikely he came to Politiko in search of Androulla to kill her. It sounds more like he came to Politiko on routine business of his own and stumbled on someone looking for him—someone he had to stop without much prior planning that would keep his own identity separate from her death. People don't just drop into Politiko on a lark—it's much too isolated for that."

"What I'd like you to do," she concluded, "is to concentrate everyone you don't need at the quarry site back onto completing Androulla's search in the area around the monastery for the one or more Hizballah guerrillas who have more than likely been living in that area. They've all got the photos she had, and your search for Androulla has pretty much indicated where she left off searching. The best thing we can do for her now is to bring her last case to a successful conclusion for her. In the meantime, I'm on my way up there. And Costas—please tell everyone they've done wonderful work in this so far and to keep it up in memory of Androulla."

And then, just before she disconnected, she added in a wavering voice, "Tell them that Androulla would have been proud of them all."

* * * *

Salem Qazzar returned to Fikardou in the late afternoon on that Monday fully prepared to resume the guise of Symeon Parikan until the next time he went down into Nicosia to finish up on the Suzanne Abu Hani case. He first, however, thought he should telephone about the developments on Suzanne's escape to ensure that his next step would be approved.

After having cleared away from the scene of the prison for nearly an hour, he circled back to retrieve his van. He had parked it several blocks over from the prison and, upon arriving back at the van, he resisted the impulse to drive past the prison again to see how much police activity had resulted from his little escapade. During his run across the courtyard and his struggle with Hamilton, he sensed eyes and muffled voices screaming at him from the prison complex windows that overlooked the courtyard. And then there was the man who had shown up in the courtyard itself. Qazzar didn't know who he was or where he had come from. He only hoped that Hamilton was already dead when he threw him into the man's arms and ran on in pursuit of Mrs. Abu Hani. Qazzar knew he couldn't go anywhere near the prison for some time. The threat was great that someone would be able to identify him.

The house and workshop were empty when Qazzar arrived home in Fikardou. He was grateful for this. He presumed his wife was visiting her family in Gourri, and he hoped she would stay there for a

198

while. He had slipped so far back into his life as Salem Qazzar that he was afraid he couldn't fully pretend to be Symeon Parikan again—especially in the presence of his wife—until his superiors in Lebanon were finished with him once more.

The first thing Qazzar did after showering, changing, and finding a new length of piano wire—he always felt incomplete without a length of piano wire in his pocket—was to call Lebanon to give his report on Suzanne Abu Hani. The Lebanon contact was much more important than the local one. He would call the local contact later. The Beirut number told him to call a Tripoli number.

His report was followed by an icy silence. Qazzar knew Suzanne's escape wouldn't go over well. He also knew, however, that he was fairly safe at the moment because he was needed. He was sure that if Mrs. Abu Hani was dead before his own unique usefulness to the Hizballah was concluded, he would probably be safe. Probably, but nothing was sure where his superiors were concerned.

"And where is she now? And why are you calling me before she is dead?"

Qazzar swallowed hard and proceeded. "That's why I had to call. When she ran from the prison, I almost caught up with her. But she ran into an embassy building. It had the flag of Syria on the gate. I would have gone on in and killed whoever tried to interfere, but I couldn't be sure what that would do to your policies. I thought I'd best let you know where she is before I proceeded."

"Yes, I see," the voice responded, somewhat mollified. "You seem to have picked up some sense of diplomatic propriety in your time with the Cypriots. Yes, in that case, I would like you to return and watch for an opportunity to get to her. I don't care who dies with her, incidentally—not even the bumbling Syrian ambassador. I would strangle him with my own hands if I could reach him. But I don't want this connected with our organization in any way. That means I don't want you to carry any identification on you that would connect you to us, and I want you either to plan so you are assured of getting away or to plan so that you cannot give information if you are caught. Am I clear on that? Remember that your wife and children are still here in Lebanon under our protection."

"Yes, of course I understand."

"And Hamilton? What about Hamilton? You mentioned that you struggled with him. I don't necessarily need him dead, but he is pesky. I wouldn't mind if he were dead."

"I'm not sure. I may have killed him. But another man showed up just as I was finishing the reporter, and I didn't have time to do them both. I had to follow the woman before she got away. I left both of the men in a heap just inside one of the passageways into the prison courtyard. With luck, Hamilton was dead. Even if he isn't dead, his throat will be too sore for him to talk for a long time."

"It's his pen, not his voice that has become troublesome," the Tripoli connection snapped. "But, no matter. And no more wasting of time. Go back to Nicosia now. Suzanne must die and as quickly as possible. She must not be allowed to talk to the police or to any more reporters."

The line went dead and Qazzar threw some clothes into a bag, dug out the secret cache of money he had accumulated over the past two years from the funds his organization had passed to him, and headed for the door.

The telephone rang. The call was from Jordan—from the other organization leader to whom Qazzar had learned to respond fully and politely.

Qazzar was confused when he hung up, but he knew better than to ask penetrating questions about what he was told to do. In this case, the job would be fairly simple and could probably be handled while he was on his way to stake out the Syrian ambassador's residence in Nicosia. But why the voice in Jordan wanted a dentist in Nicosia quietly rubbed out was beyond Qazzar's understanding. It didn't really matter to Qazzar. Now that he was back in the groove to which he had been trained, he welcomed more wet work. It aroused him almost as much as his young Cypriot wife did.

"Must have been a painful tooth extraction," Qazzar mused to himself with a few stifled chortles as he drove the van down from Fikardou and turned at Gourri on the road to Nicosia.

He hadn't gone more than a hundred yards farther, however, when the sight through his rearview mirror suppressed his chortles entirely. Five police Mercedes cars had reached the Gourri-Fikardou intersection, traveling from the Macheras Monastery area, just after he cleared it. Their lights were flashing, but this in itself didn't make Qazzar's heart leap into his throat. Cypriot police cars always drove with their lights flashing. No, what made Qazzar fearful was the decisive way in which the vehicles dispersed as they reached the intersection. Two cars turned left down toward the center of Gourri.

One car turned right up toward Fikardou. And the other two cars continued, in the wake of Qazzar's van, on the road toward Nicosia.

Qazzar had a sixth sense about personal danger. If he had not had this talent, he would not have served as a Hizballah guerrilla fighter as long as he had. His intuition was that the policewoman he had killed was picking up the search again. The search for him. And that this search had led them within his own domain, where the alterations he had made to his face and life wouldn't fool the people who had lived and worked closely with him.

It was a very good thing he had cleaned out his cache of money, Qazzar thought, as he gently accelerated, pulling farther and farther away from the police Mercedes to his rear, but not so quickly as to arouse their suspicions.

If the woman was still alive, she could identify both him and the van. Qazzar knew his comfortable life in Fikardou was over. This didn't frighten him. He had completely recast his life before. But he would have to stop at the first chance he got to call Lebanon, Jordan, and the number he had in Nicosia to warn them he was moving on and that he would call again when he could. Perhaps he now, at long last, would meet the Nicosia contact, who could be used as the conduit for information until Qazzar got resettled.

He also would have to get a new vehicle and would have to ditch this van as soon as possible. Maybe, he thought, he would now get the BMW Lenia had said she wanted. But then it really hit him that he couldn't go back to Fikardou. His life with Lenia was over. He really had enjoyed being a respected master carpenter. He wondered if Lenia was pregnant. He sort of hoped not. She had been nice to him and he didn't want to leave her with any more trouble than would naturally be caused by his disappearance.

The thought of Lenia had raised thoughts of his wife and children in Lebanon, and thence to the threats his superior in Tripoli had voiced. He focused his thoughts on the jobs ahead in Nicosia—the ambassador's wife and a dentist. Strange combination. How could they possibly be linked?

Chapter Fourteen

The headquarters building of the United Nations International Crime Investigation Service in the UN buffer zone near Nicosia had more or less returned to its usual clock-like precision. The initial shock of the murder of their colleague Stefan Gunnerson while on assignment in Malta—a death that still was far from solved by the Maltese authorities—had subsided to a dull sense of sorrow and loss. The anti-peace settlement activities had also settled down to the point where the UNICIS operations center at least could keep track of what was happening where.

Strategic to the return of the peace process from the brink of chaos had been the quickly rebounded solidarity of the region's leaders following the assassination of the Egyptian president and the attempts on the lives of several other national leaders. The strong statement that had been issued by both the PLO chief and the Israeli prime minister after they had escaped attacks had burst the bubble of the expanding, supposedly spontaneous pro-Muslim fundamentalism demonstrations that had been manifested worldwide. The Jordanian king typically said little in public about his own participation in the peace process, but he did issue a eulogy on the death of the American embassy officer, Paul Conte, that clearly reflected his strong support for a continuation of the work toward peace.

The statement in support for the process that had been issued earlier this day by the new Egyptian president seemed a bit lukewarm, but it was correctly understood by all as signaling his own support for the opening of the peace conference on the Amathus coast. And at this signal the governments of both Lebanon and Syria announced that they would send delegations to the peace conference in Cyprus. They didn't voice support for the peace settlement itself, but their declarations of participation in the process constituted a major victory for the peace forces. The Hizballah, the Muslim Brotherhood, and the Abu Nidal Palestinian faction had applied for registration at the conference, as had, strangely enough, the Kurdish Worker's Party, but no one had answered these petitions or had taken them seriously.

The people at UNICIS headquarters took considerable pride in the favorable developments today, as they knew that their own chief, Takis Koniotis, had had a great deal to do with having gained the key tacit support of the new Egyptian president.

The press of Iran, Iraq, and Libya, of course, continued to wail away concerning the evils of the Western powers and the Israeli-controlled peace process. All three nations made quite clear that they would do everything in their power to derail the Cyprus conference. To bolster the forces for peace, several high-level UN officials in addition to Takis Koniotis and including Ingrid Bittmann and Eric Isaksen were traveling to the region or were already in the region to beg, cajole, reason, and threaten, if necessary, all of the central players back into formation.

The governments of Lebanon and Syria had made it just under the deadline for registration for the conference, and their embassies in Nicosia were already on the road to Limassol to try to find prestigious hotels that would clear their regular bookings during the busy season and house their government's officials.

It was late afternoon as the embassy representatives of the two tardy governments were speeding to the southern beaches. At the same time, as the operations center of the UNICIS was humming along as if no longer concerned that it would be the center of the most significant Middle East peace conference in history within a week, the center's chief, Thomas Jameson, was gently returning the receiver of the telephone on his desk to its cradle. The missions of the embassy representatives and the telephone call he had just received were much of the same fabric.

He didn't want them calling him here at UNICIS headquarters, and he had tried to tell them so—in polite terms, of course, because he didn't want to lose them as sponsors. And if he did this for them, he would now have passed the point of no return in his commitment.

What they had asked him to obtain was intriguing, and he had no trouble figuring out what they intended to do with the information. They had asked him for a list of the accommodations of the delegations coming to the Amathus coast conference and for the names of the specific conference rooms where the various meetings were to be held. He was to concentrate on where the highest-level leaders were going to be meeting in camera.

Both they and he knew that only the service's chief, Takis Koniotis, had the full information on these matters, and Jameson was perfectly aware that he himself was the best-placed asset for getting at these plans without revealing that they had been compromised. If Koniotis suspected that the plans had been stolen, he, of course, would simply change them and Jameson would have to start all over again to steal them.

Jameson waited until he saw the unit's deputy chief, Safa Ziya, depart for the day. He was, most certainly, frightened about what he had promised to do, but he was exhilarated as well. Koniotis had not taken his covert talents nearly serious enough. If he had been given his due, it would have been he who would have been sent to Malta, not Gunnerson. And *he* would not have botched the job and wound up dead on the pavement.

With Ziya gone, he was the senior officer present, and he could go just about anywhere he wanted to go without arousing suspicion—just as long as he acted like he had the authority to do what he did.

He would start with Koniotis's office. Jameson picked up a stack of papers and marched confidently into the chief's office. Once there, he turned on the light and moved behind the desk. He opened several file drawers and acted like he was filing papers where they belonged. As he opened the drawers and ran his hands down the files, for all intents and purposes looking for the proper file in which to put his papers, his eyes raced over the topic recorded on the file tabs.

Nothing on the peace process events. One of his operations center officers—one of the very attractive and friendly youngsters who had been signaling interest in Jameson for the past two weeks—passed by the windowed office on the way to the coffee pot and waved to the supervisor. Jameson waved back and smiled warmly, striking the perfectly confident pose of being clearly within the bounds of his duties.

As he waved, he had been reaching for a file drawer near the floor. It didn't open. When the ops officer had passed by, Jameson inspected the drawer more closely. it was locked. All of the file drawers had locks on them, but only this one seemed to be locked. All of the drawers also had tabs on them, loosely identifying the categories of the files in the individual drawers. This one had a tab, but nothing was written on it.

Until or unless he found a better candidate, Jameson was ready to assume that this was the drawer he wanted. He looked out onto the unit's main working floor to see who could be watching. He didn't bother to scrutinize the darkened inner windows of the other executive rooms along the side of the bigger room, as he thought all of the senior officers had gone for the evening. No one seemed to be watching. Still, filing papers in open drawers in Takis's office was one thing. Trying to force open one of the drawers—and in such a way that Takis wouldn't know it was forced—was quite another.

Jameson started opening drawers in the desk, looking for keys that would give him quick and noiseless entry to the locked filing drawer. There, in the front corner of the center drawer, was a key ring with what looked like the whole set of keys to the filing cabinets.

Did he dare start trying to find the right key? No, the ops officer had returned with the coffee and was entering the door of Koniotis's office, obviously prepared to take this opportunity to chat up Jameson. There wasn't anything else Jameson could do for the moment. He shut the desk drawer, gathered up his paper, and strolled back toward the Operations Center area with the other, younger man.

There would be another time, perhaps even later tonight, when he could safely come back and try the keys. If not tonight, surely tomorrow night. His sponsors weren't expecting overnight service, and he was safe as long as no one saw him.

But someone *had* seen him. Safa Ziya's companion, John Patterson, the UNICIS head of research, had been sitting in his own, nearby, darkened office. He had been thinking out a problem, and he often did this while sitting quietly in the dark. He also had not gone home with Safa, as he usually did, precisely because he was trying to think out a research problem. He had told her he would have one of the service's drivers take him home to the apartment in the Turkish zone of Nicosia after he had worked his problem out—or when he had gotten tired of trying to work it out.

While Patterson sat in the dark, he was staring out into the central room, not really focusing on anything in particular. When Jameson entered Takis's office and turned on the light, however, Patterson's attention was refocused. He had never particularly liked the retired American FBI man, with his bravado, his exaggerated fastidiousness about his appearance, and his false friendliness. Patterson had always thought that those traits were just a cover for a far different type of person underneath. Thus, he was not at all fooled or surprised when he saw Jameson starting to rifle through Takis's file drawers. Patterson had no idea what the Ops Center chief was up to, but he readily assumed that it wasn't for the benefit of the office.

When Jameson held the set of keys up only to be interrupted by the young officer who sauntered into the office, Patterson found that he had been holding his breath long enough to develop a headache. He slowly let his breath out as Jameson turned off the light in Takis's office, wrapped his arm around the younger man's shoulders in a friendly, mentoring fashion, and the two walked back into the central Ops Center room.

When all was quiet again, Patterson went to his own desk, opened his drawer, and extracted the set of keys for his own bank of file drawers. He crossed over to Takis's office, substituted his keys for the ones in Takis's desk drawer, and quietly left the building. He needed to talk with Safa. She would know what to do.

* * * *

It was late Monday morning in New York. Ingrid Bittmann was buzzing around her office in the UN Secretariat building behind the General Assembly building on Turtle Bay, gathering her notes for her coming talk with the new Egyptian president. She was very nervous about what faced her. The continued support of Egypt for the peace process was vital, and the Egyptians were lost if Sulayman didn't endorse the process. And Sulayman was both wavering and had a reputation of not approving of women in public office.

Bittmann realized her own reputation and future depended on at least getting all of the Middle Eastern leaders to the conference table in Cyprus. Once there, if they chose to cut each other up and slaughter the child of peace once again, that would probably not be held against her. No one really expected the miracle of serious cooperation among the Middle Eastern nations.

But if the process fell apart here and now, while it was still very much a Bittmann initiative—at least in as far as what the public media was being told—Bittmann would take the fall. Unless, of course, she could find someone else to take the fall for her.

Ingrid sat down in her chair. Was that a slight fever she felt coming on? And was it getting stronger? Did she perhaps need to send Eric on alone for the Egyptian portion of the visit? And, now, was her stomach beginning to act up as well? Ah, well, must find Eric.

Ingrid quickly reached over for her intercom switch, snatched her hand back, and then reached once again, but with a weaker, limp-wristed motion. Just then the intercom squawked on its own, however, and she lurched back in her chair with a sharp sense of guilt.

"Mr. Isaksen here to see you, Madam Undersecretary," her private secretary, Benjamin, voiced in honeyed tones from the intercom.

"Yes, send him right in," Ingrid answered, gazing around the room as if a shawl and a bowl of chicken soup would leap into her hands to help illustrate her sudden illness.

Eric Isaksen strode into the room all business.

Ingrid started to speak, in a childlike, pained voice, "Eric, about Egypt—"

"Looks like we can forget Egypt, Ingrid," Isaksen responded brightly.

Bittmann was feeling better already and sat straighter in her chair, inviting Isaksen with a hand motion to continue.

"Takis Koniotis has been very busy in Cairo during this morning, their time. We have a new commitment from Sulayman not only to appear at the Cyprus conference but also to support the peace settlement as long as it doesn't change radically from what his predecessor supported. Haven't you heard anything from this, Ingrid? Immediately after Sulayman gave a supportive statement, the Lebanese and Syrians registered for the conference. Didn't you have your television sets on in here? Haven't you read the press file as it has come up?"

"No, I've been busy keeping the building together while the secretary general was traveling from Timbuktu to Mandalay," Bittmann answered sharply, with a touch of hurt feelings. "You know what I think of having that bank of televisions on all day. I can't think with all of that racket going on. I need someone I trust to keep me informed on such happenings," she concluded, giving Isaksen a coquettish, meaningful look.

"I suggest we bypass Cairo and go straight on to Jerusalem today and then to Beirut," Isaksen continued, although he did move closer to Ingrid and sat very near to her on her desk. Ingrid started playing with the crease on one of his trouser legs, and he casually reached over and fingered the lace ruffle on her blouse. "Koniotis has taken care of our needs in Cairo for now, and although Damascus and Beirut have agreed to come to the conference, they are far from giving us support at the conference. I've already asked Koniotis to go to Damascus after he's finished in Amman. I think a little attention from us would do some good. But first Jerusalem. We have to balance our visits. And, having talked with the prime minister's husband about the visit on the telephone this morning because the prime minister wasn't available, I'm anxious to see Rachel Gilat. Moshe was absolutely rude. I know he's pressuring his wife to abandon the peace process, and I think she might need a little support from us."

"But what about Amman?" asked Ingrid, bidding for the easiest target in the region.

"Koniotis is on his way there now. He and his wife, who is accompanying him, were good friends of Paul Conte, the American who got killed during the assassination attempt on the Jordanian king. They have been invited to the memorial service for Conte, and I'm sure they can play on the king's sympathy through the Conte affair enough to keep him in line for us. You know Caitlyn Koniotis. She's a well-known archaeologist and is smart and beautiful to boot. I'm sure the Jordanian king will be impressed."

"More impressed than he would be with me?" Ingrid asked with a pouty expression. Isaksen leaned down and gave her a long, lingering kiss, his fingers straying away from the lace, to more strategic areas under her blouse.

"I'm not sharing you with any king, my love."

But then he sat back up, his other hand taking Ingrid's hand, which had also strayed away from his trousers creases, and putting it back in her lap.

"Right now, I'm afraid, you need to come give your press conference, and then we'll need to leave for the airport for the flight to

Israel. I took the liberty of having reservations made. Benjamin can have the ones to Cairo canceled."

"Press conference?" Ingrid asked. Sometimes Eric moved entirely too fast for her to keep pace. And sometimes he presumed a bit too much.

"Certainly." Isaksen smiled broadly, as he took the text of her opening comments out of his briefcase. "You do want to talk to the press about your successful negotiations behind the scenes to win over Egyptian president Sulayman, don't you?"

When Isaksen pulled the press conference document out of his briefcase, he mistakenly extracted two rather than one folder. Luckily, he glanced at the one he was handing Bittmann, because he had to do a slight-of-hand maneuver to slip that one back into his case and to hand the other one to the UN official.

It would not do, he thought bitterly to himself, to hand Ingrid the secret press release he had sent out hours earlier correctly fully crediting Takis Koniotis for having won over Sulayman.

* * * *

Demetris Mattas was staring intently into his computer screen, willing the right words to appear that would highlight his "I was there" information on the day's events at the central prison while not losing the breezy, satirical style of his *Simerini* "Under the Grapevine" political column. The copyboy—or, in this case, the copy girl—passed by his desk for the third time in two minutes, a constant, purposeful editorial desk reminder that he had missed the deadline for his column. Mattas didn't mind much having this new copy assistant come by his desk so often; she was definitely much easier on the eyes than her predecessor, who had been sacked in some sort of scandal involving leaking the paper's research and close-held story sources to other newspapers and even to a couple of embassies.

Yes, the world of the print and broadcast media was a highly politicized and cut-throat business, Mattas thought. He saw more intrigue on any given day than half of the intelligence agents he knew experienced.

This thought brought him, in logical progression, to Alec Stuart, who both was known to him as a British spy and had been involved in the prison courtyard escapade of earlier today. Mattas wondered if Stuart had stepped forward yet as having been on the scene during the attack and Suzanne's escape. Mattas himself had been in the prison's press room and had seen much of what happened from that room's window onto the courtyard. He heard Suzanne scream and reached the window in time to see the two guards on the ground in the corner passageway across from where he was standing at the window. He saw Suzanne head to the corner of the courtyard next to the building in which he was standing and just out of the range of his vision to the right and at the base of the building. A man was racing across the yard from where the guards were sprawled on the ground, and Willie Hamilton was moving to cut the man off.

Mattas could barely make out signs of a struggle between Willie and this man by forcing open one of the press room windows and screwing his head around to the right as far as it would go. And then, suddenly, Alec Stuart was in the courtyard as well, racing toward the two fighting men. Then . . . nothing. Mattas no longer could see the men or any other sign of activity, and the courtyard was bathed in suspended silence for what seemed to be hours but what must only have been seconds. Then people started to pour out of the prison building and into the courtyard.

When Mattas reached the courtyard, only the bodies of the two guards remained. Everyone else—Suzanne, the assailant, Willie Hamilton, and Alec Stuart—were gone. Presuming Willie had run off to register yet another news scoop for the *Cyprus Mail*, Mattas had also left for his own paper. Damned if he would be stuck in a police interview room all evening while Willie was filing the story.

As Demetris handed the hard-copy printout of his column for the next day to the sweet young thing standing expectantly beside his desk and punched the filing button on his computer keyboard, he felt a twinge of remorse for having returned to the paper to write up his story before contacting Maria and telling her what he'd seen. But only a slight twinge. He knew he would be seeing Maria at home this evening. He could tell her everything then. He really did wonder, though, if Stuart had returned to the prison to give a statement.

His wondering was stopped by a telephone call from one of his informants. It, funnily enough, was the very same fired copyboy who Demetris had just been thinking about earlier. The young man had remained in the "information" business after he was sacked by the newspaper, and, ironically, the newspaper was now one of his primary clients.

What the man had to tell Mattas canceled his intent to go right home and tell Maria all about the prison courtyard events earlier that day. He grabbed his coat, stopped at the coffee bar for a foam cup full of hot coffee and a lid, and headed for his automobile. The

216

information that had been passed to him was that Suzanne Abu Hani had escaped to the home of the Syrian ambassador.

"Should have guessed," Mattas muttered bitterly. "Bet she won't stay there long, though, and I'm going to be on the scene when she flees again."

* * * *

The object of Mattas's thoughts was even then, as he surmised, sitting on the back terrace of the home of Syrian ambassador to Cyprus Munir Nahlawi and was, as Mattas also surmised, planning her next flight plan.

Three people—Suzanne, Nahlawi, and Nahlawi's wife—were sitting, silently—one could even say morosely—at opposite corners of the terrace n the gathering gloom. It had been Nahlawi's elderly wife who had given Suzanne the less-than-enthusiastic reception at the front entrance earlier in the day. The woman had shrewishly returned to the attack when her husband arrived an hour later.

Now all three were tired of fighting. They sat in their respective corners, breathing heavily, waiting for—but not really wanting to hear—the bell for the next round.

Into the silence, the ambassador quietly said, "Let's go up to bed. This will all sort itself out in the morning."

"But It's much too early for bed," Mrs. Nahlawi responded.

But then she looked up and saw that her husband had directed this comment to a different corner. He was approaching where Suzanne sat and was offering her his hand.

The bell for the next round of fighting was heard throughout the town.

217

Dr. Theocharis Thoma was nearing retirement. He had actually been nearing retirement for over a decade, but he had only recently been able to bring on two new, American-trained dentists to come into his practice and continue to bring the money into the firm that would support his retirement. He had lived well for many years— even better than his lucrative practice among the country's wealthy and foreign community supported. In all, Dr. Thoma had put in nearly forty years of service—first as a private dentist primarily to the families of the colonial British administrators, then as the government's official dental surgeon, and then, for the past fifteen years, once again as the favored dentist of the cream of Cypriot society and of the foreign diplomatic and business community. Yes, Dr. Thoma intended to continue to live well after he had filled his last tooth, which he planned to do within two-month's time.

As chance would have it, though, Dr. Thoma had already filled his last tooth.

As usual, he was the last one to leave his plush Evagorou Street office in a high-rise building near the old city walls of Nicosia. The doctor always remained in the office for several hours after the last patient and the last of his office colleagues left for the day. Although he had brought in new help to handle the patient load, he always had done all of the practice's accounts himself, and he intended to go on doing the firm's accounts after he had retired. He didn't want anyone going around looking into the income figures and finding that the doctor's gross income far exceeded payments from patients.

In the Monday evening twilight, Dr. Thoma opened his fifth-floor office door and turned to lock the office for the night. As he did so, a figure moved quickly and quietly from the adjacent stairwell and pushed the aging dentist back into his reception area. Even as the entry door was snapped shut again, the assailant was already wrapping the third loop of his length of piano wire around the dentist's throat. There was practically no rush of pleasure to this particular job at all. Dr. Thoma had been so surprised and was so feeble that he didn't put up any resistance.

After he was done with the dentist, Salem Qazzar went back to the office area and pulled out drawers and emptied boxes as he had been instructed to do. It was supposed to look like Dr. Thoma had been killed during a burglary, perhaps by someone in search of money or drugs. Qazzar had been instructed not to take anything with him, but he saw a miniature set of false teeth on the desk in one of the offices and couldn't resist taking it.

On to the Syrian ambassador's residence, Qazzar thought, as he quietly let himself out of the office and carefully descended the stairs to the street below.

As he sauntered off toward the BMW he had "acquired" earlier in the evening and that he had matched with registration tags he had taken from a demolished automobile in the back lot of the dealership, Qazzar placed both hands in his trouser pockets. In one pocket, he lovingly fingered his new length of piano wire, while in the other pocket he played the miniature set of false teeth as if they were castanets.

Chapter Fifteen

The entry of Mr. and Dr. Koniotis into the network of undulating hills of the Jordanian capital city of Amman was not quite as Caitlyn had envisioned her first visit to the ancient Roman caravan city she had known as Philadelphia from her archaeological studies would be.

After landing on Tuesday morning at the Queen Alia International Airport, named after the first, well-beloved wife of the current Jordanian king, who had been killed in a somewhat suspect helicopter crash two decades earlier, Caitlyn insisted on approaching their hotel via Al Hashimi Street, which ran between the well-preserved Roman amphitheater and both the ancient citadel and the less-ancient Raghadan royal palace enclave. In the bustle of a busy city and the jumble of cookie-cutter boxy buildings, Caitlyn wanted both to start off her first visit to Jordan with a sense of the area's rich cultural past and to come immediately in touch, via a drive past the palace complex, with the reality of Paul Conte's death. It had not yet been four days since Paul's death there in the Raghadan Palace. It was still very hard for Caitlyn to accept that it had really happened.

Caitlyn had always intended to visit Jordan. A must on any archaeologist's list were the excavations at Jerash, some thirty-five miles to the north of Amman. She also wanted, of course, to see Petra, the "hidden" city carved into canyon walls—and there was Mount Nebo, the spot, in the biblical country of Moab, from whence Moses reputedly spied the promised land and subsequently died and was buried in a hidden grave on the mountain itself.

But, alas, she would have to see all of this in a subsequent visit, as she had been told that Takis's business here would not take long and she knew that the time would be filled with visiting with and consoling Ellen Larkin and attending the memorial service for Paul. She hoped she would have more time to spend on the archaeological wonders of the region when they flew on to Damascus the next day.

None of Caitlyn's archaeological curiosity was to be assuaged on this initial visit to Jordan. Even her desire to see the ancient center of Amman en route from the airport had to be aborted, because they ran into thick, angry crowds that spilled out onto the streets as they drove east on Quraysh Street not far from where it merged into Al Hashimi Street at the Roman amphitheater.

After warning Takis to place his camera on the floor of the Mercedes limousine so as not to antagonize the crowd further, which had noticed the presence of an automobile of the royal household by the emblem on the door, their attendant ordered the driver to turn north on Husay Street and on to the hotel district beyond the Jamal Abd Nasir Interchange,

221

"I'm sorry," he apologized, "the city market surrounds the amphitheater area, and it's a bit too crowded in that district this morning for us to travel through."

"But the crowds looked angry," remarked Takis. "Is marketing not a happy experience in Amman?"

"Well, to tell the truth, this is a very conservative section of the city, and there is a bit of unrest at the moment."

"Oh?" asked Takis pointedly.

And with increasing embarrassment, the attendant further elaborated. "Yes, I'm afraid many people in Jordan are not pleased with the king's policies on the Middle East peace settlement."

The rest of the short ride to the hotel was conducted in a heavy, uncomfortable silence.

* * * *

The meeting that was being conducted at the moment in Jerusalem between the UN officials, Ingrid Bittmann and Eric Isaksen, and the Israeli prime minister, Rachel Gilat, just a very short distance from Amman in space but a universe away from Amman in mind-set and cultural orientation, was not going at all well either.

It hadn't even started well, although not through any fault of either the UN officials or the prime minister. The blame for this could be laid squarely on the doorstep of the prime minister's radical rightist husband, Moshe Gilat, who was very pleased to take responsibility. For Moshe, who had intercepted the telephone call from Isakson informing the prime minister he and the UN undersecretary were coming to Jerusalem to meet with her on the coming Cyprus peace conference, had purposely neglected to tell his wife about the call. He had also used the agents he had placed on her staff to ensure that no one else told her the two were coming, and he had even unsuccessfully tried to convince her that she needed to go to the Red Sea resort of Elat in the south for a few days for a rest before facing the grueling peace conference negotiations.

Moshe's manipulations had ensured that what was already normally a tedious and insulting entry process at Tel Aviv's Ben Gurion Airport was particularly annoying to Ingrid Bittmann, who was extremely upset that she hadn't been met by someone important from the government and whisked around immigration control. And for her part, the telephoned announcement that the two UN officials were waiting in their American Colony Hotel suite for an appointment to see her today had caught the prime minister at her offices in the Knesset, the Israeli parliament, deeply and irritatingly embroiled in putting out brush fires within her own party ranks, flames that prominently featured her policies on the Middle East peace settlement.

To save time and also because she didn't want the media to hear about an unannounced meeting between herself and high-level UN officials that would certainly be misconstrued as secret talks and be blown out of proportion, Gilat suggested that she meet Bittmann and Isaksen at the American Colony. As she had had a luncheon engagement with her husband, she called to tell him where she was going—but not why—and she was driven out to the old colonial hotel not far from the city walls in what had been, as the hotel's name implied, the section of the new city in which most of the American residents had congregated in the early decades of the twentieth century. She took only Sergey Stepanov, the chief of her personal bodyguard squad, with her.

Having reached the hotel, Gilat and Stepanov went up to Bittmann's suite, which turned out to have a balcony that extended over the hotel's entire entry and reception area. To discourage listeners, Rachel Gilat had insisted that they all sit at the table on the balcony. Stepanov refused to sit, but spent the brief span of the meeting hovering over his employer and scanning the surrounding area for possible sources of danger.

The already-doomed talks suffered a further shot to the vitals when the two women, the prime minister and the UN official, took an instant dislike to each other. Ingrid Bittmann was primarily to blame, as she launched immediate into an instructional monologue on the combined strategy of the forces intent on reaching a final, lasting peace agreement at the Cyprus conference. Gilat spat back with a statement that neither she nor Israel were part of any coalition in the negotiations, that she would not take instruction from a representative of any other political entity, and that the extent to which she and her government were supporting the peace efforts devolved entirely from the long-term interests of Israel and the Jewish people.

Isaksen, as usual, was all smoothness and started to interject himself between the two. But the shot or the engine backfire—no one was sure what it had been—saved them all. At the cracking sound, Sergey Stepanov descended upon and enfolded the figure of the prime minister like a Dracula in a Grade-B horror film and dragged her back into the hotel room and away to her waiting car, leaving Bittmann and Isaksen gasping for breath and understanding at their table on the pleasant balcony of the rambling American Colony Hotel. None of the four actually believed there had been a shot, but each of the four was just as pleased as they could be to have had such an ill-fated meeting ended so decisively.

* * * *

Caitlyn was waiting in the lobby lounge of the Amman Marriott Hotel for Ellen Larkin to appear. The day after Paul died, Ellen moved to the Marriott from the Regency Palace just across the street. She said she couldn't remain in the hotel where her last memories of her fiancé had been formed. Ellen wasn't in her room when the Koniotises checked in, and Caitlyn was waiting for her friend's return to the hotel here, near the entryway.

Takis had already gone off to his meeting with the king. This was merely a formality, Takis had said. As a matter of face, the king would want to be included in any round of visits to regional heads of state, but any "bolstering" of his resolve to support the peace process would be a waste of time. The king was both a Muslim and a friend, in so far as that was possible, of the West. In addition, he was a survivor. His policy decisions wouldn't be based on any principles cast in concrete but, rather, would evolve from how well the talks went at the conference. He would lean toward peace and the West as much as possible, but not so far that it caused him to topple off his throne.

As Caitlyn sat on a sofa, reading the hotel's monthly glossy magazine, she glanced occasionally at all avenues of approach, wanting to be sure to intercept Ellen as soon as her friend appeared. It was thus that she saw a tall, elderly, distinguished-looking gentleman who she thought she recognized descending the hotel's central staircase.

225

The man was extremely handsome and might have been a male model in his earlier years. The only flaw Caitlyn could discern in his appearance was a pale strawberry birthmark that ran from his left ear down into his impeccable shirt collar. But even that one small flaw seemed to emphasize the perfection of his other facial features. Try as she might, Caitlyn couldn't place him in her mind's eye. She must have been staring at him, because he became aware of the stare and returned an amused, interested look that indicated that he possibly misjudged the intent of Caitlyn's gaze. The man walked with elegant, slow steps, back ramrod straight despite his advanced age, over to the reception desk, briefly talked with the desk manager, took on a look of concern, and moved quickly out of the hotel's front door.

Caitlyn couldn't remember where she had seen—or met—the gentleman before, and it was irritating her that she couldn't dredge up a name from the far recesses of her brain. She was usually quite good with names and faces. She couldn't stop turning names over in her mind. Maybe the desk manager could tell her.

She walked over to the reception desk and asked the supervisor if he could tell her who that man was.

"Oh, that was Mr. Piccard. He's one of our regular visitors."

"A Piccard!" Caitlyn thought. "Yes, that must be it. Now that I think of it, he reminded me of Jacques Piccard. But he's dead. I wonder just how many Piccards there are wandering around the Middle East. And what they are up to. According to Takis, they couldn't be up to anything good."

But Caitlyn was snapped out of her thoughts because she suddenly realized that the desk manager was still talking to her.

226

"Excuse me, what was that you just said?" she asked.

"I said that it was funny that you asked me who Mr. Piccard was, because he asked the same thing about you just now."

This really did start Caitlyn's mind to working, but, as she turned to return to the sofa and contemplate what she had just learned, there was Ellen Larkin, standing just inside the front entrance, looking delicate and vulnerable and badly in need of a friend.

* * * *

Three automobiles with diplomatic registrations left the driveway of the residence of the Syrian ambassador to Cyprus in quick succession. Neither the terrorist, Salem Qazzar, nor the journalist, Demetris Mattas, who had been so intent on watching the residence that they had not noticed each other, wasted any time on the third car. This one transported a tearful Mrs. Nahlawi, undoubtedly on her way to cry on the shoulder of her dear friend, the wife of the Indian ambassador, in her residence next to the city reservoir on top of the Monte Parnasse ridge.

On instinct, Mattas followed the first automobile. It was a small sedan and appeared only to be occupied by a servant on his way to the market, but Mattas thought the departure of all three vehicles at the same time was suspicious, and he was banking that Suzanne was hidden in the backseat of the first vehicle. Being impressed with authority, Salem Qazzar assumed Suzanne was hidden in the second automobile, a luxury, chauffeured BMW with the Syrian ambassador in the backseat.

About fifteen minutes after all of these automobiles drove off, a fourth Syrian embassy vehicle, a closed van, drove up to and stopped in front of the steps up to the front door of the residence. A figure separated from the shadows of the front entryway porch and glided down the path and into the back of the van.

A nice ruse, but all in vain. As the van turned onto Ayiou Pavlou Avenue and moved toward the old city of Nicosia, another watcher turned over the ignition in a nearby parked automobile and followed the van at a distance. The van crossed the bridge over the temporarily trickling river, turned right past the law courts at the Municipal Park circle, and glided through the Greek checkpoint at the only regularized diplomatic crossing point on the UN buffer zone, the one that extended between the walls of the old city and the formerly grand Ledra Palace Hotel, which stood proudly, but pockmarked with bullet holes, in its splendid buffer zone isolation. The pursuing vehicle hesitated momentarily at the circle just this side of the Greek checkpoint and then followed the Syrian embassy van into the buffer zone.

* * * *

The memorial service for Paul Conte was very moving—and quite unusual, especially as it concerned the setting. When Ellen Larkin returned to the hotel—from finalizing the arrangements for Paul's final trip back to the United States the next day and getting her own tickets on the same plane—she and Caitlyn had first gone to the hotel bar for a stiff drink and then, thusly bolstered, went up to the Koniotis suite for a good cry and a mutual consolation session. In the process, the strange brush with the Piccard family that Caitlyn had experience earlier completely slipped her mind.

When Takis returned to the hotel an hour later, he joined in with both activities. As he had surmised, there were no surprises in his meeting with the king, although it had been a friendly and cordial meeting. Takis had left feeling that he could count on help from the Jordanian secret service in ensuring that the Cyprus conference was able to open.

Increasingly Takis was coming to believe that he needed to forge a network of cooperation in the police investigative services of the countries of the region if the Amathus coast peace conference was to come off without a hitch and if any settlement that was signed had a chance of bearing fruit. If he was able to form this type of cooperation for the conference, perhaps he could then fold it into a backbone in this region for the work of UNICIS.

In the late afternoon, the palace car returned and took the three friends to the memorial service. After a short drive, the limousine pulled up in front of the impressive national mosque, the King Abdullah Mosque, which was named after the king's martyred grandfather. The parliament building—the building the king had built when he granted a limited mandate of representative government to the people—loomed across the avenue.

As impressive as the central mosque structure was, the memorial service was not being held there. Upon entering the courtyard of the complex, the three were escorted to a miniature version of the mosque that sat off to the side. Moving inside, the three encountered a small audience hall, with a central throne surrounded by divans and Louis XVI upholstered chairs. This was where, their escort told them, the king received well wishers after he had attended Friday prayers. They didn't remain in the reception room, however, but descended a stairway to the left of the room, where they found an even larger lounge area. The escort whispered that this was where the royal family waited while the king received people upstairs.

And this was where Ellen, Caitlyn, and Takis waited. The company of those waiting grew as official and personal friends of Paul Conte and the government leaders of Jordan gathered for the ceremony. Then, within the great flurry of a host of late arrivals, the king and queen and their entourage were there, and everyone was swept into a large, circular conference hall, with tiers of plush seats and wood-grained surfaces and plush carpet underfoot, on the walls, and even on the ceiling.

The escort once again provided an explanation in hushed tones. This was the Islamic Parliament hall, and it was located directly below the huge King Abdullah Mosque and was, incidentally, connected by tunnel to the Jordanian parliament building across the street. It had been King Abdullah's dream that a unifying representative assembly of all Muslim nations would form—around the Hashemite dynasty of King Abdullah, of course—that would meet to debate and rationally settle on a common Muslim line on international policies. When the current king built the national mosque for his grandfather, he built it to encompass the old man's complete dream. There had, in fact, been many interesting and significant regional sessions in this conference room, but none as yet that would acknowledge that the world revolved around the Hashemites.

In spite of—or perhaps because of—the setting, the memorial service for Paul Conte was quite moving. The only interruption of mood that Caitlyn experienced throughout the ceremony came near the end when she permitted her eyes to wander around the hall. And there he was, in the very back and across the hall from her. The Piccard who she almost, but not quite, met in the Marriott lobby lounge earlier in the day.

* * * *

It had been so simple. God, he was good. Thomas Jameson almost fell out of the tub chair in the Milano Café in his efforts to pat himself on the back. And he was getting plenty of help from his contact, who had been very, very pleased with the Xerox copies of the file Jameson had just handed across the table.

"Just about everything you asked for is there," Jameson noted, with a tone of great pride in his voice. "Delegation assignments, meeting rooms, known arrival dates and flights. Names of the advance people."

"Yes, thank you. Our people will, of course, be very pleased. No indication you were detected, I trust?"

"No, none. After you called last night, I checked out Takis Koniotis's office and discerned where he was keeping the information. I went back today, found the keys to the cabinet, extracted and Xeroxed that information, and put everything back in place without anyone noticing what I was doing. I'm a senior officer there, as you know, so, as long as Koniotis is out of the country, all I had to do was act like I had authorization to do what I did."

"Yes, yes. You did a wonderful job. As I said before, my people will be very happy. You have been a very good friend to us. We will not forget this."

"Do pay special attention, by the way, to what I circled there on the third page," said Jameson in a stage whisper, puffed up and conspiratorial.

"Ah, yes. The key national leaders will be scheduled to meet in the Kumar's Conference room of the Amathus Beach hotel, I see. Very good. Just what we were looking for."

"Then, perhaps if you could turn to the fifth page and look at what I've marked. There, right there. See?"

"Yes. A room number and a notation that a conference table and extra security would be needed. Hmm. I wonder . . ."

"So did I," Jameson whispered with barely contained excitement. "You don't suppose they might be pulling a switch on us, do you? Telling nearly everyone, but confidentially, of course, that the most important leaders will be meeting in an Amathus Beach Hotel conference room as necessary, when they actually will be meeting upstairs in one of the suites?"

"Yes, I see the possibilities. Very, v-e-r-y good, Mr. Jameson. We'll just have to take that into account as a possibility, won't we? We are very pleased to have you on our team. You know, I'm sure, how important it is for us not to be sold out by such a conference. I must go for now. Please keep your head down and your tail end safe. You have become an extremely valuable asset to us."

Chapter Sixteen

"Ugh! What time is it, and where are we?"

"Ugh, yourself," Caitlyn responded, as she rose from the bed and drew back the drapes, letting both the sunlight and the street noise from the over-two million people of the world's longest continuously occupied city stream into the Meridien Hotel room. "It is half past seven; time to get up; and, if it's Wednesday, it must be Damascus. Come on, up, up, up, UP," Caitlyn prattled gaily as she fought her husband for the bedcovers.

"Cancel Wednesday," Takis muttered, as he buried his head under the pillow. "I feel like I traveled the world in the last three days."

"Well, you *have* traveled a good portion of the ancient Middle Eastern world in the last three days. Come on, now. You mustn't keep the bloodthirsty absolute dictator waiting. Your head will join that of John the Baptist's over in yon Omayyad Mosque if you are late for your appointment."

"I believe I've told you before not to be playful about the Syrian president," Takis said wearily as he sat up on the edge of the bed and attempted to shield his eyes form the early morning light. "And leave it to you to know where John the Baptist's head wound up. You know you're just calling him that to make fun of what a couple of your less-knowledgeable friends say." And then he swung Caitlyn around by the elbow so that she was looking into his face and mouthed and mimed the phrase, "The walls have ears."

Caitlyn chortled, mouthed a "S-o-o sorry," and headed for the shower. She turned just as she reached the door and clearly and loudly enunciated, "A little paranoid today, are we?"

Two hours later, Takis was cooling his heels in the reception room in a nondescript Russian-built block building that clashed seriously with the nearly 5,000 years of accumulated architecture of the city beyond these walls. The Syrian president was making a point concerning who was waiting upon whom. Caitlyn, along with the suave male escort so kindly provided by the Syrian Foreign Ministry, was touring the old walled city.

When Takis was finally ushered in to see the Syrian president, he was treated to the leader's own studied view of the benevolent grandfather routine. Takis was not taken in at all, but he did acknowledge a begrudging respect for a man who had remained in power for twenty-five years, the longest of any Syrian leader in modern history, and who had steadily, if slowly, improved the lot of his people and maintained a certain acceptable level of stability, even if it brought to mind the cynical management text negative goal of "keep them sullen but subdued." Regardless, the Syrians and their president were potential "spoilers" if not key elements of a Middle East peace conference and thus had to be consulted and cajoled.

This morning the Syrian president wasn't making it easy for Takis to do either. He would say something supportive of the current Middle East peace efforts and then he would pull back. He would say he would be helpful to the process and might even, himself, show up for the Amathus coast conference in Cyprus due to open in the coming days. And then he would say he wasn't sure a delegation would appear at all and that maybe he would be in London for his medical checkup at that time.

At length the leader's comments on the conference and the peace process appeared to be becoming ever more critical, and Takis, feeling he was losing ground, decided to introduce a new tack.

"You know, Your Excellency, that I'm not part of the actual peace negotiations, and I don't have any responsibility for seeing that a conference is successfully concluded."

The president's eyes narrowed in interest, and Takis plunged ahead.

"My job—and the reason I'm traveling around to the various capitals of the region is to ensure that the conference is safely concluded." He continued, "Are you in favor of order and stability? Which choice would you take between a conference that went through its paces peacefully without a settlement and one where all of the delegates were gunned down short of any resolution of the issues?"

"Yes, of course," said the Middle East champion of strict—very strict—order and stability.

235

"And would you really prefer to have warfare within the region or to continue down the path of peace—armed and sullen peace, if necessary, but peace just the same—that permits further economic development?"

"I hardly need respond to that," the Syrian huffed.

"Well, then," said the UNICIS chief, "do you really want there to be bloodshed at the Cyprus conference? Do you really want to see leaders assassinated and/or toppled en masse by this process—to see the instability that this would create?"

"No, not really," answered the president, fully aware that he could be one of the ones toppled just as he, the then-defense minister, had toppled his own predecessor during a period of regional unrest.

"Let me repeat then. All I'm looking for in this round of visits is support for a safe conference—if there is to be a conference at all. From my perspective, I have no problem if the conference results in no progress in the status quo or even if the conference is called off altogether. But what I need, for the safety of all leaders, including yourself, and all individuals involved in this process is active help from your police and investigative services to ensure that this process doesn't ignite a brush fire across the region that envelops us all. Can you commit to the UN effort to this extent, Mr. President?"

The president contemplated his hands for a brief moment and cheerily responded, "Yes, of course. Syria is a responsible member of the United Nations, and we certainly can support and help your security efforts for the conference—should there be a conference, of course."

"Thank you, Your Excellency. I have decided to call a conference of the highest-level security services officials you can send to Nicosia during the coming weekend. Can I count on you sending an official to meet with us, one who will be directed to help make the conference venue safe for all?"

"But naturally," the Syrian president said with a little smile. He always enjoyed clever maneuvering—even when it boxed him in. "We would be happy to help."

And then, after a bit of warming chitchat, the president bid Takis good-bye and a safe journey back to Cyprus. Just as Takis was passing through the doorway, though, the conversation instantly went from warm to frozen as the president said, with a dead-eyed smile, "Oh, and Mr. Koniotis, please tell your lovely wife that I only thirst for blood on Mondays."

Despite being entirely nonplussed, Takis immediate tested the boundaries of the Syrians' willingness to cooperate by asking the official who was escorting him from "the presence" if he could be given access to a telephone to make several calls throughout the region. The Syrians showed that they were willing to go at least this far with him by taking him immediately to the central telephone exchange and permitting him to dial through to security service contacts throughout the Middle East region.

By the time he left for the Meridien to check up on Caitlyn's morning, he had either firm pledges or promises to search out pledges from every major conference player to have an empowered security services delegate present at the Nicosia Hilton on Sunday morning to discuss the sharing of information on the opponents of the peace process, especially the ones who were willing to turn to violence to obtain their ends, and the networking of cooperation to counter such threats. If Safa Ziya were here at this moment, he would have kissed her for suggesting that he provisionally book rooms and conference facilities in the Hilton for this weekend. Now he knew what he needed the space for.

Takis had one unpleasant surprise during his telephoning, which came when he got through to Israel, no easy feat from Damascus. He was shunted around from official to official and finally ended up talking to someone from his own past, someone unpleasant. Of course, Sergey Stepanov wasn't any less surprised or more pleased at being connected with the former chief Cypriot police investigator than Takis was in finding himself talking with someone who had once been suspected of being involved in various international crimes in Cyprus. Stepanov was now the head of the prime minister's personal security in Israel, but he had once been closely connected with Russian mafia operations in Cyprus. Stepanov did agree to come to Cyprus for the conference, but only if his capacity as an Israeli official, with full diplomatic immunity, was recognized—which meant he couldn't be arrested or even questioned in connection with his past association with Cyprus. Takis had to agree to this, even if reluctantly. The network wouldn't be effective without the participation of the Israelis.

Meanwhile, Caitlyn had been busy drinking in the sights and sounds of a city that had been around so long that it had the dubious honor of having been conquered by some of the ancient world's most renowned leaders, including King David, Nebuchadnezzar, Alexander the Great, Saladin, and Tamerlaine. Only in such a cultural melting pot

238

as Damascus could you have a mosque that prominently housed the tombs of both John the Baptist—head only—and the scourge of the crusaders, Saladin.

After strolling through the mosque and the nearby Azem Palace, Caitlyn and her escort moved into the covered Souk al Hamadiyeh, one of the most extensive and most colorful open markets in the Middle East. It was for the purpose of visiting this souk that Caitlyn needed this escort. Although Damascus was a city of wide-ranging cultural tolerance, with the attire of women safely walking the narrow streets ranging from the full purdah of the visitor from Iran to the thoughtless halter top and shorts of the visitor from Sweden, the souk was a bustling, close-air, noisy, dirty center of exotic commerce that offered everything from inlay work, copperware, silks, and carpets to, some claimed, blonde women—and boys—from Europe and America. In the case of the beautiful, blonde wife of the visiting UN official, the Syrian Foreign Ministry was taking no chances, so Caitlyn had a free guide for the morning.

Caitlyn loved all of the exotic goods that were on display in the souk. She loved to haggle, which was a must, and the shopkeepers were having a terrific time themselves playfully haggling with this beautiful American who could converse in almost passable Arabic.

She stopped at one shop and admired the damask silk tablecloths for which the city was famous worldwide. Out of the corner of her eye she caught sight of a particularly bulky, disheveled merchant in the cooper shop next door shuffling toward her and pulling at her elbow.

"Some nice copperware, pretty lady? A special price for you and for—"

Caitlyn had started to turn, in sudden irritation. The grating voice sounded familiar. It reminded her of someone and events that had decidedly been unpleasant. But she had only half turned, because another tall, thin merchant from a jewelry store was dangling beaded necklaces in her face. The copper merchant hadn't even finished his sales pitch, and when Caitlyn turned, he was gone. But he had left in his wake a clanging of copper pots that added delightful texture to this teaming market place.

This was the chaotic context of Caitlyn's visit to the old city of Damascus, and she was so tired and loaded down with new-found treasures when she reached the hotel and plopped down at Takis's side in the lobby bar that she didn't even respond immediately when he told her he had rearranged their travel so that they could leave for home tonight. He had a lot of work to do at UNICIS headquarters before Sunday, including checking with John Patterson on how their worldwide hookup to police databases was moving along.

Caitlyn was fine one moment and then she was gagging on her drink.

Takis gave her a look of concern, but she was already rising and heading for the shopping arcade.

"Would you believe it?" she tossed over her shoulder as she rushed off toward the hotel gift shop. "I found all of that good stuff in the souk, but nothing for the twins."

* * * *

Maria Solonos was spending her Wednesday morning in the Nicosia police headquarters building busily putting together the various eyewitness accounts to the murders of Suzanne Abu Hani's guards at the central prison the previous Sunday and Suzanne's subsequent disappearance. Luckily, she could take time away from the Androulla Varnavidou murder case to turn to this one. The patrols had had sent out to the region around the Macheras Monastery had run evidence of a hidden Hizballah terrorist to ground in the small showcase village of Fikardou. Although the terrorist seemed to have gotten away for now, the villagers of Fikardou and nearby Gourd were being very cooperative. The village girl the suspect had married said her husband had left on a carpentry job in the Paphos area, so an intensive search was already under way on the western end of the island.

Maria herself, however, didn't give much credence to the theory that the terrorist would be found in Paphos. She was becoming increasingly sure that her own investigation into the attack at the prison would link up with the disappearance of the Hizballah terrorist suspect. She needed some strategic pieces of the puzzle to fit into place, but she had already gotten some tentative identification of recent photos they had taken from the Fikardou village house of the missing terrorist as being the same man who killed the guards and attacked Willie Hamilton at the central prison.

What Maria couldn't understand, though, was why key witnesses of the prison attacks hadn't stepped forward as yet. Even Demetris had not returned home to tell her what he'd seen and what he knew until the previous night. She wouldn't be speaking to him at all for not having come forward sooner, but he was fully cooperating now, and he seemed to be the most observant witness she had so far, even though he had not had a full view of the action from the press room at the prison. She would just have to snub him after she had wrung everything he had remembered of the event out of him.

Demetris, who was now sitting in the central squad room and giving a full statement to a detective, had been the first witness to place Alec Stuart on the scene. He also had voluntarily told her that Suzanne had escaped to the residence of one of her former lovers and dupes, the Syrian ambassador, Munir Nahlawi, a development that he was quick to assert he had learned from an informant he could not identify, and that he had not reported to Maria earlier because he had staked out the residence in hopes of seeing where Suzanne would go next. He was embarrassed to admit that he had guessed wrong on how—or if—she had left the residence.

Maria had, of course, immediately called the Syrian ambassador and asked him if he was harboring a murder suspect, but Nahlawi had denied it and had invited the police to inspect the house, which he voiced as over and above what they could expect considering his house technically was Syrian territory. She had sent a team over to do just that, but, of course, she knew that, if he made the offer, it meant that Suzanne no longer was there—or was too well hidden for their search to ferret her out.

What Maria really couldn't understand was why neither Willie Hamilton nor Alec Stuart had stepped forward as yet to report what they had seen and done. They were the only two people—living people—in the courtyard with the assailant after Suzanne had escaped.

She was beginning to worry about where they were. She was not as worried about Willie, who was most likely off pursuing some angle of the story as Demetris had done, but it was unlike the diplomat, Alec Stuart, not to fully cooperate with the police. Or at least that was her first thought. Now that she thought about it, though, she remembered instances in cases in the past in which it seemed like Stuart had more information than he was readily sharing.

She really wanted to talk with Willie, though. She wanted to know what angle of the story he was now following. Whatever it was, it doubtlessly would fill in an important missing piece of the puzzle. Willie was an excellent investigator; he must be following an important lead. But, more important, she needed to find out if Suzanne had told him anything before the attack and her escape. Maria was convinced that Suzanne held some vital information concerning the Hizballah, information that connected with Cyprus and/or the coming Middle East peace conference on Cyprus, and she was willing to bet that someone had tried to kill Suzanne to keep her from revealing that information. Under that sort of threat, Maria was hoping that she could find Suzanne and that the woman would reveal what she knew in exchange for protection.

The answer to one of Maria's quandaries walked into her office at just that moment.

A visibly tired Alec Stuart almost literally lurched into Maria's office and plopped down into the "guest" chair. He apologized for having only now come to see her about the attack at the prison, but he said he had followed both Suzanne and the assailant to the Syrian embassy. The assailant had left, but he had stayed on, returning to his nearby apartment only long enough to retrieve his automobile and grab some bread and a six-pack of beer. He said he had seen the assailant and Demetris Mattas come back to watch the house as well.

When all of the vehicles left the next morning, the assailant and Demetris chose to follow two of the vehicles. He himself had been parked at such an angle to the house that he had seen the figure lingering in the shadows of the entryway. So, he remained after the other vehicles paraded off, and he was rewarded with the appearance of a van and with witnessing Suzanne's second escape. He said that he followed the van across to the Turkish side, but he lost it in the traffic on the Turkish side of Nicosia. He drove around the north from that time to this searching for Suzanne—to the point of almost having been stranded over there by running out of gas—but he hadn't found a trace of either her or the van.

Maria made a mental note to set up a meeting with her Turkish Cypriot counterpart at the Ledra Palace Hotel in the buffer zone as soon as possible to have an arrest order put out for Suzanne. She made a second mental note to telephone the Syrian ambassador and to lean on him to tell her where Suzanne had been taken. The Syrian ambassador had been skating on thin diplomatic ice for several years. It was perhaps time to present a case for having him declared persona non grata. Maria wondered just how long such a spoiled wheeler and dealer would last in the stringent environment in his home country.

But Maria had two more question for Alec before she sent him off to make a statement to the detectives.

"What about Willie, Alec? What happened to Willie? We know the assailant was choking him and then threw him into your arms at the mouth of the passage through which Suzanne escaped. But none of our witnesses can tell us what happened after that."

"Well, what does Willie have to say?" responded Stuart. "I just let him fall to the ground and continued on after Suzanne and the assailant. I just assumed Willie followed after us when he got up but that he was too roughed up and old to keep up the pace—or that he needed medical attention and stayed in the courtyard."

"We haven't heard from Willie since that day, Alec, and that worries us."

"Maybe he's off working on the story. You know how tenacious he is."

"Yes, we thought of that as a possibility too, of course."

"But maybe . . ." Alec was finding it hard to verbalize the thought. "You know the attacker had a very nasty choke hold on Willie with a thin wire. I think Willie had been more or less holding his own when I got to him, but he had to have been cut up pretty badly. Maybe, just maybe, more damage was done to Willie than I thought. Do you suppose he might have started out after us and fallen by the path someplace? You know, it's pretty overgrown behind the prison complex."

Maria sighed. "Yes, you might be right. If so, he's been out there far too long. I'll send someone out there to look just in case."

Maria started to pick up the telephone receiver, but she was interrupted by an incoming call. It might have been telepathy or it

245

might have been coincidence, but it most definitely was a worried Ginger Hamilton.

"I'm sorry to call you, Maria," Ginger whispered through what sounded to be tears, "but I couldn't think of anyone else to call. It's William. He hasn't come home since Sunday. I've read about what happened over at the prison. That's where he was headed the last time I talked to him. I know he's famous for staying away from home for days at a time. On some story of his or some drunken binge. But for the past two years, he's never stayed out without telephoning me. I know everyone remembers the fights we used to have and that those sometimes kept him away from home for days. But, Maria, we haven't been fighting. I swear we haven't been fighting. And we even discussed where we were going to eat when he got home from his interview at the prison on Sunday. Oh, Maria, I'm so worried."

"So am I, Ginger," Maria responded gently. "We have people out looking for Willie now. I promise we'll call just as soon as we know anything. Please stay by the telephone. I'll have someone come by and give you an update on what we know before this evening, I promise."

When she disconnected, Maria's eyes locked onto Alec's. They were most probably thinking exactly the same thing. It had just been too long. Up to now Willie had led a charmed, if somewhat battered, life. But the charm may have just worn off.

Stuart got up to go give his statement to the police detective waiting just beyond Maria's door, but Maria touched his arm.

"One more thing, Alec, if you would. Would you look at this photograph and tell me whether this might have been the assailant at the prison?"

Stuart looked at the photo and Maria thought she saw some momentary sign of recognition or of special interest, but then his eyes became guarded and he handed the photograph back.

"It could be. But I'll have to confess that I was too much in shock over having stumbled over the bodies of the guards and then seeing Willie being attacked to pay too much attention to the assailant's features. All I can say, I'm afraid, is that I can't think of any features I saw that indicate the attacker was anyone else. Sorry."

"That's all right. I understand perfectly." And, in fact, she did. She had seen Alec in action more than once; he was about the last person she could think of who would be in shock under attack to the point of not identifying his attacker. She'd have to think about why he was holding back.

And then, when he was almost gone, she said, "Oh, one more thing, Alec. Why did you come to the prison in the first place?"

"I was afraid you were going to ask me that," Alec answered sheepishly. "I went to the prison to try to see Suzanne, of course. I know I threatened to do her bodily harm if I ever saw her again. I mean she played me for a fool, spied on my country through me, and even tried to kill me. But Suzanne is not someone you get over quickly, if at all. I'm sorry to say that Suzanne may be a virus from which one never recovers."

"Thank you; I just wondered," Maria said in a distant voice. She was sorry now that she had asked. And she was not thinking of

Alec's addiction to Suzanne, a woman who had treated Alec as badly as any woman possibly could and who apparently still owned his heart in spite of her treachery. No, she was thinking of Demetris. Had he been irrevocably infected by this Suzanne virus as well? And, if so, what did this mean for Demetris and herself—and what did this mean for Suzanne? Were they all trapped in Suzanne's web? Even Suzanne?

Chapter Seventeen

If Suzanne Abu Hani had been in the mood to appreciate beauty, there would have been plenty for her to appreciate on that Thursday morning in mid April, as she sat near the edge of the stone terrace and stared out over the scenic northern coastline of Cyprus. From here on the terrace of the highest house in the artists' village midway up the northern slopes of the Kyrenia mountain ridge, Suzanne could see all the way from the picturesque harbor town of Kyrenia toward the east, with its bulky double castle—a Byzantine structure locked inside a Venetian shell—nearly to Lapithos to the west, site of one of the island's wealthy ancient kingdoms. If she looked above her and to the east, she could see the royal chamber area of the crusader St. Hilarion castle, looming between the horns of one of the highest peaks in the mountain chain.

Looking straight out onto the narrow northern coastal plain, Suzanne could see down through the village of Karmi to the distant village of Ayios Georgios at the Mediterranean's edge. This view was filtered by a curious set of three stately funeral cypress trees that rose

249

up to the level of Munir Nahlawi's mountain hideaway from a garden a bit farther down the slope. Two of these trees rose in their natural thin, spiked glory. The third tree had been cruelly chopped off in mid height, a graphic and constant reminder that one could not escape the real world, even in a peaceful mountain aerie such as Karmi.

The tree had been cut off during the Turkish invasion of the island in 1974, when a shell being lobbed toward Greek encampments in the mountains strayed into Karmi. The shell itself was lodged in the wall of the house bordering the terrace, just beside the main entry, which provided access to the country kitchen. Both a telling commentary on the state of affairs in Cyprus and an interesting welcome to the Nahlawi village home.

Suzanne was amazed that the mountain slopes had looked more or less like they had when she had been a regular—and secretive—visitor to this house in earlier years. She had known there had been a devastating fire that had raged for more than two days across this side of the Kyrenia range during the summer before the last one. The fire had blackened most of the mountain slopes and had even reached the sea at a couple of places. But when Suzanne gazed out over the slopes now, in the area that had suffered the worst damage, she wouldn't have guessed that it had recently been devastated. The vegetation had come back up, and the bougainvillea and jasmine vines and oleander bushes were already in full glory even though it was early in the season for them to be blooming. Nature certainly was resilient to the matches of men.

Suzanne was depressed, however, and didn't feel the least bit resilient at the moment. This was quite a new feeling for a woman who had always been the ultimate survivor. She felt lost and lonely and at odds. She felt strangely safe here, at least for the moment, however. With Munir's help she had made it to the Turkish zone, cut off from the Greek zone to any but the diplomatic community. Even if the authorities in the Cypriot Republic—and her own immediate enemies in the more far-flung region of this end of the Mediterranean—were guessing she had entered the Turkish Cypriot zone, surely they couldn't know that she was hiding here, in Munir Nahlawi's secret hideaway, at the top of Karmi—or do much about it even if they suspected as much.

Suzanne doubted that Munir had even told his diplomatic colleagues or his own wife about this trysting spot, where Suzanne and Munir had spent so many hours—blissful for him, trying for her—in the lovemaking that had made the foolish old pig Suzanne's slave. And not only Suzanne's slave at that, but the dupe and unwitting agent of her husband, the then-Lebanese ambassador Ayman Abu Hani, as well.

For, in order to better her life and to escape the civil war–torn city of Beirut, Suzanne had prostituted herself for her scheming and ambitious husband. She had been as much his dupe as had been the people she had ensnared for Ayman—Nahlawi, Alec Stuart, the commander of the terrorist brigade that had operated here at Abu Hani's command two years previously, and even that bitch Ingrid Bittmann, who had been UN coordinator here for a period. Suzanne could see the evil in her husband now, and she had no doubts what he intended for her—what he'd already tried. She no longer was of any use to him, and she knew too much about his activities.

But she was a survivor, even though the parameters of her survival were narrowing. There was no doubt about that. But she wouldn't just sit here and wait for her fate to catch up with her. She sighed, took one more look at the lobbed cypress tree, and entered the house.

Nahlawi's mountain hideaway was functional, but it was no palace. It was newly whitewashed and clean inside and had a new red tile roof, however, thanks to the refurbishing following the brush fire two years earlier, which hadn't spared the structures at the edges of Karmi. The plaster-covered stone house had been constructed in the shape of an L, with the backbone of the L dug into the mountain slope that rose steeply at this point. The large terrace fit neatly between the two wings. There was a guest room with its own small bath above the kitchen. This room was reached by means of an outside staircase on the western wall of the kitchen, beside the small, rutted parking area that could accommodate three automobiles at the highest point up the mountain that the winding village street reached. Suzanne was occupying the guest room, because she couldn't stomach sleeping in the first-floor bedroom she had had to share with Munir Nahlawi. She hadn't run to him for affection; she had run to him for survival.

Suzanne walked into the kitchen and picked up the telephone, a luxury in the mountain village even for an ambassador. After ringing the telephone operator for help, she was finally connected with the Turkish Cypriot police headquarters down on the central plain in Nicosia. From thence she was shunted from connection to connection until she reached someone who began to help her unravel the whereabouts of Safa Ziya.

252

Yes, the angry male voice said between sneezes—he apparently had a very bad cold—he had shared an office with Ms. Ziya when she had been a chief investigator for the police department. But she had moved to another job now. If Suzanne would hold, he would, he said after a short conversation on who she was and where she was, connect her with someone who could tell her where Safa had gone. For his own part, he stated strongly and unnecessarily, he didn't care where Ms. Ziya had gone, as long as she didn't return. After the disgruntled official rang off, he delivered his own vengeance on Ziya and others like her by calling the number he'd been paid to call if he got any whiff of where Suzanne might be in the Turkish zone.

Suzanne was then connected with Safa Ziya's former investigative assistant, who explained that Ms. Ziya had moved on from the Turkish Cypriot police department to the new UN investigative service, which was headquartered in the buffer zone outside Nicosia. Suzanne responded that this was even better and that, if the former assistant, Tansul, could get in touch with Safa Ziya, Suzanne was prepared to give herself up and pass on much significant information about threats to the coming Cyprus Middle East peace conference in exchange for immunity and protection. Tansul knew who—and what—Suzanne Abu Hani was, and everything happened pretty quickly after that.

Tansul called Safa Ziya at the UNICIS headquarters. Safa, in turn, asked Tansul to muster up one of her former junior police investigators, Ahmad Jallud, who knew what Suzanne looked like, to check out an unmarked police vehicle and meet her at the Turkish checkpoint within the half hour. It actually was less than a half hour when Ziya met up with the police detective and the two roared off on the fifty-minute cross-mountain drive to Karmi.

When Suzanne replaced the receiver, she rose, and in a more peaceful mood than she had experienced in several weeks, slowly mounted the stairs to her room above. She needed to shower and prepare to greet the former senior investigator who she greatly respected, and who she had once greatly feared.

Having showered, Suzanne was standing in the middle of the small guest room. She had powdered her body with perfumed talc and was starting to dress. She was humming an Arabic melody to herself and was facing away from the windows that opened to the roof over the lounge and their probing sunlight.

He was on her in a flash, one arm snaking around her throat, a hand clamped tightly over her mouth. He brutally dragged her across the room and pushed her to the floor and onto her back between the bed and the wall, hidden from view from the window—straddling her body and increasing the pressure, ripping, lifting, opening, thrusting. The struggle was short and largely uncontested, as it had caught her completely by surprise. Suzanne was not having a good day.

* * * *

Down in the Greek sector of Nicosia, Maria Solonos was also not having a good day. As her searchers had just discovered, Willie Hamilton had, in fact, had an extremely bad day—but not recently. As Maria and Alec had feared, Willie had never left the area of the central prison complex the previous Sunday. The police team that Maria sent out the previous evening had decided it was too dark then to thoroughly cover the overgrown area behind the prison and had returned with Thursday's light.

Willie's body was near the beaten-down pathway between the rear of the prison and the street that Suzanne had escaped down on Sunday. But he had fallen far enough away from the path that it had not been easy to spot him. Evidently, as Alec surmised, Willie had tried to follow the others but had only made it this far when he had succumbed to the beating and choking he sustained at the hands of the assailant who had already killed two guards.

At least this was how it appeared at first and how it might appear to someone quick to accept the most likely explanations. But Maria had not been trained to accept evidence at face value, and when she arrived at the prison complex and checked the crime scene out for herself, she was less happy about the evidence dangling in front of her face than she had been before she arrived on the scene.

After inspecting the area, talking to the members of search party, and standing for several moments in deep contemplation, she walked slowly back to the police car and attempted to place several calls. She wasn't able to find Alec anywhere. He hadn't reported in to work that morning, he didn't answer at his apartment, and he hadn't been seen that day at any of his favorite pubs. She left word everywhere for Alec Stuart to telephone her as soon as possible, leaving both her office and home telephone numbers.

Now she had to make the telephone call she had been dreading for days—and she suddenly realized that she had known for days that she would have to make this call.

"No, I can't do it this way," Maria decided, as she disconnected right after the first ring.

Instead, she got in the automobile and stoically drove out toward Strovolos to break the news to Ginger. The wiry little scrapper Willie had gotten into one too many scraps.

* * * *

As Ahmad Jallud and Safa Ziya turned off the northern coastal road and up toward the Kyrenia Mountains in the village of Ayios Georgios, Safa asked her former promising young protégé whether he had heard from his uncle, the copper merchant, Mehmet Tosun, of late. Ahmad had almost gone the route of international crime, as his uncle had done, but had been pulled back when, two years previously, he helped close the case of the Hizballah terrorist band known as the Mouflon Brigade. In that incident, although an involuntarily enforced member of the band himself, he had helped save two of the kidnap victims, Caitlyn Koniotis and the UN official Eric Isaksen. As a reward, he was assigned to Safa Ziya as a police trainee and was proving to be very good at and faithful to his new profession.

It would have been very easy for him to have gone the other way in the world of international crime, though. He had originally lived under the wing of his not-altogether-evil, but not-altogether-scrupulous uncle here on the Turkish side of Cyprus. Mehmet Tosun had been a smuggler and forger of ancient artifacts and was forced to escape from Cyprus, with his nephew in tow, when his partner decided to reduce the size of the partnership.

Ahmad said that he did hear occasionally from his uncle, who still appeared to be in Damascus after having had to leave Beirut as well under a death threat. He was still trying to sell copperware in the bazaar.

As they approached Karmi, the two recalled the day that Ahmad's uncle conducted a tour of the ancient Greek ruins at Salamis, on the east coast of the island, for a group of archaeologists and latched onto and deeply irritated Caitlyn Koniotis.

They were still laughing at their shared memory when their glee was cut short as they rounded a particularly narrow roadway near the Treasure House Restaurant, which marked the lower reach of Karmi village. At this juncture they were nearly forced off the road by a vehicle moving quickly and recklessly at them. As Ahmad struggled to keep the police vehicle on the road, the experienced investigator, Safa Ziya, had the presence of mind to take down the registration number of the offending vehicle.

"A diplomatic tag," Ziya muttered to herself. "It might be from the Syrian embassy. I hope Suzanne hasn't changed her mind and taken a powder." And then in a louder voice, "Did you get a look at the driver or any passengers, Ahmad?"

"I'm sorry, Ms. Ziya. I was too busy trying to stay on the side of the mountain. I think there only was a driver, though."

Safa grunted approval. She hadn't seen that much herself, and she hadn't been the one fighting with the steering wheel.

When the two reached the top of the road and explored the silent village house of Munir Nahlawi, they found that, although there was considerable powder strewn around the upper-level guest bedroom, it hadn't been something that Suzanne had "taken." Suzanne wasn't in the condition to take anything.

"Looks like she was raped and strangled," Ziya said with a sigh, huffing as she raised herself off her knees from the side of the bed.

Ahmad was doing his best not even to look at the body. For sure, he no longer was a novice policeman and had seen a good many dead bodies, but he had painful memories of having seen Suzanne in the nude in his previous life, and he was fighting to keep some very bad memories from intruding into his current life.

Safa Ziya moved down to the lower level to take advantage of the presence of a telephone. She knew that her good friend and colleague Maria Solonos had been counting on Suzanne to provide all sorts of insights into what some of the forces opposed to the Middle East settlement were up to. For that matter, and for the same reason, her own chief at UNICIS, Takis Koniotis, would be equally frustrated and disappointed. Safa just hoped that the news that John Patterson had to give Takis on his computer database project and what she, herself, had to tell Takis about the other matter would make up for some of the disappointment.

* * * *

A couple of hours later, the Hizballah mastermind, Ayman Abu Hani, who had been waiting impatiently beside the telephone at his seaside villa near Tripoli, Lebanon, got the call he had been hoping for. Suzanne was dead—truly dead this time. This time he would even receive photographs. And, no, it had not been an easy death.

258

"And what about our other asset on the island?" Abu Hani moved on to other matters, his mind now free from the main threat to his program. "Have you made contact recently?"

"I'm afraid we'll have to discuss the future of the other asset," was the concerned response.

* * * *

"What a great place," Salem Qazzar thought in awe, as he moved around his new hiding place. "This guy must really be rich and powerful."

Once Qazzar got in touch with his local contact, he quickly found himself in safe hands once again. And the funny thing was that he was just a stone's throw from the central prison complex in Nicosia, where Qazzar's current troubles had all begun earlier in the week.

Qazzar was told to go to the outskirts of Nicosia and to ditch the BMW he'd stolen—after rubbing it down to get rid of any fingerprints, of course. He was told then to walk for at least an hour around the suburbs until he could get a taxicab whose driver wouldn't place him anywhere near where the BMW had been abandoned. He was to take the taxi to the Nicosia General Hospital near the old city's Paphos Gate and then he was supposed to walk the short distance to an old mansion on Averof Street. One of the French doors at the side of the house would be unlocked and there would be plenty of food on the shelves and beer in the refrigerator. He was then to wait there until his local contact arrived.

Qazzar found the mansion, arriving there as he had been directed. It obviously had been one of the largest and most beautiful homes in that section of the city many decades previously, and it had been restored and furnished to perfection. The grounds were lush, with mature plantings that almost totally hid the house and the secret of its luxury from the street. Qazzar was afraid to touch anything. It made him nervous to walk round in such wealth and to have to avoid knocking anything onto the floor. Since he had arrived, he had just been walking from one room to another, not settling.

As he walked, he played with the objects in his trouser pockets, as was his nervous habit. His length of piano wire became tangled in his pocket, and he took it out to rewind it. At that point, he found himself facing the kitchen door and suddenly felt very hungry. He absentmindedly placed the length of piano wire on the dining room table and moved into the kitchen. He opened the refrigerator door and poked his head inside.

Ah, a bottle of beer. That was even better than food. He'd toss off a bottle of beer while he was checking out the food opportunities.

The piano wire—his own length of piano wire—went around his neck as his hands were busy with the top on the beer bottle. One, two, three loops, pull back hard, and you're dead.

Salem Qazzar had finally encountered his local contact personally.

* * * *

Safa Ziya hadn't gone back to the UNICIS office, but the UNICIS office had established through their own switchboard a phone patch between the international investigations divisions of the respective Turkish Cypriot and Greek Cypriot police departments, which were normally cut off from contact with each other by the division of the island, even though the two buildings, both in Nicosia, were almost within sight of each other.

Because of this connection, Ziya had managed to quickly get in touch with both Maria Solonos and Takis Koniotis, now groggily back on duty from his whirlwind tour of Middle Eastern capitals, to tell them of the death of Suzanne in Karmi and to request an immediate check on the diplomatic registration number on the vehicle that had nearly forced them over the side of the mountain in lower Karmi.

Maria got back to Ziya very quickly via the connection, which was also being monitored at UNICIS headquarters by Koniotis.

"The automobile was registered to the British high commission," Solonos reported. "We're checking with the high commission now."

"Damn," exclaimed Ziya. "I thought it would be a Syrian embassy car. Maybe the automobile doesn't have anything to do with the killing."

"What was that?" both Ziya and Koniotis heard Solonos saying in a muffled voice, evidently to someone else off line in her office. "Oh, my god!"

And then, back on the line, in an excited voice, "And then again maybe it *does* have something to do with the killing, Safa. The high commission just reported that Alec Stuart is signed out for the vehicle with that registration number."

Koniotis and Ziya whistled in harmony over the line.

261

"Safa," Maria quickly continued. "Did you or Ahmad get a good look at the driver of the automobile? Was it Alec? I know he's been on the Turkish side recently. He told me that just an hour ago when he was here in my office."

"No, I'm sorry, Maria, neither of us can recall anything about who was in the vehicle. Ahmad was trying to keep us from crashing, and I was busy getting down the registration number."

The three agreed to put out an arrest notice on both sides of the island for both the embassy vehicle and for Alec Stuart.

Maria provided a precautionary note: "We should tell all our officers not to use strong-arm tactics in picking up Alec—especially if he isn't found with the vehicle we're looking for. And I'll have to get an arrest waver from the British high commission before we can detain him at all. This all sounds just a bit too pat for me. Everyone knew Alec and Suzanne had been lovers and that he had threatened to kill her when he found out how she had used him—and that she had actually tried to kill him. But we've also all known Alec for a long time, and we should continue to give him the benefit of the doubt."

All agreed, and just before the three disconnected their telephone conference, Takis said, "There will be at least one good thing that comes out of Suzanne's death. Now that we have this three-way telephone connection set up between the international crime investigation units of the Greek and Turkish Cypriots and the UN, I have no intention of letting the circuit get closed down again. From here on out, we've got instantaneous connections, and we should each assign a twenty-four-hour watch on the telephone. Agreed?"

He was echoed across the line of many years of distrust and enmity with an answering "Agreed" from Greeks and Turks alike.

Chapter Eighteen

Friday morning breakfast on the terrace at the Koniotises' Makedonitissa ridge-top villa. The coffee was weak, Takis had burned the eggs, the twins were having a food fight, both parents would be late in getting to their respective offices, the telephone was ringing, and ominous rain clouds were swiftly scuttling over the Kyrenia range and toward the capital. Boy it was good to be home. Caitlyn wasn't sorry she had taken the Middle East capital tour with Takis, but she was grateful to be home and to have her life returning to normal. And, yes, this was certainly normal, she thought, as she grabbed for the toast basket and dodged the first drops of a rare rain shower while racing for the telephone.

Caitlyn was glad she had gotten to the telephone before it had stopped ringing. It was Ellen Larkin, calling from Ottawa. She had thoughtfully waited until it was a decent hour in Cyprus to call. It was 1:00 AM where she was. She wanted Caitlyn and Takis to know how grateful she was that they had come to Amman had been with her for Paul's memorial service. Paul's burial had gone as well as could be expected, and Ellen was gratified to see that his hometown had given him a hero's sendoff.

Ellen's big news, which Caitlyn heard with delight, was that her Foreign Office had agreed to let her stay on in Cyprus and had even agreed with her that she needed to get back to work in time to help cover the Amathus coast peace conference that was due to open the next Tuesday.

"I know this is very soon after Paul's death to be going back to work, but I need to lose myself in action for a while."

"I completely understand," Caitlyn responded. "It will be good having you back in Cyprus. Let me know what flight you'll be coming in, and I'll be there to meet you."

Takis appeared in the house then, herding the squealing twins toward the playroom. They had wanted to remain outside and play in the raindrops. Raindrops were a real novelty in Nicosia. With a minimum of explanation from Caitlyn, Takis took the telephone receiver and talked with Ellen.

"You sure you couldn't get back here by Sunday rather than Tuesday?" he asked. "I've arranged to have all of the security services of the big players meet first and try to forge some sort of cooperation in investigating terrorism and international crime. I sure could use your help."

"Yes, I'm sure I can get there, Takis." Ellen responded. "I'll leave as soon as I can get a flight reservation. And thanks. I need the work just now."

Takis went on to fill Ellen in on what had happened with the Suzanne Abu Hani case over the past couple of days. He only held back from telling her about the death of Willie Hamilton. Ellen had been a particular fan of the feisty *Cyprus Mail* reporter, and Takis thought Ellen would be better for a few more days of healing from Paul's death. But he told her that Alec Stuart, her British counterpart, was missing and needed to be found as soon as possible to clear his name of suspicion in the death of Suzanne.

"I don't know if it would help, Takis," Ellen said with a bit of hesitancy, "but I've heard rumors that Alec has another house in Nicosia, a nicer house than the sloven flat he lives in to keep up appearances. You might check to see if he's there."

"Another house? Keeping up appearances?" Takis asked in confusion.

"Y-e-s," Ellen continued, and Takis could tell that she was struggling with herself about whether she should reveal professional secrets. But she eventually decided to reveal all. She fully supported Takis's attempts to forge strong cooperation between the investigative services of the UN member states, and she couldn't hold back now—especially when Alec's reputation was at stake.

"Takis, Alec Stuart isn't the coarse-talking, dockworker, elbow-bender he appears to be in public. That's his cover. That's what gets him accepted here and keeps people from realizing that he has the breeding and sharp mind to fully qualify him for the position as the high commission's chief spy. He's actually very well educated, quite rich, and the son of an English earl to boot. He has the messy flat near the high commission offices in the Ayios Pavlos section of the city near the central prison. But my sources say he also has restored an old mansion nearby and that he spends his private hours there. They say

266

he has a telephone hookup that permits him to take his calls at either residence."

"So you're saying Alec may be at another residence? But if so, he must still know that Suzanne has been killed and that the Cypriot authorities want him to come in and make a statement. You said he could answer his phone at either residence, and the police have been bombarding his flat with telephone calls."

"He may just be very scared, Takis, and may be trying to build up the courage to come in—or is trying to clear himself before he surfaces. He may, in fact, have trouble providing an alibi. But if someone is trying to frame him for Suzanne's murder, they probably would try to see to it that he didn't have an alibi for the time he supposedly was up in Karmi. He's our friend, Takis. We need to have a little faith in him."

"Thanks, Ellen. You're right, of course. All the more reason we need you back with us as soon as possible.

When he disconnected, Takis immediately called Maria and asked her to have records checked on the residences in the Aylios Pavlos section of the city to try to isolate one that might be owned by Alec Stuart. Maria was very surprised at what Ellen had told Takis about Alec's life.

"As both you and Ellen have said, Maria," noted Takis, "we do need to keep an open mind on Alec. But we're beginning to see that he's a much different person than any of us have thought him to be. I find it all very disturbing."

* * * *

Maria had been equally disturbed just before Takis telephoned and, after having set a check of the Ayios Pavlos residence ownership records in motion, she returned to her disturbing thoughts. She also made a decision, one that might change entirely the direction in which she had been hoping her life was headed.

Maria called in Costas and asked him to go over to the central prison.

"Please take this statement with you and go to the press room in the prison complex and determine if what this statement says was seen from the press room windows of the assault on the prison guards and Willie Hamilton last Sunday could actually have been seen from there."

"But, Maria. This is Demetris Mattas's statement."

"I know it is," Demetris's lover said with a firm set to her jaw. "But something is wrong with someone's statement. You saw Willie Hamilton's body. He didn't sustain that kind of damage and then run on for a good distance and conveniently keel over far enough off the path for his body to be hidden for several days. Either one of the people who have been claiming to have chased after Suzanne Abu Hani killed Willie and hid his body before they moved on, or someone from within the prison got out before everyone else reached the courtyard and moved Willie—dead or alive—to the pathway in back of the prison."

At that moment the object of Maria's reluctant, and possibly life-changing decision to go with her professional instincts over her heart was quietly and stealthily departing the grounds of an old mansion on Averof Street in the Ayios Pavlos section of the city.

Demetris was quite pleased with himself. This was all working out quite well, he thought.

* * * *

Just after Takis left for the office and just before she herself was able to break away from the twins and Takis's aunt to depart for her own office at the Cyprus Museum, Caitlyn received a telephone call that was to haunt her for the next two days. The manager of the Old Mill Restaurant in Kakopetria telephoned her. He said he didn't quite know himself why he was calling her about the issue, but something kept nagging after him to do so.

On Wednesday he had been called by the Piccard shipping company offices in Limassol and told that someone was coming up to Kakopetria to stay a couple of days in Eleni Piccard's apartment above the Old Mill Restaurant. This person was not to be bothered, he was told. He thought it quite peculiar and, indeed, there had been a luxury automobile parked in the restaurant's lot for the past day and a half, there were occasional sounds of footsteps and running water coming from above the restaurant, and one of the cooks had claimed that she had seen a figure at the private entrance to the stairwell leading from the balcony at the restaurant level to the apartment above. The restaurant manager didn't know why he thought Caitlyn would want to know this other than the interest she had shown the previous week when she and her husband visited Kakopetria, but he felt compelled to telephone her.

A small matter. A matter that was none of her business, certainly. But a matter that also, strangely, seemed to be compelling her to visit the loft above her bedroom again to go through Eleni's papers and mementos. Surely a waste of time. Caitlyn had been through that box dozens of times. Perhaps rather than hanging on to that box, Caitlyn should bury it, bury it deep, just as Eleni and her family had been long buried. Perhaps it was just that they all had died so tragically and that Caitlyn was sensitive to that tragedy. But it was time to put all of that aside. She wouldn't give in to the urge. And she would forget all about the telephone call to inform her Eleni's Kakopetria apartment was occupied.

But saying you are going to forget about something is a lot easier than actually doing so.

* * * *

When Takis arrived at work that morning at the UNICIS headquarters building in the UN buffer zone, his second day back at work, but the first day he had time to review what had been happening in the office since he left for his tour of the region's capitals, he made the rounds of the separate departments. Safa Ziya accompanied him.

When they got to the research lab, they were met by an excited John Patterson. Patterson's excitement soon spread to Takis Koniotis. Takis was shown the work Patterson and his computer specialists had done on connecting into the police investigation and immigration databanks of a good many of the world's countries and independent crime research agencies. Interpol had already been developing such connectivity, but the position of UNICIS as a United Nations agency had helped to make many more databases become available—with the caveat, of course, that only UNICIS could connect to and dip into many of the very secret and highly sensitive computer files.

Patterson's people had concentrated on personalities in their initial indexing of the system and had developed a list of 154 identity points—from features, to nationalities, to countries visited, to language capability, to known and suspected crimes and methods, to personal habits, to associates, and so forth—of a "personality print" that could be quickly queried and massaged by the computer. With time, Patterson said with great enthusiasm, they could zero in on international terrorists and criminals almost as quickly as these individuals could start their planning for crimes.

"And, in fact, Takis," Patterson whispered, as he guided the UNICIS chief away from the main work floor, "with what I added to the system yesterday, we might even be in the position already to give you a step up on those on their way here to try to spoil the Amathus coast peace conference."

"What do you mean?" Takis asked sharply. Safa Ziya joined them, placing her voluminous body between the two men and the internal window between the research lab and the central office space. Thomas Jameson was just a short way away, on the other side of the glass, and was straining, while attempting to look totally disinterested, to hear—or read lips—concerning what was happening in the research lab.

"I know it's illegal, Takis," Patterson cajoled, "but this is a war we are fighting."

"Out with it, John," Koniotis pleaded.

"It's the Piccard shipping and travel agency empire. You keep saying you know they are expediting the travel of terrorists and probably even have moved into laundering their money. You also say

271

you intend to target them for investigation. But there's so much involved in setting up this new UN investigation service that you haven't been able to do anything about the Piccards."

Patterson swallowed hard and continued, "Well, I have, I'm afraid. We have managed to break into their computer systems. We have the potential of knowing almost everything they know about their activities—at least what they put into their computer databanks."

"You what?!" Takis whooped. Thomas Jameson's head snapped up and he began to look very concerned. Safa Ziya put a warning hand on Takis's arm, and her chief calmed down.

Takis wasn't mad, however. He was ecstatic.

Patterson finished with the introduction to the issue. He would have to brief Takis more fully on the intricacies of the process later. "The bottom line, Takis, is that we can merge our growing criminal and terrorist personality isolation computer model with the Piccard company files on clients and transactions. We believe that, starting today, we can identify many if not all of the undesirables the Piccard company might be helping to get to Cyprus. With your permission, we'll turn it on now and see what we can do."

"Go! Go now," Takis commanded. "I won't get in your way. Just see if you can get me some names. If we can pick off a few terrorists heading our way this early in the game, maybe we can give our opponents enough of a pause so that we can bring this conference off."

Takis turned to leave, but Safa restrained him. "There's something else, Takis. Something else very important. Something happened while you were gone. We need to talk about it now, and we need to talk about it right here, while it appears we are still reviewing the work of the research lab."

* * * *

"I don't know. Something's going on in the research lab, and they won't let me get at it. Something's going on and I don't like it." Thomas Jameson sat up in his Milano Café tub chair, elbows on table and hands fingering his beer glass. The music from the piano and electric guitar duo across the room was loud and both off key and off the beat.

"They don't suspect you, do they?" his contact asked nervously. "They aren't beginning to keep anything from you that you once would have been told, are they?"

"No, no, of course not. Like I told you, I've had years of training in this. They don't suspect a thing."

Which was true. They no longer suspected, they positively knew. And it was at that precise moment that the Cypriot International Investigations squad, led by Maria Solonos and accompanied by Takis Koniotis and representatives from the Cypriot Foreign Ministry descended on the table in the Milano Café. The music skipped a beat as the two men at the table tried to stand but were forced back into their chairs. A detective waved at the music makers to continue, and, miraculously, when they resumed playing, they had picked up the proper beat and moved appreciatively closer to the proper key.

Thomas Jameson started to bluster indignantly. His contact, his eyes narrowed, had hunched over and seemed to be pretending that no one could see him.

"Save it, Jameson," Koniotis spoke over the blustering in an angry, but controlled and authoritative voice. "We will certainly want to know what you have to say—and probably much of what you don't want to say—later at the police department."

"But, as for you, sir . . ." Takis rounded on Jameson's contact.

Having discovered he wasn't invisible to the police squad, the man stood up with a great show of dignity, pulled at his shirt cuffs as if that was all it would take to straighten his crookedness, and spoke in a calm voice. "I have diplomatic immunity. I believe I will leave you now."

He turned to go, and the detectives who had been hovering around him moved off to give him room at a signal from the Foreign Ministry official.

He had only taken one step when Takis spoke. "Yes, certainly you may leave. You don't have far to go, either, do you? The Israeli embassy is just across the street. You do need to get back to report, don't you? But this wasn't an official operation, was it? Who sent you? It was Moshe Gilat, wasn't it?"

At that the agent did turn to Takis in shock and gave him a revealing look.

"Yes, I thought so," said Takis. "We will, of course, be contacting Gilat's wife, the prime minister, in the morning. I'm sure by then Mr. Jameson here will have told us quite a lot that will come up in a family discussion later in the day. As you said, we can't—and won't—detain you. But I strongly suggest that you be gone from Cyprus by morning. There's a flight to Tel Aviv in just four hours. You can easily make that flight. If you stay here, I'm willing to waver that Rachel Gilat will have removed your immunity before the next flight to Tel Aviv leaves Cyprus."

As they were leaving the Milano, Takis asked to borrow the cellular telephone in Maria's police car and requested permission to call Jerusalem.

"I have no real desire to talk to Sergey Stepanov," he said, "but if I want the Israeli security official to appear at the Hilton on Sunday and to cooperate with our efforts, I'll have to start including him in our network. It won't do for him to hear this from Rachel Gilat first. And for all we know, Moshe, with his connections, could hear before either the prime minister or Stepanov do, and he might take preemptive action. It doesn't seem to matter to him that he's undermining his own wife. She could be in personal danger as well."

Chapter Nineteen

There was no doubt about it. The old colonial mansion on Averof Street in Nicosia was indeed the house of the British high commission's Alec Stuart. The contrast between the elegance, neatness, and good taste of this house and the grubby bachelor's apartment just one block away that Stuart had offered up to the world as his actual residence was like day is to night.

Chief police investigator Maria Solonos had finally given up waiting for Stuart to show up voluntarily the previous, Thursday, evening and had gotten a search warrant served out on his flat in a rundown building on Rupel Street. As she was prone to believe Alec to be innocent of complicity in Suzanne Abu Hani's death until and unless she was convinced otherwise, she now primarily was worried about his safety. If Alec was being framed for the death of Suzanne, why wouldn't the real killer have gone the extra length of killing Alec as well and making it appear that he had committed suicide in remorse for Suzanne's murder?

There was no doubt that Stuart had been assigned the automobile that Safa Ziya had seen leaving Karmi. And Maria had seen him alive after that—he had been in her office shortly before Safa contacted her about finding Suzanne dead. But then he had disappeared.

But there had been no sign of Alec at his publicly acknowledged residence, the flat. It had looked like he had left the flat in a great hurry and in mid meal, but from what Maria had heard from Alec's close drinking buddies, his flat always looked that way.

Luckily, just when the police thought they had reached a dead end when they were unable to find a clue as to Stuart's whereabouts at his flat, they found out about the other house. It was the tip-off from Ellen Larkin matched with the sleuthing of Demetris Mattas, who had found it on his own before they did, that led them to the mansion, but the successful search of the city records had been concluded soon after as well.

Having been told of Stuart's lineage, Maria's early schooling had clicked in and she had broadened the search of the deed records. This broadened search revealed a deed to what was an Averof Street lot with an inhabitable, derelict dwelling on the official register. The deed had been issued to Stuart's royal grandfather some fifty years previously, when he was the British colonial supreme court chief magistrate for the colony of Cyprus. He had been assassinated by Greek Cypriot rebels as he had been sitting in his courtroom, a story from her school days that Maria had retained through the years for some inexplicable reason. Perhaps the story had been connected in some way with her own early decision to go into police work.

They had easily found the property—Mattas had already been there and checked the place out—but it no longer supported a ruined house. True, many of the once-glorious British colonial-style mansions on this street were swiftly moving toward the definition of dereliction, but this one had been lovingly and quite expensively restored. The building looked small from the street and was largely obscured by the copious, yet well-groomed surrounding garden. It looked like a one-story bungalow, but, when Maria entered from the corner, stone-carved entry porch and encountered the foyer with its sweeping staircase and gigantic overhead chandelier, she saw that the building opened toward the back into two floors. There also was an above-ground basement level below the main floor. There were ten major rooms in all, with several more small serving rooms. The rooms were quite tastefully decorated with Cypriot and British antiques, Persian rugs, and Oriental bric-a-brac that Stuart must have collected during his many years of service in East Asia.

For this undoubtedly was Alec Stuart's home. There were family photographs on the tables and grand piano of people who obviously, from the distinctive features being handed down through the generations, were related to Alec. And in the study, awards and degrees in Stuart's name were mounted on the walls, and his personal papers were in and on the desk. Maria was having trouble reconciling these two very different sides to Alec Stuart's life, though.

At length they found the body in the back of the garden.

There had been some effort to cover the body with dirt from the garden, but the ground had been so dry and hard from the scarcity of rainfall that the murderer must have quickly realized that the body couldn't be buried at the house. Thus, it had been hurriedly covered with dead palm branches and vines. Apparently the killer planned to return when convenient and take the body elsewhere for disposal.

When Maria was called to the garden, she was sure that it must be Alec—that her fears had been realized. The body looked so forlorn, dirty, and cast off as she approached it, stretched out full length along the back corner of the garden wall, its face to the wall.

It was such a shock when they turned the body over—not just because she quickly realized with a flood of relief and confusion that it wasn't Alec but also because she instantly recognized the victim from the photograph she had been scrutinizing for the past several days. The hunt for the Hizballah terrorist, Salem Qazzar, was over. Maria's spirits hit the ground—not only because the death of the terrorists closed out her avenue to understanding what the Hizballah was trying to do now in Cyprus, but also because she had hoped somehow that Qazzar could be linked to the murder of Suzanne and thus clear Alec of complicity in that death. Finding Qazzar dead didn't necessarily free him of blame in the Abu Hani murder, but finding him dead in Alec Stuart's secret garden didn't exactly make Alec's case for innocence look any better either.

After noting the piano wire still strung around the terrorist's throat—the evident cause of death—Maria directed that he be searched.

This was when the just-slammed door to a solution to the case was nudged open once more.

"Hello, what's this?" queried Loucis, the senior detective of the scene. "How peculiar. Haven't seen anything like this in a victim's pocket before."

Maria whipped a handkerchief out of her pocket and took the object. She walked over into the sunlight and examined it closely.

"Oh, my," she exclaimed, and Loucis rose and came over to her—and saw the small set of model teeth she was holding in her hand.

"You see that inscription there? That name? Does that ring a bell?"

"It certainly does," Loucis responded with surprise.

* * * *

Ingrid Bittmann awoke in the late morning. The shades were drawn in the room of the refurbished luxury St. Georges Hotel on its downtown promontory between the Rue Ahmed Cahouqi and the blue Mediterranean. But she could tell that the sun was rising high and was strong by the rays of light penetrating through the cracks in the drawn curtains at the balcony window. She turned slightly to admire the handsome profile beside her. He was sleeping peacefully. She gently explored with her hand—not enough to wake him but enough to bring a smile to his lips, heavier breathing, and an arousal response that assured her that he would be ready to meet her needs when she chose to awaken him once again.

She wasn't sure whether she herself was ready for another round of the earlier morning's pleasure, however. Her head felt quite groggy from the previous evening of debauchery—she could not define it in any more socially acceptable or less pleasurable word—at

280

the Casino du Beyrouth to the north of the city, with its gambling rooms, first-class nightclub floor show, and free-flowing champagne.

Ingrid and Eric Isaksen had arrived in Beirut, Lebanon, the previous morning, and the reception the Lebanese government had provided them had been a very pleasant change from the virtual snub they had received in Israel. The Lebanese were working hard to improve their image in the world following a fifteen-year devastating civil war that had turned their capital, Beirut, from the Paris of the Middle East into a virtual hell on earth. In the last three years they had launched an ambitious and extremely costly reconstruction and revitalization plan for Beirut, and they had largely succeeded in reopening the flow of tourism.

The Beirut government had not quite yet succeeded in proving its stability or even that it was able to maintain political control in Beirut, however. The traditional strains between Christian and Muslim were on simmer, but they were still on the stove. The Israelis and Syrians both meddled capriciously and outrageously in Lebanon's affairs from the west and north, respectively. And there was always the threat of the Iranian-controlled Hizballah, always claiming it was withdrawing from Beirut, but never actually doing so.

In this atmosphere, the consultative visit by two senior UN officials was a real shot in the arm, both as a visual recognition of the official government of Lebanon as a legitimate player in not only Lebanon but also in the region as a whole and as a boost to international recognition of the safety of travel to Lebanon. The authorities had made the most of the Bittmann and Isaksen visit in both the media coverage they accorded it and in the sensual, deep-red color of the carpet they rolled out for the two officials.

Ingrid Bittmann had bitten hard on both approaches, to the sheer delight of her hosts. After the frosty reception she had received in Jerusalem, which had been engineered by Moshe Gilat, the welcoming arms of the regenerated Beirut had caused her to take a quick and definite pro-Arab turn in her views on the Middle East peace process. And the special entertainment the Lebanese had laid on had certainly hit her personal pleasure spot as well.

She made her decision that a fuzzy head would not be permitted to intervene in the pleasure of the moment, and she therefore increased and focused her fondling of the body next to her to a point that he half woke enough for biological functions to proceed. Ingrid rolled on top of her partner, positioned herself strategically, and the natural rhythmic movements, awash with harmonious moans, began once again. Outside the drawn drapes, the reemerging Pearl of the Mediterranean bustled along optimistically in the early morning sunlight reflecting off the crystal-clear sea.

As a city attractive to commerce and tourism, Beirut had everything working in its favor for thousands of years. It had a perfect location at the foot of the Lebanon Mountain range on a peninsula jutting into the Mediterranean, and it had evolved into a fine European-style city with a sophisticated, yet casual, ambiance and with beautiful architecture and wonderful parks and gardens. It also had a fascinating history. It had enjoyed prosperity and acclaim as a pleasant place to visit and to live under the Seleucids, the Romans, and Byzantium. Although it had eventually been overrun by the Arabs, their reign was more or less benevolent and the city continued to thrive. The crusaders seized the city in 1100, and the crusader family, the Lusignans, established on the nearby island of Cyprus, ruled the city for two hundred years. Although the Ottoman Turks subsequently seized Beirut, it was never henceforth to lose either its French or its Christian character.

But tragedy caught up with most of the major cities of the Middle East at some point, and most even had been totally abandoned to the elements for centuries at a time. Modern Beirut's ill fortune was to have had its historical tragic moment much delayed. Between 1975 and 1990 the city was caught up in an internecine war between Christians and Muslims, exacerbated by its strategic location in the broader war that was raging around and across it between Arab and Jew. A tenuous cease-fire had been struck in 1990, which led to a tentative peace and which had now led to the government's attempt to regain a commercial and touristic foothold in the region.

The club that Ingrid Bittmann and Eric Isaksen had been taken to the previous night was meant to convince the two high-ranking UN officials that Lebanon had returned to the footing of being a good financial investment for international banks and the UN Development Program. They seemed to have succeeded beyond their hopes in this area—particularly with Bittmann—even though the Casino du Beyrouth itself reflected the recent tragedy through which the city had lived. Badly damaged in the civil war, the entertainment complex overlooking the sea to the north of Beirut had been used as a headquarters by the Christian militia throughout much of the war and had sustained much shell damage in the fighting. Even now, after having reopened following a $25-million refurbishment and the addition of a 200-room luxury hotel, the complex wasn't escaping the effects of the complicated, touchy political situation in Lebanon. The complex was owned by Ayman Abu Hani, mastermind of the Hizballah organization, and had been financed through the fine old French shipping family, the Piccards.

Despite the delightful sensations that were assaulting other parts of her body, Ingrid's head was throbbing so badly from the effects of her previous evening at the Casino du Beyrouth that she was almost grateful when the knock came on the connecting door of her room.

"Just a minute. Coming," Ingrid called as she rolled off of Benjamin, wrapped herself in a negligee, and headed for the door to let Eric in.

Her personal secretary dutifully rose from his side of the bed, padded over to the other connecting door, and was gone. All in a day's work. Another dictation session had been successfully concluded.

Chapter Twenty

It was 9:31 AM on a Saturday morning in the third week of April, the morning before the security preconference was to begin in preparation for next Tuesday's opening of the Amathus coast Middle East peace conference summit. The computer bank in the research lab at UNICIS headquarters in the UN buffer zone on the ridge overlooking Nicosia was whirring, and a small army of UN criminal investigators was busy with the telephones.

Once the unit's chief, Takis Koniotis, adjusted John Patterson's search strategy for the movement of international terrorists toward Cyprus to try to disrupt the conference's proceedings, the research lab and the criminal investigators had to work overtime and reinforcements had to be brought in from Interpol, the United States, the United Kingdom, France, and Germany. The Canadians had consented to Koniotis's request for the services of Ellen Larkin, who took over as chief of operations in the wake of the arrest of Thomas Jameson.

Koniotis himself went on the road starting from the previous evening to meet, greet, house, and cajole the arriving security conference delegates. His wife, Caitlyn, was pressed into service to help with the meet and greet duties for the less-troublesome delegates. Under the circumstances, Koniotis only had time to call in at the UNICIS operations for brief checks and reviews on how the various searches were proceeding. Although this frustrated him greatly, he was not worried about the operations because they were being expertly guided by his able deputy, Safa Ziya.

The computers were no longer whirring for, and the telephone calls were no longer directed at, the security delegates now arriving for tomorrow's conference at the Nicosia Hilton. Most delegates for that meeting were already here or on their way. The computers had worked overtime for them the previous two days. Now the computers were working to preserve the safety of the national and organizational leaders who were preparing for their travel to Tuesday's opening of the main peace conference.

It was 9:33 am on a Saturday in the third week of April, the computers in the UNICIS headquarters were whirring, and the UN criminal investigators were keeping the telephone receivers warm.

* * * *

At 9:45 AM a French ship en route from Marseilles via Beirut was docking in Limassol harbor. Almost before it touched the pier, Cypriot customs police swarmed over the side and down into the hold.

What the hold held, in addition to the manifested cheaply assembled shirts and dresses for the European market, were hand grenades and shoulder-held ground-to-air missiles, all equipment no longer in need in Lebanon. Finding out who needed them in Cyprus was going to be interesting work.

The fact that they were coming to Cyprus had been traced through the UNICIS computers, whose search had been significantly helped with the tap in to the Piccard Shipping Line's databanks. Strike One in favor of the UNICIS research lab. The computers whirred and the telephone calls continued.

Between 9:34 AM and 4:17 PM, in what would eventually prove to be the other half of the Limassol arms seizure story, five Libyan "college" students arriving from three different cities on the flights of three different airlines were intercepted at Larnaca Airport immigration. They all claimed they were arriving in Cyprus to start their studies at a Nicosia college specializing in hotel catering. The fact, however, that all five "students" were well into their twenties, that the college they claimed they were entering had closed down more than a year previously, that they all had listed the same fleabag hotel in Nicosia as their destination, and that they were all documented with Swedish passports with consecutive numbers and were carrying crisp new U.S. dollar bills, also with consecutive numbers (as well as being forged), pretty much indicated that the Libyans' strong suit was direct action rather than espionage.

Patterson's team had linked its new personalities file database with Interpol's database on missing blank passport documents as well as with its tap into the Piccard Travel Agency database. Strike Two for the people in the UNICIS research lab. The computers whirred and the telephone calls continued.

At 1:17 PM a small Syrian vessel nosed into the new harbor at Kyrenia, in the Turkish zone of Cyprus. Ahmad Jallud and a squad of Turkish Cypriot police were there to greet it. There was a small smattering of gunfire to celebrate the docking of the ship. Jallud's men left the party far more pleased than did the scruffy Syrian crew. The Syrians had brought several cases of high-powered rifles in their personal baggage.

At last, it seemed, Syrian ambassador Munir Nahlawi would be eating his last Cypriot meze soon and would be shoving off for his homeland.

In this case, the computers had melded the UNICIS personalities profile with the arms shipment databases of various secret services as well as the Lloyd's of London insurance database. The latter file kept track of destination ports.

Strike Three in favor of John Patterson and his crew at UNICIS. And still the computers continued to whir and the criminal investigators continued to telephone.

* * * *

At 10:15 that Saturday morning Takis Koniotis was sitting in the office of Maria Solonos—his own former office—in the Nicosia Police Headquarters building. He was touching base with her on the protections in place for the security conference at the Nicosia Hilton the next day and was reviewing the status of various Cypriot police investigations that seemed to be connected with his own Amathus coast peace conference concerns.

Their discussions zeroed in on the deaths of Suzanne Abu Hani, Androulla Varnavidou, Willie Hamilton, and the terrorist Salem

288

Qazzar and the seemingly connected disappearance of Alec Stuart. And in a somewhat bizarre twist in the story, they also discussed the murder the previous Monday night in his office of the Nicosia dentist Theocharis Thoma.

"Everyone else fits logically into the circle somehow except the dentist," Maria was saying. "Suzanne Abu Hani knew too much about the activities of her husband and she was killed—after at least two attempts on her life, the attempt that washed her up at Cape Greco and Qazzar's attempt to kill her in the courtyard of the central prison. Androulla was killed for getting too close to ferreting Qazzar out. Willie was killed because he got in the way when Qazzar was trying to kill Suzanne. Lord know why Qazzar got killed, but winding up dead in Alec Stuart's secret garden brings Alec into the picture once too often."

"Alec is implicated in this too many ways, and he still hasn't been found and still hasn't turned himself in," Maria continued. "I'm trying to keep an open mind about his involvement, but he certainly could have killed Suzanne. Everyone heard him threaten her life when she escaped from here two years ago. And an automobile assigned to him was at the scene of the crime. He was conveniently in the courtyard when Willie was killed—and there are questions about when and where Willie died that don't add up with Alec's statement. And then there is the issue of Qazzar's body being found at Alec's house, a house that very few people even knew about."

"Here, let me read the folder on what you found at the house," Koniotis requested. He spent several minutes going over the file.

At length, not being able to hold herself longer, Maria burst out, "We've learned from various sources that there is another Hizballah agent in place in Cyprus, Takis. Not just Qazzar or even another one of the Mouflon Brigade band that might have been left behind. We're led to believe it is someone with power and authority. You don't think, do you, that it might be . . . that it might be Alec?"

"I don't know," Koniotis responded bleakly. "But that's always a possibility. Certainly not one I want to believe, of course. But maybe they're just referring to Munir Nahlawi. We can be pretty sure he's been mixed up with these terrorists since the beginning."

And then he changed the subject. "But what about this dentist and how he fits in—and why you have decided he fits?"

"I have no idea *how* he fits in, but we do have pretty strong evidence that he was murdered by Qazzar. He was murdered with Qazzar's signature weapon, a thin wire, and we found a novelty set of false teeth in Qazzar's pocket with Thoma's name on it. The dentist's assistant confirmed that Thoma kept such a pair on his desk and that it was there the evening he died. She claims she dusted the desk right before she left and she remembers the teeth being there. She said they always gave her a repugnant feeling. As far as the investigation police could ascertain, although the office was ransacked, that set of false teeth was the only object that was known to be missing. Takis, you don't suppose that Thoma could have been the other Hizballah plant, do you? He was the dentist to many important people in the Cypriot and foreign community."

"It's possible, perhaps," Koniotis answered with a tone of skepticism. "Not too likely, however. I knew Thoma, of course, He was my dentist as well. But he didn't socialize outside the office and he didn't seem to me to be too curious about people during office visits. It's pretty difficult, you know, to spill secrets with your mouth full of cotton balls, a drain, and a drill. Still, it's possible he was involved with the Hizballah, and he *did* get murdered for a reason, we must presume. I suggest you have your own people go through his papers for clues."

This turned out to be a good move. Later in the evening Maria called Takis with some very startling news that had been gleaned from the meticulous records Dr. Thoma kept in his office, information that explained a lot, coming from files that Qazzar's superior should have had the foresight to tell Qazzar to seek and destroy while he was still in the dentist's office.

"Shouldn't we do something with this right away, Takis?" Maria queried.

"Yes, but as far as I am concerned it will have to wait until after the Hilton conference tomorrow morning. I don't think it will matter much if we move today or even tomorrow. This is already decades old. But I've indicated where we might begin the search. I suggest you send a team there now to see if I'm right, and if I am, to establish surveillance until we can get there."

* * * *

Moshe Gilat had been on pins and needles for two days. Rachel had walked out on him. She claimed she was going to take him up on his suggestion that she go off to Elat for a couple of days alone, without him, but he had known even then, from the look she gave him after her conference with Stepanov, that she had found out about Jameson. He, of course, hadn't known whether she'd found out about his own involvement until the agent returned from the embassy in Nicosia and told him the worst. He was personally implicated in trying to find out secrets on where peace conference delegates were to be accommodated and where they were to hold their meetings on the Amathus coast.

Well, so what? he thought. Rachel had known all along that he opposed the conference. And she wasn't being a dutiful wife for standing in his way. Who was the real prime minister of Israel after all? He loved Rachel, but he loved Zionism more.

Thus, when Rachel finally called him and told him she was back in Jerusalem and wanted to meet with him in her office, he went. He went, after first putting one of his old pistols in his bulky pocket. He had struck for the Jewish State before and he was prepared to strike again. Nothing was more important than the full integrity of Zionism and the Jewish State.

But Rachel wasn't at her office, and the gun in Moshe's pocket made it all the easier for Sergey Stepanov and his security detail to turn Moshe over to the criminal authorities.

Even in defeat, however, Moshe had his style. He eyed Stepanov with a knowing look that challenged him with the thought that Moshe Gilat had not yet fired his last Zionist arrow.

Stepanov permitted the old man his one last David and Goliath image, however, and restrained from telling him that the security chief knew exactly what Moshe was thinking. Stepanov's regular driver, the driver who was supposed to take him to the airport in two hours for the flight to the security conference in Nicosia,

Cyprus, had taken ill. Stepanov hadn't even been told that the driver was being replaced, and he hadn't known the replacement driver.

But the computer banks at UNICIS headquarters outside of Nicosia did know about the replacement driver and what her plans for Stepanov's drive to the airport were. The replacement driver had now, in her turn, already been replaced. Stepanov was going to drive himself to the airport, because his replacement driver had been arrested had been relieved of the handgun she'd been carrying, and already was babbling of the plot that Moshe Gilat had embroiled her in.

It was 7:23 PM on a Saturday in the third week of April. Strike Four in favor of the folks at UNICIS.

Strike Four? But there are only three strikes in the American game of baseball. True, but the hunt for terrorists descending on Cyprus was not really a game. And there was no telling how many there were to find.

However, the UNICIS computers kept whirring, and the UN criminal investigators kept their telephone receivers warm.

* * * *

Caitlyn and Takis Koniotis fell into bed exhausted that night. They had had their fill of meeting and greeting and depositing regional dignitaries, and they both realized that the formalities of this day paled in relation to what they both would face when the main conference started in three days. They both needed their rest badly, but both had other, oppressive issues on their minds in addition to the looming conferences. Takis was not so preoccupied with his own worries not to notice that Caitlyn looked like she was carrying the burdens of the world on her shoulders.

"What's the matter, honey?" he asked, as he moved into the bed and cuddled up beside his wife.

"It can wait," she responded. "You have too much on your plate now, and I haven't even fully resolved what the issue is. Anyway, It doesn't have anything to do with the conferences—or the family. The conferences are more important now. Just concentrate on them."

The lights went off and Takis immediately went to sleep, but Caitlyn didn't. She remained awake, stewing, and trying to ignore the call to look through Eleni's box in their loft one more time. She tried closing her eyes tight and controlling her breathing. It must have worked to some degree, because she was more than half asleep when the vision of Eleni, standing at the edge of a wood and beckoning to her, whispering something, something just beyond Caitlyn's grasp. She woke with a start, startled to hear her own voice whispering "do it." And when she heard that—from herself—she realized that this was what Eleni was calling to her in the dream.

Losing the struggle, she quietly got out of bed, reached for the flashlight on her nightstand, and climbed up the ladder to the loft. What she saw this time when she sifted through the mementos caused her to descend the ladder, flip on the master switch on the bedroom lights, and disturb Takis's sleep.

Takis awoke to a photograph being suspended by jittery hands in front of his face.

"You see that, Takis? It's him. I've just realized it's him. The evidence is right there."

"Yes, I know it's him," Takis said dreamily, trying to grab and photograph and make it hold still.

"I should have known some time ago," Caitlyn continued, oblivious to her husband's response. "Oh, how awful. No wonder she's been trying to signal to me. How could this have happened? What does it . . . You know? What do you mean you know?"

"I mean I know. Just figured it out earlier today. Don't have time to do anything about it tonight, and I didn't want to upset you. After the conference. After the conference I'll go do something about it."

"After the conference? I? You *do* mean *we*, don't you, Takis? I have to see this through. You can't leave me out of this now."

"Yes, love. I know better than to try to keep you away from something like this. Now put that awful photograph down and turn off the lights and come to bed. Tomorrow's another day. Everything will work out. After the conference we'll . . ."

And Takis was asleep and Caitlyn realized that there was no moving him for the rest of the night. And strangely enough, knowing the worst, Caitlyn was now able to sleep as well. She drifted off to sleep muttering to herself, "That poor woman. All that time, wasted. And I wonder about her . . ."

* * * *

The automobile of the chief of the Egyptian security service rolled up toward the Gulf Air-Cyprus Air flight GFYC033 airplane waiting on the tarmac at the Abu Dhabi airport, just about ready to be boarded for its scheduled 10:32 PM departure for Cyprus' Larnaca airport. A uniformed man walked out from the airplane and waved the sedan to a halt. He stood in front of the hood, holding his hands out in a "stop" motion, while looking over his shoulder at the aircraft.

Moments later two figures in ground crew suits were manhandled out of the belly of the airplane and hustled into an idling van. A short while after that, a large package was handed down from the same compartment with considerably more respect and care than the men had enjoyed. It too was placed in a vehicle, a heavily armored vehicle, and was slowly driven away, not toward the terminal, but toward a remote, deserted section of the airport.

The uniformed man turned, smiled, and directed the Egyptian security service chief's automobile to proceed toward the airplane. They all had their ears tuned to the anticipated sound from across the tarmac that arrived as a muffled boom of an explosive device safely being exploded.

At 2:05 PM on the following Sunday morning, the delegate of the Jordanian security service, clothes askew and a silly grin on his face, answered the door to his Nicosia Hilton hotel room. The voice had said it was room service, but he didn't remember having ordered any room service. Maybe the woman had, he thought. What he remembered was a fine night at the Crazy Horse nightclub, a diversion he was not permitted when he was in Amman, and a taxi ride back to the hotel with the most exotic little Far Eastern honey he had ever seen. Also the easiest pick up he had ever managed.

As he opened the door, the Malaysian beauty slipped into the bathroom, where she failed to see her intoxicated Arabian prince being jerked out into the hallway and his mouth covered with a waiter's tea towel.

When the Malaysian beauty, who was a Muslim fanatic in her real life, emerged from the bathroom, attired only in a nasty-looking knife, she was confronted, not with the Jordanian chief of security, but with four of Cyprus' best International Investigations Unit detectives.

The strikes kept coming for the people in the UNICIS research lab, and these dedicated folks kept on working through Saturday night and into Sunday morning. The computers whirred and the investigators talked on the telephone.

Chapter Twenty-One

Sunday's all-day regional security conference at the Nicosia Hilton started off slowly, but it finished just fine. As the United Nations International Crimes Investigation Service director, Takis Koniotis, knew would be the case, the officials who showed up at the conference were, on the whole, initially quite suspicious of and guarded with both him and the other delegates. This was the nature of their business, of course, and the attitude was to be expected. It could also be expected that such deeply engrained attitudes would make genuine cooperation improbable, and most assuredly so on the short, two-day deadline facing Koniotis for having the services working together.

But Koniotis had been just as sure that these attitudes needed to change in order for the world's legitimate governments to be able to control the burgeoning terrorist and criminal world, which had taken advantage of the old-world isolation of states to expand their operations across international lines. Koniotis, in his previous position as a Cypriot police inspector, had seen this phenomenon of the internationalization of terrorism and crime take advantage of the two isolated entities on his own island of Cyprus. From that perspective he had also been able to see how the forces of evil took advantage of the closed investigation systems of separate states as well. This simply had to change. The nations had to wrest back their control of peace and stability. And here and now was as good a place and time as any to start reestablishing that control.

As expected, during the initial, introductory morning session, the assembled delegates sat in self-important silence, knowing and false smiles on their faces, prepared to provide honeyed rhetoric without substance. Such was the nature of their customary "international cooperation" style. After the first coffee break, however, Koniotis purposely popped their assorted bubbles.

The first presentation by the UNICIS staff was of their program for information sharing and mutual support for the apprehension of international terrorists and criminals. UNICIS itself would act as a clearing house for information and would, with the authorities already provided by the UN Security Council resolution that established the service, issue international arrest orders that would empower individual UN member states to hold suspected persons and goods until their own legal mechanisms could take effect. Several of the larger powers had already set up information-clearing houses on terrorism, illegal arms shipments, and the narcotics trade. All had agreed to dump their information into the UNICIS databases and to update that information frequently. The only caveat was that UNICIS was to control the source of information and was not to permit others to tap into its own central databases. The police, customs, immigration, and security of all UN member states would eventually be expected to freely submit information in these areas directly to UNICIS via computer systems that would be provided and financed by the UN Development Program. Until the system could be established worldwide, the Middle East would serve as the test bed. This decision was driven by the immediate needs arising from the coming Amathus coast peace summit.

Naturally, the delegates from some of the European countries and from the United States, who had also been aware of and were cooperating with the program, launched into cries of outrage and anguish against the attack on their individual nation's sovereignty.

Koniotis called another break. During that break, his staff set up charts depicting all of the terrorist operations they had caused to be interdicted just over the last three days in conjunction with the preparations of the Amathus coast summit. He had these charts set up in full view of the delegates as they milled around waiting for the session to resume. As these charts included actions taken to ensure the presence of more than half of the delegates in the room at this presummit meeting—with some of the life-saving interdiction that had been facilitated not having been previously known by the individual who benefited from the operation—it was a greatly changed, and more sober and serious, group of delegates that reassembled after the break.

Koniotis's staff spent the rest of the morning going over each chart in detail and specifying to the extent that their agreements with the original sources of the information permitted exactly how the information had been put together by the UNICIS computer programs.

As Koniotis released the delegates for lunch, he pointed out that he had the assurances from each government involved that the delegate who had been sent to today's meeting had been given full authority to set up cooperation in the international investigation sphere. If any did not, in fact, have that authority, he said, they should use their lunch hour to obtain that authority from their government on a genuine basis. If their government was not willing to cooperate—in fact, not just in theory—the delegate simply was not expected to return to the afternoon's session and Takis would inform all other governments and the media that country was not prepared to cooperate and thus was not included.

Koniotis went on to clearly state that any country that didn't have a delegate at the afternoon's session or that subsequently was deemed to be withholding information that was necessary to the safety of the conference or any representative or leader attending the conference would not be accommodated in the Amathus coast area during the conference and would not be protected by the international security forces at the conference. Then he released them with the silent prayer that most of them would return. This was the ultimate gamble. If the governments of the region were not prepared at this juncture to cooperate on personal security at least, then the whole process was a sham. But if that was the case, perhaps this was the best time to know it.

During lunch, Maria Solonos, who was Cyprus' delegate to the security meeting, received a telephone call concerning the surveillance request Koniotis had made the previous day. She reported to Koniotis as he was reiterating to the Syrian delegate that what he had just told the delegates was exactly what he was going to do and that, yes, he had the Security Council's blessing and authority to do this.

When they were alone, Maria told Koniotis that his notion had been quite correct and that, in fact, the surveillance team's efforts had achieved even more than either one of them had envisioned. Koniotis then asked her to break away from the conference, go to the scene herself, and expand the surveillance team into a cordon so that there was no chance of escape. He and Caitlyn would come there that evening. He was sure they were getting to the end of the trail on several of their concerns.

By the time the meeting resumed following lunch, Koniotis's plan had broken the back of the traditional intransigence of the region's security services. All of the delegates who had been in the morning session reappeared, and all spent the remainder of the afternoon being very helpful.

It was a visibly ecstatic Takis who appeared in his Makedonitissa mountain-top home for a quick bite to eat before he and Caitlyn had to rush off again. He was not fooling himself that the region's countries would be completely forthcoming with their information and cooperation, at least in the initial months, but they had collectively moved farther toward such vital cooperation in this afternoon than they had in all of the years since the recarving of the Middle East in the years following the two world wars.

No matter what the results were of the main Middle East peace conference, the meeting today of the security forces alone represented a gigantic step forward toward peace and stability in the region.

The six-floor front of the Old Mill Restaurant and Hotel in the Troodos mountain village of Kakopetria was eerily lighted up as the Koniotis Jaguar drove up into the small stone forecourt between the old structure and the noisily flowing millstream. Several police vehicles were parked in the area, their revolving blue roof lights adding to the usual spotlights on the building's façade in such a way that one would almost think a movie was being filmed. One of the police vehicles had been parked astride the narrow lane leading from the main street to the restaurant, and it had to move aside for the Koniotises to drive into the lot.

As she got out of the old Jaguar, Caitlyn looked up to the top of the structure. Eleni Piccard's apartment was fully lighted as well. Takis came around the automobile, took her by the elbow, and started to lead her toward the small elevator that would take them up to the restaurant level. From there they would have to climb another flight of stairs to reach the flat. Caitlyn shuddered and held back. Takis misunderstood her action.

"You've decided you don't want to go up there?" he asked in obvious relief.

"No, of course not. It's not that. I just don't want to use the elevator. Eleni was murdered in that elevator."

"Ah, yes, I keep forgetting you avoid it. I guess I hope that someday you'll forget that as well."

And so they climbed the several flights of stairs that hung onto the north wall of the old stone warehouse building. They were both winded when they reached the restaurant level, which was

303

unnaturally quiet for this time of the evening. People were sitting at the chairs near the balcony tables, to be sure, but there was no meal being served at the Old Mill tonight. All of the people present, with the exception of the flustered restaurant manager, were police officers and investigators. Maria was there. She came up to Caitlyn and Takis, and the three murmured in low tones until Takis had gotten his breath. Caitlyn was in much better shape for climbing, because her job in archaeology entailed much movement over rough terrain.

When they agreed they were ready, Takis pushed open the door to the stairs leading to the flat above—Eleni Piccard's old flat—and called out a greeting and an explanation of who was coming up, as the couple ascended the treads.

"Yes, please do come in, Mr. and Mrs. Koniotis," a cultured, foreign-accented voice responded from above.

As Caitlyn and Takis entered the main lounge of the flat, they encountered two people, sitting calmly on facing sofas, just as if they were enjoying a chat and an after-dinner drink, which, in fact, they were. The only incongruity in sight was that one person had a nasty-looking handgun leveled at the other.

"Well, hello, Caitlyn and Takis," the elegant elderly man said in a cheery voice.

"Hello," Takis responded. "You seem to know us, but I don't believe we've formally met you. Mr. Piccard, isn't it? Mr. Guy Piccard?"

"Ah, so you've found me out, have you? Very clever of you. If I've told Ayman once, I've told him a hundred times that you were much too clever to live, Mr. Koniotis. but Ayman is such a sentimentalist. He always said the beautiful Mrs. Koniotis would not look good in black. Speaking of whom, we almost did meet the other day in Amman, didn't we, Caitlyn?"

Caitlyn frowned and started to speak, but Takis beat her to the podium.

"What I can't understand, Mr. Piccard—Mr. GUY Piccard— is why you are looking so well this evening. The last we knew, you had been dead since 1974, killed during the Turkish invasion of Cyprus along with your son, Pierre. Murdered by your nephew, Jacques Piccard, we were led to believe, and your bodies stuffed into a remote dungeon in Kyrenia Castle, where your bones weren't discovered until just over two years ago. We were there, just down the valley, in the new Kakopetria church, when your devoted and grieving widow, Eleni, reinterred your bones. But here you are, looking well and fit. How strange."

"Hardly well and fit, of course, but, yes, here I am. Did my nephew ever confess to having murdered me, Mr. Koniotis? I think not. And did you ever actually find any proof that he had? Again, I think not. What I think is that you all let Eleni's emotions carry you away and that Jacques was facing so many real charges that there was no real reason for him to belabor his innocence in the killing of his uncle and cousin."

"But I don't understand," said Caitlyn through clenched teeth, trying to retain control. "Why did you let everyone think you were dead? And where have you been, and why didn't you let Eleni know you were alive? She pined so much for you and your son. How could you let her go for twenty years not knowing you were alive?"

"Eleni pining?" Piccard laughed out loud, a process that ended in a hollow cough. "Not for me. Maybe for Pierre, but not for me. And Pierre died soon after we got to Marseilles. He had never been a strong boy. Always was susceptible to any and all viruses in play. And then when he died, there was no pressing reason to contact Eleni. Yes, maybe if he had lived, I would have contacted her. Maybe not, though," he added, a playful tone in his voice.

"But pining for *me*? Ha. She's the whole reason I left Cyprus in 1974. She was having an affair with that politician, Nicos Petrou, who later became the Cypriot president for a brief time. He was looking into my business dealings in Cyprus, itching to further his political ambitions by ferreting out the, shall we say, creative operations of the Piccard Shipping Corporation. And Eleni. Eleni was helping him. They had long been lovers, ever since they grew up together right here in Kakopetria. Eleni married me both to punish Petrou for marrying a foreigner while he was in France and to get out of Cyprus herself. I married Eleni to get the Piccard businesses *into* Cyprus."

"No," Piccard continued, "I would not have told Eleni I was still alive. I had planned too carefully to convince her and Petrou that I had died. It's true that Jacques was in Kyrenia when my son and I 'disappeared' during the Turkish invasion. But he was there to help us get away. I went straight to Marseilles, where I continued to control the Piccard holdings in Cyprus even after I was gone from the island. Eleni always fancied that she controlled the Cyprus end of the operations, but she only truly controlled her handicraft center and the philanthropic foundation—and as you surmised some time ago, there were once activities going on at her handicraft center that even she didn't know about. I continued to control the shipping company and the hotels. And you said she 'pined' for me. When she grew tired of Petrou, she moved on to a Canadian diplomat. And who knows how many other lovers she entertained as she 'pined.'"

Piccard coughed, a deep cough that almost made him lose a grip on his gun. Almost, but not quite. He used the interlude to motion Caitlyn and Takis to the third sofa of the set on which he and the other person were sitting.

"But, please do tell me how you knew I was alive. I would be amused to know where I let my guard down. I've spent so much effort and money protecting my death."

"Two things, actually," responded Takis calmly. "One was the photographs. That's quite a distinct birthmark you have on your neck. Caitlyn saw you in the photographs Eleni left behind. You knew that Caitlyn inherited Eleni's residence outside Nicosia, I presume."

"The photographs? I destroyed all of the photographs after Eleni died. I returned to Cyprus then. I searched the house in Makedonitissa and the flat here in Kakopetria, and I destroyed all of the photographs."

"Unfortunately for you, that's not quite true," Takis replied. "A box of Eleni's mementos was hidden behind some construction material in the loft above the master bedroom of our residence. Caitlyn saw those photos and then she saw you in Amman and it all clicked together. Not immediately, though, I'm sorry to say."

"Granted. An unfortunate oversight, Mr. Koniotis," Piccard conceded. "But I believe you said there was a second slip."

"Yes, there was. And it was one I wonder about. When you had the Nicosia dentist, Theocharis Thoma, murdered last week, you should have had his office searched better, not just messed up to make the killing look like a burglary."

Guy Piccard lifted his eyebrows. He was beginning to understand.

"Dr. Thoma kept meticulous records, Mr. Piccard," Takis continued. "Not only did he list all of the regular bribes he was receiving from you—by name, incidentally—but he also noted why he was receiving the bribes. He was both your dentist when you were officially alive and the dental surgeon general of Cyprus when your bones were supposedly found. That put him in the perfect place to verify the teeth of the two sets of bones found in the dungeon of Kyrenia Castle two years ago as those of you and your son. On this basis, no doubt was cast on the theory that the two people who died in Kyrenia Castle were the two missing Piccards. No one need have looked at the charts except the family dentist and the dental surgeon general, in this case one and the same person, and apparently a person who could easily be bribed. Dr. Theocharis Thoma. Tell me, Mr. Piccard, who were those two people who were found in Kyrenia Castle?"

"I haven't the vaguest idea, Mr. Koniotis. There were so many people who went missing during the Turkish invasion. I don't know who they were and didn't even think of there even being bones that could be identified as mine until those were found in the castle two years ago."

"So, you didn't kill them or have them killed?"

308

"Certainly not. What do you take me for, a barbarian?"

"Well, I'm not quite sure what to take you for, Mr. Piccard. Why did you find it necessary to have Dr. Thoma murdered this late in the game—it only brought attention to yourself. And what are you doing sitting here, pointing a gun at our friend over there? And what are either of you doing here, for that matter? Surely you know the building is surrounded by the police. You could have cleared out days ago."

"Yes, I admit the killing of Dr. Thoma was a mistake. The terrorist fellow was conveniently here to do Ayman's and my bidding, and it seemed a good opportunity to tidy up loose ends. But, if I had waited just a day, I would not have ordered the killing. It's quite ironic."

"What do you mean, 'waited just a day'?" Caitlyn broke in.

"You've heard my cough. I'm dying. The end will come quickly now, and I only learned about it from my physician the day after Thoma was dispatched. And that explains the rest of this as well. I'm dying and I'm tired of Abu Hani and his game, and he and this monster over there are responsible for the death of Suzanne. I loved Suzanne. She didn't love me back, of course, but Ayman made a prostitute out of her and it's time for the ledger to be balanced. I knew you people were out there. I called this man up here yesterday explicitly so that we'd both be here for you in a neat bundle. This came as a bit of an unwelcome surprise to him, as you can see, and I've had to keep him in check with my little persuader here for most of today. He, of course, is the other Hizballah agent you were looking for. Rest assured that there are no more in Cyprus. If your precious peace conference is disrupted now, it won't be by any members of the Hizballah hiding on the island."

At this, Alec Stuart started blustering for the first time since Caitlyn and Takis had arrived. Up until then he had sat with the frightened look of the captive innocent on his face, the captive innocent just waiting to be set free of this mad man by Koniotis and the police below.

"He's crazy, Takis," Alec blathered. "He's trying to cover for the Hizballah. He's only trying to protect the real hidden agent in Cyprus. And I didn't kill Suzanne. You know I couldn't kill Suzanne. I loved her."

"Oh, cut the routine, Alec," Takis shot back "You've been caught in a few too many lies. Your story about Willie Hamilton's death doesn't jell. Your embassy automobile was at the scene of Suzanne's death, and you were one of the few people who could have gone over to the Turkish zone and killed her anyway. We've found your grandfather's house. We've found the telephone bills from that house to Ayman's telephone number in Lebanon. That information, plus a lot more derogatory information about your pro-Muslim fundamentalist activities is beginning to pop out of our new computer system at UNICIS. And we've found Qazzar's body at your house, with your fingerprints, and only your fingerprints, all over the shovel that was used to attempt to dig his grave. You've pretty much dug your own grave, my friend, and I just don't want to hear any more of your dissembling."

"My house?" Stuart squeaked. "Your computer told you about my house?"

"No," responded Takis. "Demetris Mattas told us about your house. An informant of his gave him the address, and he went in and saw all of your framed awards and diplomas in the study. We were well on our way to finding out about the house anyway, though. For once he told Maria directly so she didn't have to find out about it by reading his newspaper column in tomorrow's *Simerini*. Once we knew about your grandfather, we were able to track the house down in the deed records as well. If Demetris hadn't told us about your house, we would have known within hours anyway. Ellen Larkin knew you had the house too."

Stuart's face took on a wild, hunted look, and he fell back into the sofa and buried his face in his hands.

Piccard spoke with tired tones into the silence. "Would you mind very much taking this gun? It has become very heavy, and we've been sitting here, waiting for you, most of the day. I suddenly feel quite weary." At that, the old man seemed to become very small as he handed the gun to Takis, withdrew into the sofa cushions, and nodded off into a state of semiconsciousness.

Once Takis had the gun, Alec seemed to perk up. He sat up straighter in the sofa and took on an almost cocky expression. Now that his real character had been exposed, he seemed almost anxious to discuss his exploits.

"Oh, Alec. Where did it all go wrong? When did this start?" Caitlyn was grasping for understanding.

And Alec was suddenly prepared to help her understand. He seemed to have lost all intention of defending his innocence.

311

"Where did I go wrong, Caitlyn? I don't quite know how to answer that. First of all, I have never owed the Cypriots anything. They assassinated my grandfather. I've tried to honor his memory by restoring his house. But I avenge him every day in some little way that sticks it to the Greek Cypriots. And as far as going wrong in aiding the Hizballah, I'm sure Takis's little computer can tell you by now that I am a Muslim myself. Converted years ago when I was serving in Singapore. All Muslims aren't Arabs, you know; in fact, most Muslims aren't Arabs. I believe in what I've been doing for the Hizballah. The Hizballah is serving true Islam."

"And where did it all begin, you ask? Where should I begin? Is the American economic officer, Jill Murray, far enough back, or should I go all the way back to the honorable Nicos Petrou?"

Caitlyn gasped, and Alec stood and started to strut about the room. He almost seemed to be enjoying himself now.

"Well, let's see. Nicos Petrou's wife, who was handling the travel arrangements for terrorists before the Piccards took on the chore, ordered her husband's death some five years ago. He had found out what she was up to and was gunned down in front of the parliament building in Nicosia. Nice touch, I thought. I arranged that, even though Nora Petrou was never to learn that I was involved. I liked that scenario so much that I helped arrange the exact same death for Petrou's son because he too had found out what his stepmother was doing."

Alec was near the door to the staircase now. But Takis raised the gun in warning and they were all able to hear the murmurings of police officers below, so Alec took a swing back toward the sitting area.

"Then there was Jill Murray. At first you all thought Jill and I were having an affair, but I convinced you we weren't. In fact, we were both assigned to try to find out what was happening on the island in terms of arms and narcotics smuggling. But Jill was just too smart. She was beginning to connect names to operations, names that were on my special associates file. Names like the then-French ambassador to Cyprus, Jacques Piccard, the favored nephew of yon drowsing Guy Piccard. Guy was already one of my main employers at that time, so I arranged to have Jill killed to protect Jacques Piccard. And I later had to kill Jacques Piccard's partner, the deputy UN coordinator, Victor Gorodov, myself at Curium, also to protect Jacques Piccard. You both remember that night at Curium, don't you? You were both there. You just didn't know I was there."

Caitlyn and Takis did both remember. This was all very confusing and shocking to them. Jacques Piccard had eventually been blamed for both of these killings, and there seemed to be no doubt about his guilt at the time.

"Ah, I see that you both do remember. Then you'll also remember that when we finally trapped Jacques—in the restaurant just below us—I managed to be wounded by Jacques himself. Everyone thought he was trying to kill Eleni Piccard. That was true. But he was, in fact, also trying to kill me. He was a little piqued with me, you see, because I was busy turning the blame for some of my own activities on to Nora Petrou and him. Well, I mean, they *were* being legitimately blamed for several serious crimes. I saw no reason for Jacques not to carry some more of the burden, especially since, as eventually happened, a Piccard returned to France in chains is a Piccard free as a bird in Switzerland."

"And then I was a good boy for a while. I wasn't even involved in your kidnapping by the Hizballah band, Caitlyn. Not my style at all. That was wholly the product of the brigade commander's overactive mind. I possibly could have done more to get you freed, but the Hizballah was my employer. And then there is Qazzar. You were closing in on him, so he had become both expendable and a possible danger to our cause. Not much more to that story. Was sorry, however, to have to sully my house with a body. I'll admit I miscalculated by not planning ahead on getting rid of the body, but I assumed that no one knew about my house anyway, so that would be a good place to store him for a while."

Alec's wanderings had taken him to behind the sofa and next to the doors out onto the balcony. Takis was not particularly concerned. There was no exit off of the balcony, they were at the roof level, and the balcony below, at the restaurant level was well covered with police officers.

"And Willie, Alec? What about Willie?" Takis asked.

Alec gave a pained expression. "I liked Willie, really I did. I didn't want to see him dead, particularly. At the same time he was just too sharp. He was always making good assumptions out of very thin evidence. But the courtyard was just a case of survival. I had no idea whether Suzanne had time to tell him anything before Qazzar appeared on the scene. I knew that if she wanted to do maximum damage, she need only whisper my name to Willie. No, I'm sorry to

314

say Willie wasn't completely dead when he was thrust into my arms by Qazzar. Chances were good that he was irretrievably on his way to death, but I had to finish the job. I had to be sure. But I didn't enjoy having to finish off Willie myself. Funny thing about the courtyard. Qazzar never knew I had come to make sure he did the job. He honestly thought I was trying to save Willie and Suzanne."

"And speaking of Suzanne, Alec," Caitlyn was now asking. "You said you loved her, and yet you did kill her, didn't you?—and brutally."

"I'm sorry to have to offend your tender ears, Caitlyn, my love, but I lusted after Suzanne. I didn't really love her, it was more of an obsession with her. True I was mad enough at her to kill her, but, in the end, I killed her just to keep her quiet. It was pure and simple. And it was her own fault. It's true we were lovers when she was here in Cyprus and Ayman was the Lebanese ambassador. But I didn't know at the time that Ayman hadn't told his wife I was the Hizballah's secret agent here. Both Ayman and I were furious when we found she was trying to steal British secrets from me—secrets that Ayman received directly from me on a regular basis already. She even tried to kill me when I caught her at it. Ayman really gave her the whip when she finally returned to Lebanon for endangering me and almost uncovering my activities. She was marked for death from that point on. Ayman made two bad mistakes, though. He told her who I really was at that point, and he let her escape alive."

Everyone in the room seemed exhausted. Everyone but Alec, that was. There didn't seem to be much more to say. Caitlyn and Takis felt like they were moving in a pool of water, slowing down their metabolism to protect themselves from all of the evil that was being revealed to them.

"Oh, I almost forgot. There's Stefan Gunnerson in Malta."

Takis and Caitlyn were speechless. They now had heard just too much.

"Yes. You sent me to help Gunnerson, Takis, little knowing that my business in Malta was with the very people Gunnerson was sent to spy on. We decided we just couldn't use him around, so I helped him off his hotel balcony."

Takis was agape, searching for words.

Alec was leaning up against the open door frame to the balcony. He seemed to be contemplating what to say or do next—but abstractly, like it didn't matter much to him what it would be.

"Ah, smell the clean mountain air," Alec said. And then he sighed and continued. "Speaking of balconies, I think I'll just have a last look at the stars and stonework before we have to leave."

Takis and Caitlyn exclaimed in unison and cleared the sofa as quickly as they could to intercept Alec on the balcony. But Alec no longer was on the balcony by the time they got there. He got his last look at stars as he climbed up on the balcony railing, and he got his last look at the stonework as he hit the stone parking apron six floors below.

Chapter Twenty-Two

Most of the delegates to the Amathus coast Middle East peace summit conference had gathered in Cyprus by Monday night, and most of those had arrived on the southern coast, in preparation for the morning conference opening at the Sheraton Hotel's Panorama conference hall.

The Amathus coast was ready for the conference. All of the hotels that were being used had been properly refurbished and their security systems had been beefed up. Although this would, most certainly, be the most memorable international conference to be held on Cyprus, it was not, by any means, the first major international conference to grace the Amathus coast. Only three years previously, for instance, the same hotel strip had hosted the British Commonwealth Conference, complete with the imperial ship, *Britannia*, hovering off the shore in a very different kind of British sovereign invasion to that which had been experienced when Richard the Lionhearted stormed ashore almost exactly eight hundred years earlier.

By Monday afternoon, all of the major regional leaders had already arrived, because the "summit" part of the conference was actually set to begin Monday evening with the first session of national leaders at the Amathus Beach Hotel's secret conference room. Egyptian president Sulayman and his delegation were taking up an entire floor at the Amathus Beach Hotel. Grand dame of the coast's five-star hotels, the Amathus Beach was one of the oldest, having been built in 1972 in the island's first blush of realization that its destiny was to be a tourist haven. It also was one of the best-placed of the hotels, having wound up nearly in the center of the stretch of luxury resort-style hotels and almost adjacent to the ancient ruins of the kingdom that had given the coast its name.

The Jordanian delegation and the United Nations officials and staffers were just to the west of the Amathus Beach, in the Mediterranean Beach Hotel. The Americans and the segment of the international media that was on hefty expense accounts were at the glitzy Four Seasons resort hotel to the west of the Mediterranean. The newest and largest—and certainly most expensive, hotel on the coast, the Four Seasons catered to those who wanted to visit other countries but preferred never having an excuse to leave their own pampering hotel environment.

The Palestinians and most of the assorted Emirate sheikhs, the latter of whom had come to see and be seen more than to be included in a historic political settlement, were huddled together for mutual comfort at the Sheraton, where the main conference action was to take place.

Thanks to the ending of a hotel employees' strike, the Johnnie-come-lately delegations, those of Syria and Lebanon, had found accommodations at the Hawaii and Apollonia Beach hotels, the former being in the thick of the action and having been one of the main venues of the Commonwealth Conference, and the latter being closer to Limassol to the west than it was to the center of the Amathus Beach activity but nonetheless one of the better hotels in the region. The French had taken over the Le Meridien, which was the last of the hotels on the coast toward the east and also the most commodious and private. Many of the smaller conference sessions were scheduled to be held here in its La Gallerie and Daphne rooms.

Most of the rest of the minor delegations and hangers-on were booked at the Elias Beach and at the smaller hotels and rental flats on the coast. Despite the large number of people involved in the conference and the even larger number of people who had to be brought in to provide the conference participants service and security, there were still a considerable number of accommodations left over for the customary seasonal visitors to the Cyprus beaches.

Two of the major delegations were not staying on the Amathus coast at all. The British contingent was strung out across the nearby coastal city of Limassol, where they were lodging at the homes of friends or at the vacation flats they themselves owned in Cyprus. The delights of Cyprus were no secret to the British. The higher-ranked British officials were being accommodated at the Episkopi Garrison, on one of the huge British sovereign base areas to the west of Limassol.

319

And in a surprise twist, the Israeli delegation, led by Rachel Gilat, was staying, by invitation, at the Presidential Palace in Nicosia and was being helicoptered down for all of the meetings. The Israelis, almost maniacally security conscious, originally planned to house their delegation at the home of the Israeli ambassador in Nicosia. But in the wake of the arrest of Rachel Gilat's own powerful husband for subversion and the implication of an Israeli diplomat to Cyprus in that case, Rachel no longer felt safe in putting herself in the hands of her own ambassador in Cyprus. In the spirit of the new atmosphere of cooperation and openness that marked the very plans to hold a Middle East peace summit conference, the president of the strongly Greek Orthodox Cyprus had magnanimously stepped forward to offer the Israeli delegation the accommodations and security of the Cypriot Republic.

It was 9:16 PM on Monday evening, and all of the top leaders of the Middle East and the sponsor Western powers as well as the senior United Nations officials Ingrid Bittmann and Eric Isaksen were arriving at the Amathus Beach Hotel for their initial summit meeting. Their meeting was scheduled to be held in the Kamares conference room, on the mezzanine floor, which enjoyed a sweeping view of the hotel's gardens and swimming pools down to its beach and marina. As they arrived at the hotel, each leader was formally ushered to the elevators. But, of course, the elevators didn't take them to the mezzanine floor, because long ago their meetings had been rescheduled to a more secret, more secure venue.

The meeting began at 9:45 PM.

At 10:03 PM Ingrid Bittmann's private secretary, Benjamin, hustled along the hushed third-floor corridor, on his way to the suite at the door numbered 320. He was carrying a small box and a stack of papers. He was stopped frequently by security personnel who were stationed along the passageway and was required to show his identification and to state his business. His credentials were pristine; his reasons for being on the floor were that his employer, the United Nations undersecretary for political affairs, Ingrid Bittmann—and also, not incidentally, the chair for this conference—had left for the summit meeting without some papers she needed. Benjamin, her secretary, was delivering those papers.

At 10:15 PM Benjamin was permitted entry into Room 320, where, without looking, he immediately drew a hand grenade out of the box he was carrying and prepared to disengage the firing pin. However, then he looked up and what he saw gave him pause for the action that he had pledged to perform, as a martyr, for the Zionist movement. Instead of the regional leaders he had expected to see in discussion, he was looking down the barrels of five guns jutting out from bodies protected by body armor.

Maria Solonos slipped in behind Benjamin and divested him of the hand grenade. Benjamin was still in shock. "What . . . ? Where . . . ?"

"You were expecting to see someone else?" Maria asked sweetly. "I assume Moshe Gilat sent you—in what is hopefully the last arrow in his quill? No one else would believe that the leaders were meeting here. Only Thomas Jameson was given access to that false information. And he was passing his information on to Moshe Gilat's people."

Although they didn't tell Benjamin, even then, the leaders were indeed meeting in the Amathus Beach Hotel complex, but when they had entered the elevator, rather than being taken up to either the Kamares conference room on the mezzanine level or the falsified secret meeting room in Suite 320, the leaders had been taken down to the ground level. From there, they entered the hotel's health club and then they were ushered through a door and an underground tunnel that led to a one-story villa secluded on the hotel grounds but just to the west of the main Amathus Beach Hotel structure, between the hotel's tennis courts and the garden walls of the Mediterranean Beach Hotel. This was to be the leaders' very private venue for meeting with each other for the remainder of the conference.

As for Benjamin, he had fallen prey to John Patterson's continued improvement of the UNICIS research lab investigations computer program. Patterson merged in the employee file of the United Nations Secretariat, and Benjamin, an activist in the Zionist cause in what he thought was his secret life, had been the most interesting employee to pop out as also being in the central personalities database of UNICIS as a known or potential villain.

At 11:53 PM, a yacht that had been battened down and inactive at the Sheraton Hotel marina for more than three days began to show internal life. Four fighters of the Hamas Palestinian terrorist organization were stretching their limbs and trying to increase their circulation so that they could reacquire their nimbleness and quick reaction instincts following days of agonizing inactivity. It was time for another go at the Palestinian chief. They reviewed their plan one final time and quietly opened the hatch and emerged onto deck—and into the gun sights of the Cypriot police.

The computers at UNICIS continued to whir, and the investigations continued to operate the telephones.

At 3:16 AM on Sunday morning, two inflatable rafts were thrown over the seaward side of an Iranian steamer anchored off the Limassol port. Two assault teams slipped into the water and silently pulled themselves into the rafts. They paddled away from the steamer and were already in sight of the objective, the Amathus Beach Hotel marina, when they started their muffled engines and turned in a wide arc and were launched toward the beach—and into the arms of the Cypriot coastal patrol motor launches emerging from the Amathus Beach and the nearby Four Season.

And the UNICIS computers continued to whir and the UNICIS international telephone bills continued to mount.

Sunday morning dawned to yet another beautiful day on the Amathus coast. The sun was shining, the rim of the sea was awash with bathers, parasailers, and sea scooters. There were more people blissfully baking on the hotel lawns and beaches than were swimming in the Mediterranean on this late April morning. The more active beachgoers were strolling the stone walk along the rim of the sea that stretched from the Poseidonia Beach Hotel on the western edge of the Amathus Beach coast, toward Limassol, and the Le Meridien on the coast's eastern edge. The even more active were playing tennis or exploring the shops, while the most active and adventuresome were climbing the hill that supported the ruins of the ancient Amathus kingdom or were sailing in small boats off the shore.

Inside the Sheraton, in the octagonal conference room, with its sweeping views of all the seaside activity, aptly named the Panorama conference room, the delegates to the Amathus coast Middle East peace summit conference were settling in their seats, quite pleased with themselves and oblivious to the security battle raging about them to maintain their safety.

Ingrid Bittmann rose in her seat at the rostrum and pounded a gavel. The historic conference had begun.

* * * *

Ayman Abu Hani stood at the pier in Valetta, waiting for the boat to reach shore that was to take him out to one of the Libyan vessels resting at anchor off the Malta coast. It had not been a good week. He had not been able to get through to either Qazzar or Stuart in Cyprus just before he left Tripoli for Valetta. None of the measures the Valetta conference had set into motion had succeeded as yet. He kept turning on the television set in his Phoenician Hotel suite in Valetta, hoping to hear that someone had been assassinated as they left for the Amathus coast conference or that the conference site itself had been attacked. But there was only uplifting news from Cyprus on how well the preliminary meetings at the peace conference had gone and on the statements of optimism and hope that the various delegates were giving as they arrived in Cyprus. It was disgusting.

Ah, good, here was the boat now. And there was his contact nodding away to signal that all was well and that The Colonel was already in place out at the yacht. Ayman thought his agent was becoming all too obvious in his signaling and had grown more and more nervous each time a meeting had been held out at the vessel. Even now he seemed to be shaking like a leaf. Ayman decided he might have to make some changes in his arrangements. This agent didn't look like he would be able to hold together for any more meetings.

But then, Ayman thought bitterly, there might not be any more meetings. As their plans failed and as bickering within the councils of those set in opposition to a Middle East peace increased, delegations had begun to pull out. They were now essentially left only with representatives from the Libyans, the Iranians, the Iraqis, the Sudanese, the Hamas organization, the Abu Nidal Palestinian faction, and Abu Hani's own group, the Hizballah. But that was enough. If he could just keep this hard core of idealists together, Abu Hani was sure he could still mastermind the sabotage of the Middle East peace process. Today's meeting was strategic.

Abu Hani's thoughts had carried him across the waves. The little boat was now approaching a vessel. But it wasn't the usual vessel in which they met. In fact, it looked like a derelict hulk. He didn't see any of the others arriving or at the ship's railing. He must be the last to arrive today; the others must all be below already. Abu Hani looked around the little fishing boat that had picked him up for the trip out to the Libyan vessel. He was trying to catch the eye of his agent for some sort of sign of why the meeting vessel had been changed. But Abu Hani couldn't see his man on deck. He must have gone below.

When they reached the stairs to the larger vessel, Abu Hani was handed out of the fishing boat, a little roughly he thought, and the smaller boat moved back off as Abu Hani was climbing the stairs. Funny, he thought, as he reached the deck. There didn't seem to be anyone about. Strange, he wondered. Where is . . . ?

The explosion intruded rudely into everyday life in Valetta. Everyone who was in a position to look out to sea turned to watch the fireball in the watery distance and wondered what had happened.

At the railing of The Colonel's official yacht, which was standing not far off the now-disintegrating and sinking last stand of Ayman Abu Hani, The Colonel and his selected guests didn't wonder what had happened. The Colonel did so hate bunglers and failed schemers—and he most definitely hated "friends" spying on him. Lebanese could not, of course, be trusted to get any important job done. The proper way to get results was by direct action. As he raised a glass of fresh sheep's milk in salute to the sinking vessel, he invited his guests to go below with him and resume their planning for the interdiction of the disturbing movement toward peace and cooperation in the Middle East.

Gina Drew

Gina Drew is a retired American foreign service officer who specialized in investigating and countering international crime and espionage and who still travels the world in both the imagination and in fact.

Years spent working on Cyprus have left her with a deep love of this divided island and its people.

www.cyberworldpublishing.com

www.ingramcontent.com/pod-product-compliance
Lightning Source LLC
Chambersburg PA
CBHW071057250626
47159CB00002B/500